Janice Horton writes contemporary romantic fiction with a dash of humour and a sense of adventure. In 2014, after her children had left home, Janice and her husband set off to explore the Caribbean. In 2015, they returned to the UK only to sell their material possessions in favour of travelling around the world. They are currently housesitting in France after travelling around South East Asia.

 @JaniceHorton
@JaniceHortonAuthor
thebackpackinghousewife.com

Also by Janice Horton

The Backpacking Housewife
The Backpacking Housewife: The Next Adventure

The Backpacking Bride

Janice Horton

OneMoreChapter

One More Chapter
a division of HarperCollins*Publishers*
The News Building
1 London Bridge Street
London SE1 9GF

www.harpercollins.co.uk

This paperback edition 2020

First published in Great Britain in ebook format by
HarperCollins*Publishers* 2020

A catalogue record for this book
is available from the British Library

Ebook ISBN: 978-0-00-834064-3
Paperback ISBN: 978-0-00-834065-0

Set in Birka by Palimpsest Book Production Ltd, Falkirk
Stirlingshire

Printed and bound in Great Britain by
CPI Group (UK) Ltd, Croydon CR0 4YY

Chapter 1

Delhi, India

There are apparently one point three billion people in India and I honestly think every single one of them has come out to greet me as I arrive in Delhi. From the moment I step off the plane, I'm surrounded by a riotously jostling mass of people. From the baggage claim, I'm gathered up and pushed out of the bottleneck of the airport arrivals hall door and into the street, where I join an even greater surge of people with absolutely no concept of personal boundaries.

There are so many faces and the constant noise all around is totally confusing. Spicy foods, musky perfumes, and the sour scent of stale perspiration. It's so overwhelming that I'm starting to have a bit of a wobble. This is not anything like I'd expected or been promised. Where are all the rolling green mountains and the sheer tranquillity?

Where is the supernatural breeze conducive to mindful meditation?

1

Where is the calming atmosphere to help one develop enlightenment?

Where are the quiet places to chant and receive peace?

I'm suddenly having a mid-life crisis of confidence.

Oh my goodness ... I really thought I knew what I was doing in coming here.

But now I realise that I am all by myself and that I know nothing about this vast country.

I'm somehow supposed to find my way out of this mad chaos and head to a train station for the next part of this journey, but I'm gripped with a real fear of being totally lost and completely alone. Or as alone as one can be amongst one point three billion people.

What on earth was I trying to prove to myself in doing this? That I'm brave?

What was I thinking when I got onto a plane convinced I was going to a country where I could find enlightenment and learn real yoga and mindfulness? Have I lost my mind?

I look around and see that everyone here seems so much younger than me and they all look confident and purposeful. It's like they all know exactly who they are and where they are going.

Where are all the other middle-aged travellers like myself?

According to a piece I read in *The Times* this week, mid-life backpacking is supposed to have become a new trend, although I can see no evidence of it. Amongst all this youth

I feel very unworldly and conspicuous. It's like I have a sign over my head telling everyone that I am Maya Thomas – the most inexperienced experienced person who has never travelled anywhere before now – and I'm so hapless and hopeless and lost.

And, not just lost, but I also feel weak and vulnerable.

Why didn't I just stay home to feel lost? I was perfectly safe there.

And why on earth didn't my sensible sister try to stop me from doing this?

Oh, wait ... she did. But, of course, I would not listen. I never listen. I always think I know best. I'd insisted, being a mature woman, that I was capable. I'd scoffed at her safety warnings about women travelling alone and her concerns about 'Delhi Belly' being a 'Very Real Thing'.

'I've had all the travel vaccines and I'll be careful,' I had assured her with my usual adamance.

But none of that bullish confidence or self-assurance seems to have followed me here.

I try to pull myself together. I tell myself that now I'm here I should just stick to the plan and the instructions on the first yellow Post-it note in Jon's travel wallet that has written on it:

Take the bus to New Delhi train station

Except I can't see any signs or directions to a train station. I glance around, wondering whom I should ask.

3

Everyone around me seems to be busy greeting each other with the kind of physical enthusiasm that could be easily mistaken for a violent brawl, yelling and screaming in what can only be described as fervent anger.

Then I spot a young Indian woman dressed in a gorgeous yellow silk sari who is standing alone and looks to be waiting for someone. Right now, she's like my golden beacon of light.

She treats me with pity and points out a bus stop where I can get a bus to the train station.

'If you don't mind me asking, madam, where are you going by train?'

'Erm … it's a place called Rishikesh,' I told her, with a naive shrug.

'And you do already have a ticket, don't you? You did book a seat on the train in advance?'

I shake my head and something about her own head wobble tells me this is a big mistake.

I'd already looked meticulously through Jon's wallet and there was no advance train ticket.

'Oh, dear. I think you'd be better taking the bus directly to Rishikesh rather than the train.'

Despite her advice, I still feel I should stick to Jon's original plan and take the train.

So, I thank her and make my way over to hover on the edge of a crowd which I assume is also waiting for a bus to the station. When the bus pulls in, I quickly realise there is no line, no queue, no system, and absolutely no order, and so I join in with the free-for-all of pushing and shoving, spurred on by fear of missing maybe the only train that's leaving tonight.

When I make it onto the bus, I'm lucky to find a seat.

It's a seat designed for two people, but I'm soon joined on it by three others and someone's baby. Honestly, if I hadn't been hugging my backpack, the baby would be on my lap for sure.

It seems common practice for people to just pile in and sit anywhere and everywhere.

A situation that everyone seems to tolerate and accept without any complaint.

I couldn't imagine this happening in London!

It's stiflingly stuffy onboard with everybody pressed up against each other. All those standing up are holding tightly onto the overhead hand straps and have their damp and hairy armpits almost in the faces of those stood next to them. Despite all the windows being open, it's hard to breathe and once we get underway, this is made so much worse by all the suffocating diesel fumes pouring in from those open windows.

I grit my teeth and hope it isn't too far to travel to the train station.

My hair is now plastered with perspiration, my neck, my face, my head, and trickling from every pore in my body, giving me the unnerving sensation of fingers trailing down my back.

Am I being touched by someone sitting behind me?

It's impossible to know or in fact to do anything about it.

I narrow my eyes and scan those around me suspiciously and soon realise that I'm being watched and viewed as something of a curiosity. There are children and men who are staring at me intently. I'm feeling uncomfortable in every way and decide not to engage in eye contact.

Then a young man, sitting opposite to me, speaks to me directly.

'Excuse me, lady. But are you English?'

I nod my head slowly and he seems delighted.

'And, tell me, are you here from London, England?'

'Yes,' I say tentatively, as I'd actually flown out of Gatwick.

'My brother is in London. His name is Raj Patel. Do you happen to know him?'

I realise he's not joking. And, even though I do assure him that I don't know his brother, he wields his phone and says he wants to take a selfie with me. I really don't like this idea at all. I start to object, but he has twisted around so that now his head is next to mine and when we're cheek to cheek, he takes one anyway. I'm sure my face was a picture.

'My name is Albi. What is yours? Where are you going?'

'I'm Maya, and I'm going to the train station.' I reply before realising that of course everyone on this bus is also going to the train station. 'I'm travelling to Rishikesh.'

Albi looks at me with some concern. 'Maya, why? Why

are you taking the train that takes all night long when you were already at the airport and you could have flown from Delhi to Dehradun and from there reached Rishikesh by train or taxi in just over an hour? It doesn't make sense to me.'

My heart sank. One hour? Instead of goodness knows how many on a train?

But I realise, of course, that Jon's itinerary and plan for this trip was one of nostalgia. He'd obviously thought it important to replicate the exact same route that he had taken to Rishikesh in his backpacker days – almost forty years ago – a long time before there was any such thing as direct buses and budget airlines.

'Thank you, but I've been travelling all day. At least I can sleep on the night train.'

For some reason, Albi thinks this is very funny indeed and he laughs heartily.

* * *

At the train station, again there are huge crowds on the concourse and on the platforms, and especially at the ticket booths. My stomach is rolling and I'm starting to feel a bit of nausea coming on in the incredible heat and in the overload of odours. Praying that I don't faint or throw up, I make slow but diligent progress moving forward through the riot of people, and I keep asking those pushing past me if I'm still in the right line.

7

I eventually get to the ticket office window, and of course I am told the train is fully booked.

But I am informed that I can buy a 'waiting ticket'. I assume this means a standby ticket. I am also told that I really should have booked online at least one day in advance to secure a sleeper ticket.

An hour later, despite me having paid for a waiting ticket, the train, with its boxy looking carriages and traditional yellow and red livery, leaves without me. However, having watched it depart, I'm feeling terribly relieved as the train looked dangerously overcrowded.

There were hundreds of people crammed inside and the overspill were sitting on the roof, with many more passengers hanging onto the side of the train and out of the windows. As my waiting ticket would have only given me access to third class travel, I'm pretty sure that I would have been sat on the roof, where I'd have had to spend the whole journey throughout the night.

It's now six o'clock in the evening and I'm stranded in the middle of New Delhi.

Having strayed from my itinerary and with no Post-it notes in Jon's wallet offering any guidance for this situation, I'm now totally ready to explore all my other options by plane or by train or bus. But before I do, I really need to visit the loo. I've been swigging back bottled water to try and quench my seemingly unquenchable thirst and it has gone straight through me.

There's a line for the ladies' loo but I'm so relieved –

literally – when as an alternative to the typical Indian-style hole-in-the-ground, I manage to find – for the cost of a few extra rupees – a western-style toilet. Then, feeling that I need to plan my next move very carefully, I buy a cup of 'chai' – a hot milky tea that smells of ginger and fragrant herbs – from a vendor.

I sit on top of my backpack against a wall, amongst a crowd of Indian students and a posse of young western backpackers, who also seem to be waiting for their revised travel options to miraculously materialise.

With help and sympathy from the knowledgeable young travellers around me, I manage to get connected to the free internet on my phone and a young woman backpacker who is sitting next to me helps me to download the Indian Air flight app and a travel map.

Everyone is so kind. In their eyes I can see both sympathy and concern for me.

Maybe they all see me as old enough to be their mother? A backpacking housewife?

Though, as I'm actually on my honeymoon sans groom, I am, in fact, a backpacking bride.

I'm feeling a bit better now. The tea is hot and spicy. I discover from the flight app that I've missed the very last flight of the day from Delhi to Jolly Grant Airport, Dehradun, which is the nearest airport to Rishikesh, so there's no use backtracking to the airport. But someone tells me there is a coach leaving directly to Rishikesh within the hour from right outside this station.

I'm also told it's a private coach rather than a public bus (apparently buses are generally deemed risky, particularly at night, as they have a reputation for going off-road) and so it will have aircon and guaranteed seating and it comes highly recommended. I'm now sold on taking the coach. I head out to find the ticket booth feeling relieved and back on track.

I've got my ticket and find the coach is just as promised, with plush upholstered seats with head and foot-rests, air-conditioning, and on-board toilet facilities. Soon we are off and from the comfort of my window seat I have a great view of the busy streets of New Delhi in sparkling twilight. I can see buses, cars, trucks, scooters and tuk-tuks, all weaving through the slowly moving traffic. There are also lots of people going about their business and so many animals – monkeys, dogs, goats, and many cows – that all seem to be wild, stray, or wandering.

My eyes practically pop out of my head when I see an elephant walking down the street too.

An actual elephant!

And, even though my eyelids are heavy and my body is aching with travel fatigue, I fight the need to sleep in favour of continuing to stare outside at what is happening in this world, that is beyond anything or anywhere I've experienced before. My whole life I've dreamed of travelling this far and this spontaneously. I just never imagined it would be all alone and through such terrible circumstances. But, despite my angst, I'm fascinated by everything going on outside the window. It feels so surreal to be here.

I actually did it. I'm really here in India!

Then we are out on the open road and soon it is too dark to see anything outside.

Despite my best efforts, I finally feel myself succumbing to the comforting sway of the bus and the intoxicating pull of my jet lag and extreme exhaustion. I'm helplessly drifting. Spiralling down into sleep. Sinking into the dreaded dream-filled state that will once again take me tumbling back into what was the living nightmare of my wedding day.

Chapter 2

One week earlier in Sorrento, Italy

The white vintage Bentley moves slowly and purposefully through the warren of narrow streets until it
comes to a halt at the ruined shell of a thousand-year-old
abbey. I feel my heart swelling with joy and love and happiness as I climb out of the car and into the bright warm
sunshine of this beautiful day. I pause for a moment, in
the cool shadow of one of the old standing columns that
is draped in creeping ivy, and today decorated with fragrant
white roses and silk garlands. I take a slow, deep breath
and cast my eyes through rays of muted sunbeams into
the cloisters where I can see our wedding party seated and
my future husband waiting for me.

My sister, Pia, touches my arm lightly and smiles at me
reassuringly.

But I'm not in need of composure. I just needed a
moment or two to reflect on this truly special moment

in my life. A moment I never thought would ever actually happen to me.

I suppose I had started to think that fate had other plans.

I'd begun to wonder if I was maybe too set in my own ways to share my life with someone.

Or that I was being unrealistic in holding on to what might seem like impossibly high standards.

I've often been called a 'career woman' by those who might assume that being a modern middle-aged single professional female (a fund investment manager at a private bank) would be my preferred option in life over homemaking and marriage. But, of course, none of my male colleagues have ever been branded 'career men' and those who've opted to remain single have never to my knowledge been subsequently branded as unloved or unlovable.

Friends and family have always meant well, planning blind dates or dinners over the years with singletons they know, and I've always happily played along, resigning myself to the prospect of finding a life partner through mutual acquaintance. But I ask you, is it too much to ask for a good-looking man to be confident without being conceited? For an interesting man to be fun without being foolish? For an adventurous man to be both a hero and a gentleman? In my experience, yes. Until now.

Indeed, my single status to date has simply been down to a matter of personal choice.

Marriage is, after all, a serious business. That isn't to say I'm not optimistic or unromantic about the concept of love and lasting marriage because, by positive example, my parents enjoyed just that. My sister is also happily married. She once told me that the secret was compromise. And, when she asked me if I ever thought I'd marry, my reply at the time had been unnecessarily cursory and flippant.

I'd quoted from Shakespeare's *The Taming of the Shrew*.

Believe me, sister, of all the men alive
I have never yet beheld that special face
Which I could fancy more than any other!

I hadn't realised then, of course, that by fate and circumstance rather than anyone's well-meaning interventions, I would eventually meet Jon Howard. I can't help but smile when I think about the day he walked into my life. He'd made an appointment to talk to me about managing his investments and he breezed into my office that day like a breath of fresh air, with an outstretched hand. I'd greeted him with my usual candour.

What happened next was quite a shock. Literally.

I'd taken his hand in mine for the customary formal shaking and we'd both been immediately zapped with a powerful and incredibly painful static shock that caused us both to yelp and jump back in alarm. Stinging with embarrassment, I'd immediately proffered my sincerest apologies. But he'd thought it incredibly funny and had roared with laughter.

I was so taken by his infectious laughter and the twinkle in his eyes that I'd laughed too.

Then I'd offered him a choice of tea or coffee and ushered him towards the less formal comfortable sofa, where I preferred to chat with my investing clients, and I'd listened very carefully to Jon's banking requirements. He'd explained how he'd recently retired and returned to the UK after living and working in Asia for many years and how he now needed the services of a local private bank. He'd passed me a battered-looking brown leather-bound folder, monogramed with his initials. I'd opened it to find statements from his bank in Singapore, along with the bonds and certificates pertaining to his extensive stock portfolio.

I recall popping on my reading glasses and taking a moment to study the papers, on which I'd found all the documents littered with yellow Post-it notes, all containing what I surmised were scribbled personal reminders and scrawled stock prices.

Some of these Post-it notes became unstuck and scattered onto the floor.

I quickly tried to put them all back again, while Jon smiled at me reassuringly.

'Oh, just ignore my notes ...' he told me with a dismissive wave of his hand. 'They're purely for my own benefit. I'm notoriously forgetful. A lifelong trait. Not in any way an age thing!'

Despite his apparent absent mindedness, I was impressed with Jon Howard.

I peered at him over the top of his folder while he pointed out his capital investments.

He was far more interesting than other men I'd met to date or any of my usual stereotypically wealthy clients. I'm not talking about his smartly tailored attire or his expensive-smelling cologne, but his expert knowledge of wealth management and the impression he gave me of being a totally self-assured man, without being pushy or discourteous.

He seemed to be sophisticated but not at all arrogant. A gentleman.

Confident without that awful air of superiority that usually came with it.

Physically, Jon Howard was surprisingly fit and had a lean physique that defied his age.

He had me wondering if, like in Oscar Wilde's novel *Dorian Gray*, he had a painting in his attic that grew old and more wrinkled while his mortal body remained youthfully slim and taut.

Clients usually came to me for bespoke financial guidance, but Jon was already well-informed. He had done all his research. He knew exactly what type of bank account he needed and which funds he wanted to invest his money in and for how long. This made my job on that day a task of administration, assurance, and facilitation, rather than expert investment advice.

So, with our business swiftly concluded and put tactfully aside, for the rest of our allotted appointment time together, we talked about classical music, wine, and beautiful places instead. When I discovered that Jon was incredibly well-travelled, he had impressed me even more. All people who travel fascinate me. Probably because, despite suffering from an inherent wanderlust myself, the only faraway places I'd ever actually visited, have been via a book, a movie, or a TV programme. You could say that my bucket list was actually a to-do list.

And, there's just something terribly attractive about the well-travelled, isn't there?

It's that faraway look in their eyes and the dreamy expression on their faces. The twitch of a smile playing on their lips while they're being reminded about or reflecting on an exotic and distant experience. With that same look, my father used to talk to me about his experiences of travelling in Asia. He would often relate fantastical tales to me about the time when we'd lived in Hong Kong. We'd lived there until I was five years old and my own misty monotone memories of that time have, throughout my childhood and certainly through my impressionable youth, been fortified and coloured and supplemented by my father's stories.

Consequentially, I'm a real sucker for a well-travelled man with a twinkle in his eye.

The fact that Jon was ten years older than me didn't seem to matter.

I'd known straight away, from our first moment of eye contact, that I was attracted to him.

And strangely, after an hour in his company, I realised I felt completely at ease.

I was enchanted by his conversation and the confident way he maintained eye contact.

I found Jon had an incredibly dry sense of humour and a quickfire wit.

Had we ever met before? No. Never. I'm sure of it. But we'd had an immediate connection.

When he laughed heartily at our mutual banter, I found myself melting inside.

I was aware of my heart thumping in my chest at a ridiculous rate and a feeling of butterflies fluttering around in my stomach. This was absurd. Irrational. I'm hardly a swooning teenager.

When I asked him a few personal questions, he'd seemed happy to indulge my curiosity.

'I've just bought a house in Cheshire. Just outside Lymm, actually,' he told me casually.

'Oh, how lovely. That's a very nice part of the country-side. Do you have family nearby?'

His accent certainly wasn't northern. It was more Queen's English than local dialect.

'Yes. I do. I still have an aunt and uncle and cousins living in Manchester.'

I asked him from what kind of work he'd recently retired.

19

He told me how for many years he'd been an investment banker.

'In places like Hong Kong, Kuala Lumpur, and Singapore.'

The names of these fabulous-sounding, exotic places tripped off his tongue.

Discovering that our career backgrounds were similar had satisfied my inquisitiveness concerning his expert knowledge of investments and wealth management funds. And, dare I say it, sparked my interest and curiosity in him even further.

'How very exciting!' I breathed. His life sounded fascinating.

Unlike mine, I hasten to add. I'd worked in the same bank in Manchester throughout my entirely boring and monotonous career to date. I was suddenly feeling anxious about the impression I was giving him. I started to worry about my obvious lack of worldliness.

Self-consciously, I began to think that my navy skirt suit and my high-neck white blouse might look far too staid and plain to him. I dearly wished that I'd at least bothered to wear a bit of lipstick and a bright silk scarf this morning and perhaps done something different with my hair instead of just tying it back into a dreary-looking chignon.

'I've always wanted to travel,' I told him candidly while staring into his grey-green eyes.

I glanced wistfully at the antique globe on the corner of my desk, betraying my errant fantasies of spontaneous world travel. In moments of boredom, particularly on a

Monday morning, I'd spin that globe and close my eyes and then stop it turning with my finger. Then, I'd open my eyes to see and imagine where I could end up if I just decided to jump on a plane and go there impulsively, with only a few belongings thrown into a backpack. I sighed and shrugged. 'But, I'm afraid, all our banking seminars are held at our head office up in Glasgow, rather than anywhere exotic.'

'Well, working abroad is not quite as exciting as you might imagine.' He offered, perhaps somewhat kindly. 'After all, an office is an office, wherever it might be in the world!'

'My biggest dream is one day to go to Hong Kong.' I felt myself blushing and my whole body flushing hot and cold as I spoke because this felt like telling one of my most innermost secrets. 'You see, I was actually born there. My father was General Manager at the container port for ten years until 1975,' I confessed.

'An important job. It was and still is the largest container port in the world.'

'Of course, I have only vague memories, but I do remember the house we lived in was painted pale pink. It was the exact same shade as all the roses in my mother's garden. It's strange how memories work, isn't it? I can't see a pink rose without thinking of my mother and that wonderfully fragrant and sunny garden in Hong Kong. The house was on Stubbs Road in a place called Happy Valley. Doesn't that sound wonderful?'

Jon looked delighted with my personal connection and my recollections.

'Happy Valley's still there and it's still an exclusive residential area. The valley is also rather famous for its old racecourse, considered one of the few remaining Hong Kong institutions.'

I sighed. 'For me, the main attraction would be the thrill of seeing the Hong Kong cityscape with my own eyes. Of course, I've seen it on TV and in photos, but I've always wanted to go there and actually see it for myself.'

Jon studied me carefully for a moment before he spoke, and I felt my mouth go dry.

'Yes, the cityscape is spectacular. Some say it's best seen from Kowloon Island. But I say the best view is from The Peak where you can look down on the city and across Victoria Harbour in all its glitz and glory. Maya, you simply must go and see it for yourself one day.'

'Yes. One day, I'm sure I will. Please, tell me more about your experience of Hong Kong.'

He leaned in closer now that we clearly had a common interest.

'Well, it's where I first started out in the banking business in the 1980s.' He chuckled over his memories. 'We hustled like cowboys rather than bankers back in those days, but it has to be said, we had a great time and made an awful lot of money doing so!'

I found listening to Jon quite mesmerising. 'Ah, the 80s. Such a volatile decade.'

'Indeed. If working in Asia, and Hong Kong in particular, taught me one thing then it was to be ambitious. To work hard and play even harder. So, tell me, Maya … aside from Hong Kong, where else in the world is on your travel bucket list?'

'Oh, it's more like a wish list,' I said shyly, as my heart hammered against my ribs.

I found talking with Jon was having a strange effect on me. I'm not normally one to open up and tell someone I hardly know all my deepest desires. Especially not during business hours.

Yet here I was … opening my heart to a stranger.

'I've always wanted to explore India.' I confessed to him. 'To go and see the Taj Mahal, the Fort at Agra, the Mysore Palace. And I'd add all those places you've just mentioned like Singapore, Thailand, and Malaysia. I'd love to travel the whole world.'

I didn't want to admit to him that over the past few years, especially since my parents had died, I've been having serious regrets about not being more impulsive about travelling when I was younger. Lately, I'd been looking back and wishing I'd taken the time out to go backpacking before the weight of these corporate chains had anchored me here.

Immediately after finishing university and gaining my degree in economics, I'd been offered a rung on the corporate ladder at one of the most respected private banks in the country. I'd thought I was the lucky one amongst all my graduating peers, who had struggled to find vocations and so had instead taken vacations. So many of my friends had gone off travelling after graduation, whereas I'd never even been out of the UK.

So, I squirmed in my seat in anticipation of Jon asking me where in the world I'd travelled.

Despite my nightly obsession with watching the National Geographic Channel on TV and my subscription to *Wanderlust* magazine and *The Times* travel supplements, I knew that once I admitted to him that I'd never been farther than Scotland I'd appear an unworldly armchair traveller whose experiences were all imagined and shelved until an unspecified time in the future.

'Have you ever been backpacking?' I asked him, hoping that didn't sound too outlandish to a man who was wearing an antique Rolex and an expensive suit.

Jon's eyes had sparkled with amusement and enthusiasm. 'Oh, yes, although, it was a long time ago. Back then, I followed in the footsteps of The Beatles, who had famously gone to Rishikesh in Northern India to be enlightened. I was a big fan of the Fab Four and I wanted to learn about eastern culture. So, in 1979 I grabbed my guitar and a backpack and I headed out there to live in an ashram.'

'That sounds amazing and very New-Age!' I enthused.

'Ah, yes, those were the days. Living the life of a hippie and learning meditation and yoga!'

I laughed with him, but I could easily imagine him as a handsome twenty-something long-haired hippie with beads around his neck, strumming a guitar, and singing 'Hare Krishna'.

'I ended up staying in the ashram for three months. The people I met there and my experiences in India, without doubt, have had a great and lasting influence on my life.'

But then I saw Jon frown and collect his thoughts. He rubbed his forehead and, in his moment of reflection, I found myself leaning towards him and holding my breath in anticipation of hearing more of what he might have experienced in the Far East.

He shifted his seat to cross one leg casually over the other and then leaned his elbow on the arm of the sofa before reengaging me in eye contact and deciding to tell me something quite personal. 'To be honest, I also went there looking for something ...' he confessed.

'What was it?' I breathed, hoping he didn't mind me pressing him.

'Answers,' he said bluntly. 'I knew The Beatles had gone to India to heal after the sudden death of their manager. At that time, I was also looking for a way to heal. I felt I needed to make sense of the world after a good friend of mine died. I was upset and confused. I had questions about life and death. I was angry. Feeling terribly lost. I wanted answers from the universe. And, for some reason, I thought I would find those answers in India.'

'And did you?' I asked him, captivated by his honesty.

'Well, it's true to say I found something!' He began to laugh, as if trying to make light of what had suddenly become a rather deep and heavy conversation between us. 'And, to be honest, it was also pretty cool to laze around all day and night in a yoga *shala*, surrounded by candles and clouds of patchouli, listening to the wise words of a real Indian guru.'

I tried to imagine what it might feel like to sit in a real ashram with a real guru.

I imagined it to be an entirely peaceful and life-affirming experience.

'The town of Rishikesh is in the foothills of the Himalayas, on the banks of the holy Ganges river. It's a very special place to practice yoga and meditation. You see, Maya, India isn't really a country you go to see … India is a country you go to feel.'

I later found myself repeating those words to myself like some kind of mystical mantra.

India isn't really a country you go to see … India is a country you go to feel.

'Maya, my advice to you is that if you want to travel, do it. Life's short. Live your dreams!'

I listened to him, my attention rapt, and nodded in agreement.

I didn't like to admit that despite several weeks of annual-leave entitlement, taking more than one week off work at a time would be considered a lack of commitment by my superiors.

Yet, somehow, any excuse not to live one's dream seemed to sound like a feeble excuse.

I'd recently been accounting my own years. How fast they'd gone.

Soon I'd be old. How long did I have before it was too late?

How old is old? I supposed the answer lay with strength and abilities rather than actual years.

I didn't feel I could explain to Jon – a customer – how over the past couple of years everyone here in this bank, myself included, had been increasingly concerned about the rumours of staff cutbacks and branch closures. And, unlike him, despite having my own investment portfolio, I was still many years from being able to afford to retire on a full pension.

I'd been both fascinated and enchanted by Jon's stories and his life, but despite us both working in the same industry, his life and his experiences were nothing like mine. He had described to me how he'd moved up the corporate ladder quickly, while working in exciting countries and exotic cities and having adventures and escapades.

Whereas, my career path had been insipidly incremental over a long period of time. I'd started as a customer services manager and steadily worked my way up to a managerial position.

After discovering that Jon was widowed (I'd tried not to overtly express my delight at this news and to instead feign an expression of sadness and sympathy) I made sure to keep both my hands busy, shifting papers and tapping my pen, in the hope he might see I wasn't wearing a wedding ring. I do know now, of course, six months later – and from his incessant teasing about our meeting on that day – how in the very moment I'd zapped him with a bolt of static electricity, he'd noticed I wasn't wearing a ring.

It's a story he delights in telling over and over again to all our friends and family.

I'm so incredibly glad that I trusted my instincts about him that day and accepted his kind offer of dinner that very same evening. We'd sat at a cosy table in an intimate corner of a very nice restaurant in the city, eating delicious food and drinking very fine wine and we'd continued our conversation about interesting places and exotic travel, until it got so late that we were the last two people to leave.

When we'd finally said goodnight, I'd known I'd found the man I wanted to marry.

Before meeting Jon, I'd had a few boyfriends and several longer-term relationships, but they'd never reached the point of confessions of love and future commitment. I realise only now what it was that had held me back and why none of my previous partnerships worked out.

Simply put: I'd never fallen in love before meeting Jon.

I'd never met that special someone who truly connected with me on so many levels.

No one had ever before taken the incentive and encouraged me to have adventures. None had ever suggested that we go off and explore the world before our opportunity fades.

28

Instead, they'd all had the usual nine-to-five careers and weekend hobbies that didn't include me. Dating had been an exercise in time management while allowing space to pursue our separate interests and then compromising on what we might do together.

I shudder to think of how many concessions I've made in order to maintain my relationships.

Sitting in pubs for hours with a glass of warm beer while watching boring darts tournaments.

Standing on the freezing side lines at sports matches.

Of course, they sometimes later asked me (with disinterest and indifference) about the book I was reading or how my rock choir session went this week or how I'd enjoyed the classical music concert I'd attended (alone) while they'd been playing five-a-side football or out stomping their feet at the country and western club, but it wasn't the same.

Never before had I found someone who was my alterego, my soulmate, and kindred-spirit.

Just a few months after our momentous first meeting, I'd received a timely and highly lucrative offer of early redundancy from my bank, and I'd accepted Jon's proposal of marriage. He'd proposed to me in the most romantic way possible, by whisking me off to Paris – a city of my dreams – where he went down on bended knee in the Louvre.

We were both head over heels in love and we decided we wanted to marry straight away.

I'd suggested a local church in Stockport, but Jon had soon convinced me that Sorrento, in southwest Italy, was a popular and more romantic place to marry. So, on a mission to find our perfect venue, we'd flown from Manchester into Naples one weekend and Jon had hired an open-top car to drive us along the amazing coastline overlooking Vesuvius and the Bay of Naples. We'd stopped off for lunch and a spot of sightseeing in Pompei before continuing on to Sorrento, where together we found this incredibly romantic fourteenth-century church in which we could marry. For the very first time in my life, everything felt perfect.

For the first time in my life, I knew I was truly happy and deeply in love with a mature, fun, handsome, and considerate gentleman. Jon has all the qualities I could ever want in a man all rolled into one incredible person: he's a passionate lover, an honest partner, a true friend, a trusted confidant ... and today, this man will become my husband.

I venture forward, stepping out of the arched portico with my heels tapping on stone steps.

Then, suddenly, I've been spotted by the minister and the string quartet strikes up – with gusto – Wagner's 'Bridal Entrance'. And, as music fills the air, my twin nieces appear like little angels to walk ahead of me, scattering white rose petals on the old pathway.

My heart beats in sync with the tempo of the beautiful and traditional music.

The Backpacking Bride

Dah dah da dah ... dah da da dah ...

I feel like I'm floating on air as I glide along the stretch of petal-strewn carpet. I can feel my practiced Mona Lisa smile slipping away into a ridiculously wide grin, as I see my fine-looking fiancé looking relaxed and handsome and with a wealth of love shining in those sparkling grey-green eyes of his as he grins back at me. I can see from the pride on his face that he approves of my understated wedding dress and the pale pink rosebuds and gypsophila flowers gathered into my bouquet and woven through my hair, which I'm wearing loose and curled onto my shoulders, just the way he says he likes it best.

As I reach his side, he takes my hand in his and in a whisper, he tells me that I'm beautiful.

And for the first time in my life I truly feel beautiful.

Jon and I have many friends but none mutually acquainted, so we'd decided on an intimate family-only wedding. Jon's aunt, uncle, and his cousin have come over from Manchester. Jon's bachelor brother, Malcom, who is two years older than Jon and lives in London, is his best man. On my side of the family, I have my sister Pia as my matron of honour, her husband Peter, and my nieces, their eight-year-old twin daughters, Libby and Laura. All are here to share in and witness our happiness.

After our wedding in the cloisters and our wedding breakfast on a restaurant's private terrace, Jon and I are planning to stay on for a further week on a 'mini-moon' here in Sorrento.

31

We plan to further explore the islands and the Amalfi coast. After that, we'll leave on our honeymoon proper, the itinerary of which has been entirely managed by Jon and kept meticulously under wraps. It has been his top-secret project while I've been liaising with our wedding planner and busily organising our Italian nuptials.

He's described our honeymoon to me with great excitement as being something of 'a magical mystery tour' which is of course the name of a Beatles song. I didn't know *exactly* where we were heading but he had let one or two clues erroneously slip. Firstly, he'd mentioned several times since we met how he'd dearly love to go back to Asia to show me all his favourite places. For that reason, I heartily suspect that our trip might involve us exploring many of his old haunts in Singapore and Malaysia and all the exotic places that I've always dreamed of seeing one day. I'm also hoping that we'll be off to Hong Kong – I'm positively dizzy with anticipation and excitement at the very prospect!

As Wagner's 'Bridal Entrance' fades out, I arrive at Jon's side.

We turn, smiling and feeling so very happy, to look into each other's eyes.

Jon gently takes my hand and leans in to offer a loving kiss to the side of my cheek, taking the opportunity in this special moment of pause and closeness, to whisper sweet words of love and devotion into my ear before we turn together as one to face our officiating minister.

And, in that moment of silence, I hear another sound.

It's a gasp. A cry. A sharp intake of breath.

Once again, I turn to my love, wondering what might have taken him by such surprise.

The next few moments seem to play out in slow motion.

Jon is looking at me not with love and passion in his eyes but with a pained expression.

He has reached up with both hands to grip his forehead and I see his handsome face looks pale and twisted in pure agony. He's faltered on his feet. I reach out to him as his legs collapse beneath him and he falls to the floor. He's now staring up at me with wide eyes and the sharp intake of breath that he'd taken just a moment ago is now leaving his body in one long, slow sigh. I hear someone screaming and soon realise that it's me.

'No. No. No! Jon, please don't go. Please don't leave me ... not now ... not like this!'

Chapter 3

Rishikesh, India

I wake to a flurry of activity and a bevy of voices on the bus. It's still pitch black outside. I check the time. I've been travelling for five hours now and I'm relieved to see that we're pulling over into a brightly lit rest stop. I would really welcome a chance to stretch my legs and grab a cup of coffee. 'How long until we reach Rishikesh?' I ask our driver.

'Just another two hours. We'll arrive at dawn.'

I climb down from the bus and gulp in the damp night air. I realise we must be on a high road in the foothills of the Himalayas now because there's a much cooler breeze blowing. Is this the so called *supernatural air* that Jon swore to me was conducive to meditation?

I see there's a shop here to buy hot chai and coffee and breakfast items. I join the queue.

I also see that some of my fellow travellers and spiritual seekers, a motley crew of youthful hippie types, are using this time to do a quick yoga practice. I watch them curiously as they stretch and bend. One of the yellow Post-it note instructions in Jon's wallet simply states:

Yoga

I think back to my surprise when Jon had explained to me about his passion for yoga.

The first day we met, I'd already guessed that he worked out regularly and was in perfect health. I never suspected that he could drop dead due to something as terrible as a sudden brain aneurysm. I had dabbled in yoga and Pilates myself on occasion, attending classes at my local sports centre, and always thought it was a gentle form of exercise and a way for me to stay fit and flexible. But Jon had insisted that true yoga was much more than just exercise and stretching.

He said it was also a spiritual experience. That it provided a divine connection between the physical body and a person's spirit.

He told me he had first learned true yoga in India, and how it had been the catalyst to him taking up martial arts. Jon was a sensei of Aikido and Karate as well as a Tai Chi master.

All were sports that over the years had strengthened, honed, and sculpted his body.

And he credited yoga and deep meditation for his positive mindset after depression.

It obviously worked because Jon was the most positive

person I had ever met. His glass was always half full. He believed that a positive mindset attracted positive and divine energies from the universe. In truth as a practical minded and logically thinking person – with a tendency to see my own glass as half empty – I'd never really quite understood or believed in this divine connection that Jon often spoke of as it all seemed a bit wacky to me.

In my raw grief and desperation, I'll do anything to feel closer to Jon.

In the past, I've been admittedly fickle when it comes to matters of religion – I swing from atheism when all is well to praying like a pilgrim when I need something – so I suppose I can't ever expect to be 'blessed' in the way that other people believe.

I've also never believed in luck. I believe the harder I work, the luckier I will become.

But despite my real fears of the unknown and my innate scepticism of things I simply don't understand, I find myself looking forward to spending a whole week in India and learning new things. In particular, real yoga.

I'm also curious to try group chanting and sitting down to quietly meditate, as well as explore the possibility of experiencing some kind of divine connection to Jon in an authentic ashram.

I'm up for trying it all. Because right now, I'm in the deepest darkest pit of hopeless despair.

And it feels good to have a task to hold on to and to be looking forward to something.

Today I can *feel* India all around me.

Half an hour later, everyone's back on the bus and two hours later, we finally arrive in the sacred town of Rishikesh, surrounded on all sides by the rolling hills of the lower Himalayan Mountains. As we all spill out from the bus, the town is bathed in a pale pink morning light, and I can see it's all and everything that I've been promised.

The holy Ganges flows like an inky signature between the opposing banks of the sacred river, upon which stand ancient-looking flat-roofed buildings and gold domed temples.

I take a long, deep breath to appreciate the cooler air here and I gaze around in wide-eyed wonder. There are several cows and lots of dogs roaming the street and I can see a troop of small, cute monkeys sitting on a bench fastidiously grooming each other. *Monkeys!*

There are very few people around at this hour, but those who are look to be heading purposefully down to the riverbank, perhaps to meditate and to do their yoga salutations as the sun comes up on what looks to be the start of a beautiful day here in Rishikesh.

I see there's a line of rickshaws waiting to greet passengers from our bus.

I approach one of them. The driver is no more than a boy and he is sloe-eyed with sleep.

He wobbles his head when I mention the name of the ashram where I'm headed and he only wants a few rupees to take me there. As it turns out, I could have walked, because we'd only travelled for a few minutes down a dusty road in his rickshaw when he stops at a gate.

I look past the gate and along a line of mature trees heavy with clusters of white flowers and hanging grey-green foliage to see a winding dirt path leading to the same big yellow house that I recognised from the ashram website. This is it. I'm here. I'm at the famous Moksha Ashram.

The former sacred spiritual retreat of The Beatles and their entourage and also my darling Jon. I breathe a sigh of relief to have arrived. I'm just about to haul my heavy backpack onto my back again, when it's suddenly whisked away from me by a small skinny man wearing a white robe and a turban head wrap. I was so busy gazing all around that I hadn't seen him rush out of the gate to assist me.

'Namaste. Welcome to Moksha Ashram. Are you Miss Maya Thomas?'

'Yes, I am,' I tell him, appreciating the welcome. 'I'm pleased to meet you. And you are?'

'I'm Baba. We've been expecting you, Miss Maya. Please, follow me.'

I follow Baba and my backpack through the gate and along a path through the trees and then through a garden of lush and fragrant foliage until we reach an open foyer in the yellow building. When I hear the harmonious sound of lots of people chanting, I feel my heart soar and a wave of goose bumps ripple across my shoulders and down both of my arms.

Om Namah Shivaya. Om Namah Shivaya. Hara Hara Bole Namah Shivaya.

I respectfully slip out of my shoes and walk barefoot up the stone steps.

Once inside, just beyond a foyer decorated with flower-strewn Hindu statues of various spiritual deities wearing serene expressions, I see lots of people – young people – also wearing serene expressions and sitting cross legged amongst banks of candles, flowers, and smoky incense sticks in a communal area under a palm-thatched roof. This must be the *shala*. The gathering place for those staying here and where all the activities take place. The atmosphere feels harmonious and I'm delighted to find that the whole place smells exactly how I expected with exquisite notes of patchouli oil and jasmine and heady spices in the air.

I can hear Jon's voice in my head enthusing about his time here.

It was pretty cool to laze around all day in a shala listening to a real Indian guru.

Baba leads me through the building and outside again and we patter along the length of a long, mosaic-tiled terrace from which the elevated views of the valley are stunningly beautiful.

I realise that I've seen this enchanting vista before as it also features on the ashram's website.

The photo must have been taken from exactly where I'm standing right now. The view is breathtaking, with the newly risen sun shimmering on all the rooftops below us and bouncing brightly off the temple domes and the higher sections of the pedestrian suspension bridges that I can see crossing the sparkling holy river.

The river that is said to be the lifeblood of India and apparently a lifeline to millions.

Jon had once told me that The Ganges, with its source in the icy Himalayan mountains, runs for thousands of kilometres and that throughout the year it attracts many tens of thousands of worshipers and pilgrims from across India and indeed all over the world, who come to bathe in its waters, because they all believe them to be pure and magical and healing.

I shade my eyes with my hands to peer further into the distance and along the horizon to see layer after layer of mist-coated hills, every single one of them progressively more beautiful and a lighter shade of green. Then I continue to follow Baba and my backpack into a small annex room off the terrace that contains old cabinets and an untidy desk and an ancient looking computer. Filling the entire back wall is a large colourful painting of a lotus flower.

Beneath the lotus flower petals are the words: *Let It Be*.

I'm really excited to see a reference to The Beatles.

I'd expected to be greeted with images and murals of John, George, Paul, and Ringo, painted onto the walls of the ashram, especially in the foyer, but I'd only seen images of religious gods and deities instead. I can't understand why they wouldn't capitalise on their claim to fame. The ashram's close association with the Fab Four is, after all, what originally led Jon here and is essentially why I'm here too. But, strangely, except for the 'Let It Be' – which is, of course, a lovely song and a poignant sentiment – there's nothing.

I'm introduced to a tiny, smiling Indian woman who tells me her name is Swami Nanda.

She presses her palms together in front of me and bows while saying *namaste*.

I repeat the word. I've heard it before, but I don't actually know what it means.

I also bow and smile. Swami Nanda looks to be very old. I'm relieved to see there is at least one person here who is undoubtedly older than me. She has a small, round, wrinkly face and toothless smile; together with her small stature, she looks something like a happy but mischievous child. She's wearing a white cotton sari wrapped tightly around her body and her head is completely shaved. I've already assumed she must be an ashram lady monk.

I've also realised that she's the person Jon had been corresponding with by email and with whom I'd emailed just yesterday, in order to explain that I would be arriving here alone.

Although for some reason, I couldn't bring myself to tell her that Jon had died.

When Swami Nanda spoke to me, she did so in an almost inaudible whisper.

'Maya, it's nice to meet you. Welcome to Moksha Ashram.'

'Thank you,' I whispered, wondering why we were having to be so quiet when all around us there was so much raucous chanting going on.

'I expect you're exhausted from your long journey. Let's get you checked in and then I'll show you to your room. Do you have any questions? Only, once we leave the privacy of this administration room, we must continue to honour our noble silence. This means that in the ashram we are only allowed to speak after lunch through to our lights-out time at 9pm.'

I was quite taken aback. 'Erm ... excuse me? No talking ... all morning?'

'It's a ritual to help you connect with yourself and find peace while you are here.'

I shrug but accept that I can live with this rule. I did come here to find peace.

Though I'm sure I have many questions, I'm suddenly feeling incredibly tired and overwhelmed that none came to mind in that moment. So she took a copy of my passport and I'm given two sheets of printed paper and a bottle of water. I notice that one of the papers contains the programme of structured activities for the week.

I immediately spot (with a little concern) that 'morning bell' is at 4.30am.

The day starts in the *shala* at 5am with an hour of communal chanting. After which there is bell ringing (to clear the air of the chanting) followed by a class on how to breathe properly and then an hour of mindful meditation. Well, who knew there was a proper way to breathe?

Maybe I've being doing it wrong for the past fifty years?

And all before breakfast at 7.30am.

After breakfast, there's something called a 'Karmic Cleansing' followed by another hour of meditation and then the first yoga practice of the day. I decide I'm really looking forward to a good yoga stretch after sitting for so long on the bus.

After lunch, which is at 12.30pm, conversation is then encouraged.

In the early afternoon, I see a rota of activities offering more specialised forms of yoga practice, a yoga philosophy session, and something called *Satsang*. All these sessions and study classes are held in the *shala*. There is even laughter therapy. Really? Laughing as therapy?

No. No thank you. I can't imagine myself feeling happy enough to laugh ever again.

Other options on the surprisingly full programme include the study of Ancient Sanskrit and Chakra Healing with Swami Nanda and a class on Cosmic Ordering, with the ashram leader, Guru J. I'm excited to see the esteemed Guru's name on here because it's also been written down on one of Jon's Post-it notes. He's also in an old Polaroid photo in Jon's travel wallet.

In this incredible photo, Guru J has a big, bushy beard and enormous eyebrows supporting his elaborate turban. Everyone in the picture is wearing flowing white Indian clothing, yellow flower garlands around their necks, and happy smiles on their faces.

Jon, holding on to a sitar, is sitting in the middle of the group, next to the Guru.

On the back of the photo is written *Guru J Rishikesh 1979*.

This Guru is undoubtedly the very same holy man who taught Jon and The Beatles enlightenment and who will now teach me how to deal with my sorrow and grief and cure me of my terrible sadness.

Afternoons from 3pm onwards in the ashram can be spent as freely as one wishes.

Suggested activities for free time include: reading in the library, helping out in the garden, going into town, walking in the hills, meditating at the river, bathing in the river, or taking up activities in the ashram workshops that include learning pottery or soap or candle making.

'All classes until mid-afternoon are mandatory, with the exception of your first day, as we find most people just want to sleep,' Swami Nanda says with an understanding smile. 'So, take time to rest, but also try to join us on the terrace for breakfast and for your lunch. And, if you feel you'd like to take a walk with us later, we're all going down to the river to meditate.'

The other sheet of paper lists the rules of the ashram.

I glanced over this list anxiously. I hadn't expected there to be rules.

Or, at least, perhaps not quite so many of them.

I trot behind a surprisingly sprightly Swami Nanda as she leads the way up a wide and sweeping stone staircase with an impressive and elaborately carved balustrade that looks like a giant undulating serpent. Baba insists on trotting behind us with my backpack.

Along the way, I peep inside the open doors along the upper level corridor and see these are all hostel-style sparsely furnished dorm rooms, containing rows of neatly made up bunkbeds. I'm shown to my room at the end of the corridor. I'm not quite sure what I had expected. Did I perhaps think an ashram was going to be like a hotel with all sorts of holistic treatments and spiritual endeavours on offer from which to pick and choose?

I certainly hadn't realised facilities would be so basic with mandatory classes and rising at four-thirty every single morning. As a honeymoon destination it's certainly alternative! But Jon must have known what he was doing in organising this for us and I'm sure he would have looked up what authentic experiences the ashram was offering people these days. I'm feeling determined to put my own reticence and misgivings aside in order to experience this fully and to see all the things Jon had enjoyed about Rishikesh.

I was looking forward to everything Jon had planned for us on this 'magical mystery tour' and I was particularly looking forward to following all the – sometimes strange – scribbled notes and reminders on the numerous yellow Post-it notes.

And, despite Swami Nanda giving me permission to skip classes on my first day here, I'm determined to beat my jet lag and take part in this morning's activities as listed on the schedule.

After bell ringing – which I can hear has just started – I'm hoping to clean my karma and learn how to benefit from breathing properly and then I'm also hoping to discover all that lovely peace and tranquillity that was promised to me through real yoga and true meditation.

When I do eventually lie down to sleep later, I'll hopefully be able to stop having the terrible recurring nightmares about Jon's death. I'll finally be able to stop my mind from torturously replaying our ill-fated wedding day over and over again. Then, perhaps, in all the noble silence and time of quiet reflection, I'll be able to stop harbouring all these feelings of anger about being cheated in life and in love. Able to calm the relentless voice of fury in my head that demands to know from the universe why this happened to Jon and what I've ever done in my own life to deserve to feel such terrible pain and heartbreak.

'This is your room,' Swami Nanda mimes with a sweep of her hand in her noble silence.

The booking receipt showed that Jon had booked a private double room. I was surprised to see this one was hardly bigger than a broom cupboard with only enough space for the not quite double-sized bed and a small side table. There was no wardrobe and no space for one, just three coat hooks on the wall on which to hang my clothes. There was also just one small, high window, so the room is oppressively dark until I switch on the single bright bare lightbulb hanging down from the ceiling. I wonder where the draft I can feel is coming from before noticing the window has a fine mesh in its frame instead of glass.

I take a deep breath and try to push aside my detrimental thoughts and my disappointment about this looking more like a prison cell than a guest room. I decide to be thankful that it's at least a private room. I'd once shared a room at university with a friend who snored like a drunken sailor. Plus, I hadn't fancied sleeping in a dorm bunk, as I doubted I'd have been able to get to the loo in the middle of the night from the top without tumbling out of it, or to get a wink of sleep in the bottom bunk knowing that someone else was sleeping above me.

I decide it might be basic but it does look spotlessly clean and so it is absolutely fine.

After all, I hadn't come here for five-star accommodation.

I'd come here to *feel* India.

'It's perfect,' I mimed back.

The communal bathroom, however, might take some getting used to as I can see no western-style toilets. They're all Indian-style squatting latrines – basically a hole in the ground with footholds on either side. Interesting. And, for me personally, a little intimidating.

I take a quick shower to freshen up after my journey to the sound of enthusiastic bell ringing in the air. I did try to message Pia to tell her I'd arrived but couldn't get a signal or a connection and I'd forgotten to ask Swami Nanda the password to connect to the ashram Wi-Fi.

I drag on a pair of leggings and a baggy t-shirt and make my way downstairs.

Bell ringing had finished and *Ujjayi Pranayama* or 'breathing class' is just about to begin.

I'm feeling both excited and a little anxious as I cross the yard to the communal area where everyone else is already sitting cross legged on the floor in the lotus position. I slip in quietly to sit at the back to observe and learn. The lotus is a seated pose that I've attempted several times before in a yoga class but which I've sadly never managed to find comfortable.

I do wonder how you are supposed to put your left foot on your right thigh and your right foot on your left thigh, stretch open your hips and flatten your knees and twist your ankles in such a way that you look like an open flower. And then stay there, possibly for hours, while trying not to cry in agony. The lotus flower features heavily here in the ashram and in Buddhism generally. I read up on this before I came here and discovered that because the flower grows in the mud, and submerges itself every night to then remerge and flower cleanly and beautifully every day, it symbolises purity and spiritual enlightenment and rebirth. I decide to cheat with a half-lotus (right foot *under* my left thigh) instead but just for today.

I take a cue from everyone else by placing my hands lightly on top of my knees with the tips of my forefinger and thumb touching. I must look more like an old locust rather than a lotus flower with my knees sticking up and my elbows jutting out at odd angles.

I try not to mind that everyone around me looks so much younger and more flexible.

Despite feeling stiff and exhausted I try my best to relax.

Our instructor is a tall, willowy western girl with long blonde hair and lots of tattoos.

She bows to us and smiles and silently points to a white board with a bamboo stick.

Ujjayi Pranayama means: Breathe Loud and Breathe Proud!

Then with a pen she writes the word 'namaste' on the board and underlines it twice.

We all bow in response but remain silent while she then dashes off her name with a flourish.

'Hi, I'm Willow.' She adds a row of friendly kisses followed by a heart.

Then, suddenly, everyone around me starts to breathe very heavily and very noisily.

I immediately feel uncomfortable. I really hate noisy breathing. I'm sure it can never be considered polite in normal society and I can't imagine why this is supposed to be correct.

All around me everyone's sucking and gasping and rasping and hyperventilating and then blasting their sour before-breakfast breath out again to sound like a multitude of wheezy asthmatics. The guy in front of me is panting so hard he sounds like he must be imagining himself being chased by a bull across a field. The blonde instructor is looking at me specifically and she's now pointing her stick to another poster on the back wall.

This is a big poster with specific instructions on how one should breathe properly.

Apparently, the purpose is to energise our bodies and to bring our focus to our breath.

I try to do it – huffing and puffing and wheezing like I'm having an asthma attack. Then I'm so damn dizzy I almost keel over. This is totally ridiculous. Someone pass me a paper bag!

Thankfully, after about twenty minutes of this everyone starts to calm down.

The instructor once again catches my eye and she indicates another poster.

Apparently, we're going straight onto something called *vipassana.*

I see this is the much-anticipated lesson in mindful meditation.

The directions for achieving this seem simple enough. There are only six steps to follow.

SIT comfortably.
CLOSE your eyes.
FEEL. BE AWARE.
LET IT GO.
BREATHE.

Well, we've already established that I'm not sitting comfortably. The wooden floor feels very hard on my bottom and my leggings feel way too tight for sitting in lotus position for this long.

I try not to fidget. I try to relax. I try not to feel perplexed or intimidated.

I close my eyes. I try very hard to be aware. But what am I supposed to be aware of exactly?

I decide to be aware of my innermost thoughts first and then I think about my physical surroundings. I think about how thrilling it is to be in the same ashram where Jon spent three months of his life back in the seventies. The very same place where The Beatles had come to meditate and to find their peace and enlightenment.

Then I start to feel the thrill being replaced by feelings of sadness that Jon isn't here with me during this planned return to Rishikesh. I know how much he wanted to come back here to experience the same spiritual connection he had found here before and to share it with me.

With my eyes tightly closed, I try to imagine Jon is sitting next to me here in the *shala*.

I try really hard to connect with his spirit and the shadows he once left here.

In the very place where Jon had wanted me to come to *feel* India.

I know I must let it all go, but how can I ever let go of Jon and the pain I feel in my heart?

Maybe it's simply down to a matter of training and discipline?

Is that what all those rules are about?

I'm guessing that ashram life is meant to be a difficult challenge both physically and spiritually.

I know it certainly will be for me. I know I must learn to be open minded and accepting of the noble silence and all the other rules here that are meant to be of benefit to everyone.

Did I mention the second, third, and fourth rules of the ashram?

Every meal is vegan. Well, that's a challenge for me because I like eggs and cheese, and I'm actually used to eating meat with my vegetables. Also, every day is alcohol free, when I'm rather partial to a glass of wine or Champagne towards the end of the day. No stimulants are allowed in the ashram, and I'm sorry, but I simply can't live without coffee!

There's no getting around this either as apparently *the whole town* is meat and alcohol free.

I don't smoke and I've never taken illicit drugs in my life – who knew that coffee would be a banned substance?

As a coffee lover and a caffeine fiend it seems wholly unreasonable to me. A little flurry of panic sets in as I contemplate there being no coffee shops or wine bars here. No morning lattes and no afternoon espressos. No evening glass of chilled chardonnay. I'll admit to starting to feel a little disgruntled. I'm even feeling a tad rebellious.

I really don't like and hadn't expected the idea of there being so many rules.

I'm a grown woman and I should be allowed to think and do what I want!

Hadn't I already convinced myself that rules were for losers?

That those who made up their own rules were the real winners in life?

But I give myself a mental shake. I tell myself to stop sulking.

I'm flying on to Hong Kong in a week to stay in a five-star hotel for goodness' sake!

I'm sure Jon hadn't meant this to be a week of deprivation or a trial of survival.

He had meant this to be a spiritual retreat and an opportunity to connect with the mystical.

A time for us to experience something very special.

And so, for me right now, this is even more important as a place of spiritual healing.

Jon had told me that he came here when he was in pain and grieving and had needed to make sense of the world. He'd been upset and confused about life and death. He'd been feeling angry and lost and he'd needed answers from the universe. I can do this. I need this.

It's only for one week. Besides, a seven-day detox wouldn't hurt.

In learning how to believe in something, I might even be able to start believing in myself.

And, in abstaining from that glass of wine every night and eating a healthier diet and doing lots of exercise, I might finally be able to shift that stubborn weight that has refused to budge from my hips. That can't be a bad thing.

I imagine myself looking calm and svelte and trim and I feel slightly less disgruntled.

But then I realise I'm hardly being mindful or success-fully meditating with all these errant thoughts crowding my head. I'm thinking far too much. I'm having a whole conversation with myself. This must stop. Okay. Start again. What should I be aware of next? My surroundings?

I focus on the warm breeze blowing across my face and I listen to the tinkling windchimes.

I can hear birds singing in the surrounding trees. I can smell the sweet scent of incense burning in this *shala* and then ... I hear and smell something else.

It's that guy in front of me again!

Didn't anyone else notice? How disgusting!

As everyone fully embraces the mindful process, I inad-vertently join in with the hypnotic rhythm of breathing in and out, despite the smell, the hard floor, and my too-tight leggings. Ignoring the fact I've lost all feeling in my bottom, I'm soon feeling completely weightless. It's like I'm floating on air and I'm drifting off. Not into a state of mindful meditation ... but into a state of exhausted sleep.

Chapter 4

One week earlier …

I stay on in Sorrento for three days following Jon's death. After the shock and devastation and disbelief, I feel confounded and numb. I feel completely empty. It's like there's now a big hole in my chest where my heart had been. My head and my limbs feel like lead. It even hurts to breathe. My lungs feel stilted and suffocated and I'm exhausted with the sheer weight of my grief. I'd sat with Jon all day while arrangements were being made by his family to take his body back to Manchester, despite my dear sister's gentle insistence that I should go back with her to rest at the hotel. I find I didn't have the heart to leave him there all alone.

I needed to keep my vigil next to his open casket in the tiny, cold, stone chapel.

Understandably, his family want Jon laid to rest in his hometown back in the UK.

But for some reason, I'm not being consulted over any

57

of the details of his funeral. It's just not fair. They don't seem to understand that I should be his wife right now – *his widow*. Instead, they're treating me like I'm nothing at all, just a woman in love with a dead man. His family seem to have already forgotten that I ever existed.

My brother-in-law Peter and the girls are flying back to Manchester today along with Jon's aunt, uncle, and cousin. His brother, Malcolm, is returning with Pia, Jon and me tomorrow. Only, darling Jon will be travelling in a casket in the aircraft's hold.

This morning, Malcolm broached the fact that, as the marriage never actually took place between Jon and me – as if I needed a reminder – he is still legally Jon's next of kin.

He tells me that it's his duty to make the decisions he knows his late parents would have wanted and expected for Jon. I'm feeling really angry right now. I'm incensed with Jon for leaving me and I'm furious at him for not having the decency to wait until after saying his wedding vows to have his aneurysm. I'm infuriated with his family. I want to yell at them.

Now that might sound terribly unreasonable, but I feel I need to remind them that Jon and I loved each other very much and our love should bloody well still count for something now that he is dead. I should absolutely have a say in what happens to him!

I should at least be consulted on how he is laid to rest.

Jon would not have wanted traditional hymns played at his funeral.

His family want 'The Old Rugged Cross' and 'Jerusalem' for heaven's sakes, when I know he'd much prefer some Bach or a beautiful piece of Elgar.

'I'm sorry, my darling.' I say to him, as he lies in his casket wearing his silver-grey wedding suit and looking like a wax mannequin version of himself. 'I don't mean to be so terribly angry. I can't help it. It's just that I want you to have 'Air on a G String' and 'Nimrod' instead.'

I also know Jon would have wanted a citation from the Dalai Lama and not a reading from the Bible. He would have preferred a green, eco-friendly funeral with a hemp coffin rather than a traditional pine box and he'd have wanted a tree planted in his memory rather than a head-stone. It's just not fair that his family have prioritised what they require instead of what Jon would have wanted.

That night, my own body feels rigid from sitting all day in a cold chapel of rest, as I wander back through the warm and narrow streets to our hotel and lie down in what was meant to be our honeymoon bed. But I don't sleep. I lie awake thinking about what might have been.

I actually think I might be going mad. I imagine our wedding day over and over again.

But now it plays out in my mind as it was supposed to have happened and with the outcome that we'd planned together. I imagine us past that terrible moment when both our hearts had stopped beating. I imagined us standing there in the cloisters smiling at each other in the streams of sunshine of that sacred special place that we'd chosen to say our vows to each other.

And, with my eyes closed, I see how tenderly we are holding hands as Jon slides a gold band onto the third finger of my left hand. I hear our minister saying to Jon, *you may now kiss the bride,* and, with our fingers entwined and joy on our faces, I see us leaning in for our first kiss as a married couple. Then we turn together to the cheers and congratulations from our family and we walk away to the joyful music of Mendelssohn to enjoy our celebrations and a wonderful meal that we'd planned on an outside private terrace at a gorgeous little restaurant. I imagine the laughter. The speeches. The inevitable jokes. The one about how long it took for us both to find each other. The raising of glasses. The delight and all the happiness. A whole lifetime of happiness.

And then, on our wedding night, in this very same bed, we'd have made love to each other and fallen asleep happily wrapped in each other's arms as man and wife. But none of that happened. It was all cruelly snatched away from us. And I don't know why. What did I do?

Why have I lost the love of my life so soon?

I tuck up my knees and fold myself around the pillow that I'm clinging to and I press my face right into it so I can muffle the sound of my desperate screams of heartache and anguish. I'm so very lost and I feel so horribly cheated. What am I meant to do now?

And where do I go?

It's not like I can just go home to England and lock my door and hide – which is what I want to do – because now I'm homeless as well as hopeless. This is all such a terrible mess. After we'd returned from our honeymoon, I was supposed to move into Jon's house.

To that end, I'd recently sold my own house in Stockport.

Contracts were signed and exchanged. It's all done and there's no going back on it.

The people who've bought my house are moving in tomorrow.

To make matters worse, as the legal executor of his brother's estate and his financial affairs, Malcolm has asked me to return the key I have for Jon's house. He really doesn't seem to care that he's literally throwing me out onto the street. He's told me he has no choice but to ask me to vacate the house so he can ready it for sale.

He says the house has to go on the market immediately.

He says it must be sold to facilitate the paying of what will be 'substantial' death and inheritance taxes. To me, it all seems like Malcolm is keen to get his greedy hands on Jon's assets as quickly as possible. Pia kindly stepped in to help as soon as she heard this preposterous news and she has offered me a room at her house until I can get myself sorted.

Sorted? What does that mean? How will I be 'sorted' ever again?

I feel like a burden. I know it will be an imposition for her because she'll have to move both her girls into one bedroom in order to accommodate me. And, I'd only be able to take a small suitcase with me, because the bedrooms of her modern town house are tiny.

What am I supposed to do with my furniture and personal belongings?

They're already unpacked and in situ at Jon's house.

All my furniture and household items I'd wanted to keep and use in my new married life!

'Maybe I should just move in to a hotel for a while?' I suggested to my dear worried sister.

Of course Pia wouldn't hear of it. She's absolutely set on doing her best to help and support me. It's so very generous, especially as I know she's also struggling and incredibly distressed herself, after seeing poor Jon collapse as she'd reached forward to take my bouquet.

'Maya, I'm your sister and right now you need me. I'm your family!'

I'm so overwhelmed by all of this and I really don't know which way to turn.

'You can rent a storage room for all your stuff temporarily,' she told me sympathetically.

So, after flying back to northern England from Italy and spending a sleepless night tossing and turning in my niece's tiny My-Little-Pony-themed bedroom, the next morning I head downstairs, following the enticing aroma of freshly made coffee, to hear my sister on the phone arranging for a removal van to meet us at Jon's house to pick up my stuff.

Then I hear her arranging for us to go into the local estate agent together to register my interest in seeing any suitable properties on the market in this area. 'My sister's a cash buyer,' I hear her telling the agent, as if that should bag me somewhere straight away and then life can somehow resume. I know she's trying to help but how can I possibly cope with all this?

How can I even think of packing boxes right now when I'm supposed to be packing my suitcase for my honeymoon?

Chapter 5

Moksha Ashram, Rishikesh

I'm brought out of my distressing dream by the tinkling sound of a bell. I open my eyes to find that meditation class is over and my bottom is completely numb. My poor legs are aching, stiff and unyielding, from sitting cross legged on the cold floor for a whole hour.

I unfold myself and somehow manage to unlock my knees to stand and follow everyone outside onto the terrace, where I see there's one long table with bench seats set out for breakfast. I realise that this arrangement would have been conducive to some conversation, except that, of course, due to the noble silence no one is allowed to speak yet. I engage in a friendly smile to those around me, but no one seems remotely interested in making eye contact. I see everyone still has vacant expressions on their faces and dreamy looks in their eyes.

I guess they must have all successfully reached an enlightened meditative state?

Oh gosh ... I do hope I hadn't been snoring or shouting out Jon's name in my sleep.

Pia told me I'd been yelling and cursing and thrashing about in my sleep at her house.

She also told me I'd been using the really bad swear words she didn't ever expect I'd know.

Of course, the walls in her place are paper thin. In the adjacent bedroom, I'd had to listen to her and Peter talking about 'what they were going to do with Maya' and then them making love.

I take a seat on the bench and look along the length of the breakfast table to see that most people here are a heck of a lot younger than me. I'm a little disappointed by this as I was hoping there would be a good mix of ages and, in particular, a few middle-aged people like myself.

I also see there are more women than men and they look to be a varied mix of nationalities.

Interestingly, many of the girls have long tangled hair and intricate henna artwork illustrations on their faces and their hands. Several of the boys have tattoos on their arms and also wear their hair long and in braids or hanging in dreadlocks. Many are wearing attractive costume trinkets such as crystals and beads and bells on anklets that tinkle when they walk into an otherwise quiet room. Of course, real jewellery is not allowed here.

Rule #5: Leave your valuables at home.

It's a rule I realise I've already broken because I'm still wearing the solitaire engagement ring Jon gave me when he proposed in Paris. I'm loathed to take it off. In fact, I damn well refuse to take it off. There's no way. They absolutely can't make me.

Rebelliously, I quickly twist it around my finger to hide the large diamond out of sight in my palm. I'm actually feeling a bit conspicuous and out of sorts sitting here in my plain t-shirt and contrasting neon Fabletics leggings that Pia made me buy before coming here. Pia had assured me – wrongly – that these were the very latest in yoga fashion. I'd trusted her because Pia is younger than me and she should know such things.

But everyone here is wearing bohemian-style things with lots of Buddha images together with baggy cotton clothes in muted shades of dark red, deep purple and mustard yellow. Or they are sashaying around in kaftans or Alibaba-style trousers and head wraps adorned with shiny coins and trinkets. It's a look that absolutely embraces the whole ashram aesthetic.

I decide that as soon as I get half a chance I'm going shopping in town.

I imagine myself wearing a flowing kaftan dress or a silk saree and some harem-style pantaloons with a cheese-cloth blouse, sitting comfortably and bra-less in the *shala*, meditating in a serene lotus position or a soon-to-be-mastered super bendy true yoga pose.

I wonder if I can get a *shala* selfie or get someone to take my photo so I can send it to Pia?

But, of course, that would be contravening the rules.

Rule # 10: No phones allowed in the shala.

Everyone is, of course, also barefoot. There are no shoes or socks allowed in the *shala* even if your feet are cold. Mine are always frozen no matter the ambient temperature. I read that the reason we must go barefoot here is to allow our root chakras to connect with the earth.

I'm not entirely sure what that means but there's a chakra healing session later this week so maybe I'll learn more. It's optional, but as I'm sure all my chakras are horribly broken, I think I should go to it.

Breakfast is a bowl of cold rice porridge made with soy milk. It tastes okay. It has a nice consistency and a good nutty texture, although I think it could have perhaps done with a little honey for sweetness. I suppose I'm noticing all this about my porridge because, like everyone else, I'm sitting here and staring intently down into my bowl, eating in silence.

Which would have been absolutely fine except that it wasn't an *actual* silence.

I lift my eyes to glance about and see that everyone else is still either staring into their porridge or they have their eyes closed in a blissful repose while chewing it. Not that porridge normally needs chewing, but the ones with their eyes closed are really making a meal of it – pun intended – and it sounds *awful*. There's one particular guy – it's the Heavy Breather from the how-to-breathe lesson this morning – and he's sitting opposite me with his eyes tightly closed and his mouth wide open. *Chew ... chew ... chew.*

He has strings of soy milk and clumps of porridge in his goatee beard.

I look quickly back down into my bowl because I can hardly stand to watch him. I've been brought up to chew my food properly and with my lips firmly closed.

* * *

After breakfast, we all file back into the communal area for our karmic cleansing class.

I'm really looking forward to learning what this is all about.

You see, up until recently, I'd begun to believe in karma.

I say until recently because, since Jon died, I don't believe in anything anymore.

Jon explained it to me once. Simply put, it's very much about treating others in the same way you would want to be treated yourself. Basically, if you do good things then good things will come straight back at you and, conversely, if you do bad things – well, ditto – bad things will happen to you. Of course, back in the day, it was just called good manners.

Because I'm in this very special place of healing, and connected with Jon's spirit and maybe even the spirit of John Lennon too, if I can once again associate with karma, then I imagine this cleansing will wash away all the bad karma I've accumulated and make room for good and positive energies that I now need to bring into my life and my future. Perhaps if I can believe in karma once again and it has been cleansed, then I can somehow accept that Jon is dead. That he's gone while I'm still here breathing and very undead.

I also imagine that real karmic cleansing – like real yoga – is something that can only be done properly in India. And, importantly, with an authentic Indian guru like the old man sitting cross-legged on a cushion in the middle of the *shala* right now.

Along with Swami Nanda, Guru J is one of the founder members of the Moksha Ashram.

Today he is wearing a long white gown that looks like a bedsheet wrapped around his body, secured with a knot on one bony shoulder, leaving the other equally bony shoulder bare. He's very small and very thin, in a Gandhi-esque way.

I'm feeling absolutely sure that Guru J is the same Guru who once knew Jon.

He looks exactly like an older version of the person in the photo. The very same guru who also taught John, Paul, George, and Ringo, in the late sixties.

On entering the *shala* we all line up to wash our hands.

A poster on the wall shows a giant pair of hands held together in a prayer pose and states:

Wash to symbolise purity of body and soul.

Swami Nanda is being aided by Baba. He is tipping a generous splash of water from a large pitcher into a row of hand washing bowls and she's bowing and smiling at everyone and handing out soap and towels. After washing, I take my place in the circle, and this time I'm grateful to sit on a comfortable plump cushion. In front of me and everyone else there is another small bowl of water. I imagine this is holy water and I expect our karma will be cleansed with this water. I look around. I'm now really wishing I'd discreetly brought my phone along with me so I could take a quick photo to send to Pia. She'd love this. The whole room looks so pretty with lots of flower arrangements and so many candles and incense sticks and golden statues. It's so authentically ashram-like and looks like it's actually glowing.

But there's also the problem of no internet connection in the ashram.

Maybe that's *Rule #11*? Except surely there must be internet in the office?

After all, they do have email and a website and an Instagram page.

I'm wondering if it's possible to bribe Swami Nanda to give me the Wi-Fi code but then, no doubt, there will certainly be rules on the list in my room about corruption and bribery too.

Just then, Guru J presses his hands together and bows his head in a silent greeting to us all before looking up and in turn at each of us. In the hush of the room, the tension is palpable.

He begins to chant. '*Om Mani Padme Hum. Ommmm … shanti shanti.*'

I watch as he slowly lifts up his water bowl, cupping it with both of his aged and bony hands.

We all do the same. The bowl feels pleasantly warm to touch. I wonder if we are going to tip the water over our own heads in the same way as in a holy baptism? Or if we are perhaps meant to drink it and therefore cleanse ourselves of our bad karma in that way?

But what actually happened next was neither of these things.

Our esteemed guru simply cocked his head to one side and then tipped the water from his bowl into and up each of his nostrils in turn. Snorting and slurping up the water and allowing it – together with whatever dirt and mucus was up in his nose and his throat and his sinuses – to pour straight back out again into the bowl.

I will admit to being terribly shocked and more than a little disgusted by this.

To my horror, I then see everyone around me has also started to tip the water up their noses, snorting, slurping and blowing it all back out again in a gargling, bubbling blast of phlegm.

I retch. Honestly. I couldn't help it.

But then I'm spotted by our Guru as the only one in the *shala* not to have cleansed my karma.

So, in panic and fear and embarrassment, I cock my head, tip my bowl and pour the warm and very salty water over my face and up my nose – where it immediately burns all my soft tissue before flooding straight down the back of my throat.

I start to choke. I can't breathe. I honestly think I'm drowning.

I'm convinced I'm going to die a horrible death here in the ashram in front of everyone.

Until, of course, what went in – the salt water and my morning porridge – all comes rushing back out again into my bowl. When I look up, I see everyone staring at me in horror.

I'm guessing that if this is karmic cleansing then I'm thoroughly purged.

Feeling horribly humiliated and with my heart pounding and my stomach still heaving, I flee from the *shala* and run back up to my room to lie on my bed and be alone with my shame.

I curl up and let my travel-sore body sink into the thin mattress, my aching head resting on the flat, lumpy pillow. A guttural sob escapes my throat and I really wish I hadn't come here now. What on earth was I thinking? Pia was right. This really isn't my kind of thing at all.

I'd marvelled at all Jon's stories of India, but it had been from the safety and comfort of distance.

I'd had no idea what it was really like to travel so far and to land alone in a country that was so vastly different from anything I'd ever known before or could ever imagine.

I came here naively thinking I'd find a way to heal myself and move on. But now I realise I'd been desperately grasping at straws. How the hell can chanting and bell ringing help me? How can meditation calm my rage? How can yoga make me feel better about myself?

How can spending seven days in a barren commune in northern India with a load of hippies ever help me to accept a world without my Jon in it and start to live my life without him?

It all seems completely ridiculous to me now.

Just as my life without Jon seems impossible to contemplate and unbearable to comprehend.

Chapter 6

Cheshire, England

Jon's funeral took place in a small village churchyard in Cheshire. He was buried in a family grave with his mother and his father. The day was grey, misty, and miserable and everyone stood around grimly mumbling their prayers at the graveside under black umbrellas.

I fell into a deep mind-numbing depression after the funeral service.

Somehow, I had to continue to live. But how? It all seemed impossible.

How could I ever get over this and move on? I doubted I ever would.

I'd grieved before when my parents had died but this was entirely different. My parents had been elderly and sick. They'd both needed years of constant care and loving attention from my sister and me until we'd had to make the heart-breaking decision to move them into a nursing home. So, when the dreaded day finally came and they died naturally and peacefully in their sleep within weeks of each other, there had been great sadness and grief, but there hadn't been the shock and anger that I'm experiencing now.

There was a quiet feeling of inevitability and acceptance with their passing.

We didn't feel they'd been taken away from us unfairly or unexpectedly.

We'd mourned their loss, but we also celebrated their long and happy lives.

They hadn't been stolen away from me too soon and before their time like Jon.

After Jon's funeral, I'd gone from angry and depressed to raging and rampant in my despair.

I'd howled like a wounded animal and I'd cursed at the universe.

I'd begged to know what I'd ever done in my life to deserve this terrible loss and misery.

I'd always tried to live by the set of values instilled in me by my loving and worldly wise parents who brought my sister and me up to be honest, trustworthy, and caring.

Not that I'm claiming to be perfect. Far from it. I know I'm not. I have my faults.

I'm aware that I'm sometimes an overly observant person, a personal trait brought to my attention through my workplace appraisals and evaluations. I've been advised that in its positive form this allows for acute attention to detail but can alternatively make me appear overly critical of people and situations and therefore I can be perceived as disapproving.

To be honest, this has also been mentioned by one or two previous ex-manfriends, but it has certainly never been my intention to appear abrupt or seem judgemental. On the contrary, I've always tried to be a helpful colleague and a true friend. I've honestly never knowingly lied. I've never broken the law. I've never even had so much as a speeding ticket. I've always tried to do my best. I've been a loving daughter. A good sister. A generous aunt. A loyal friend.

I regularly give to charity. I despise and petition against unfairness and inequality.

So why has my one chance of love and happiness been taken away from me so cruelly?

Was it wrong to try to be a good and decent person?

Can we conclude that playing life by the rules is for fools?

My dear father used to say to me that no good deed ever went unrewarded. Well, I'm sorry Dad, but that's just bullshit. I've seen some rotten people making up their own damn rules and thriving on it. Proof is everywhere. People lie and steal and betray and even worse, and yet they do very well indeed. So where is this thing that some call karma and the universal power that some call faith? What is there left for me now? What am I supposed to do next?

I can't go back and yet I can't move forward.

I'm stuck all alone in a foreboding place between life and death.

Jon is gone and for the life of me I really don't know what to do about it.

* * *

A few days after the funeral, I was surprised to see Jon's brother Malcolm calling at my sister's home. I'd already returned the house key he'd so insensitively asked me to relinquish. Pia had led him into the kitchen and then she'd made herself scarce. It was early afternoon and I was sitting having my umpteenth cup of coffee while still in my dressing gown, looking a terrible, trembling mess with my puffy face and lank, unwashed hair.

'What can I do for you Malcolm?' I asked him in a voice that even to me sounded surly.

'Maya, I've brought you something. I know Jon would have wanted you to have it.'

He slid a brown leather wallet across the worktop towards me. I recognised it immediately.

Jon's old monogramed business portfolio.

I reached out to it instinctively, and tentatively touched it.

My fingers caressing the cover instantly reminded me of the day Jon and I first met.

Such a wonderful day and not that long ago. Six short months. That's all.

'Open it.' Malcolm commanded.

I did. Inside I found a neat stack of printed papers. Only

this time, they weren't bank statements or stock investments or bond certificates, but receipts and travel confirmations. I'd caught my breath and quickly closed the wallet again. The leather made a sound like a hard slap. It felt like a slap to my face. I uttered my thanks to Malcolm. He told me he 'must get on' and left me with a folder filled with ruined hopes and broken dreams.

I stared at it for a while, morosely, and focused on the monogramed initials on the cover so intently that it was as if through the sheer force of this tangible connection to Jon, I could somehow manifest him back from the grave. Eventually, I mustered up the courage to open it again and to scrutinise the itinerary inside. Then I saw that flights were booked and hotels reserved in our names. Seats on planes and beds in hotels that would now be cold and empty.

Cold and empty like my life.

When Pia returned to the kitchen, I was a shuddering, raging mess again.

'Look! Just look at this. It's so unfair!' I yelled, consumed with anger, slamming my fist down on the countertop. 'It's our entire honeymoon itinerary. All the places I've ever dreamed of visiting. All places in the world that Jon knew so well and said he longed to show me.' My voice cracked as I spoke but still the tears would not come.

It was Pia who had pointed out to me that I was yet to cry a tear over losing Jon.

'You need to cry, Maya. You need to let go and allow yourself to be sad about losing him.'

But I was far too angry to be tearful. Tears were for sad people not mad people.

'He promised me a honeymoon that would be a magical mystery tour,' I explained.

Pia looked a little surprised by this. 'Goodness. Really? How? What does it mean?'

'It means our first stop would have been India. We were to stay at the same ashram where The Beatles had once stayed and where Jon had stayed in the seventies to grieve and to reflect on the death of his dear friend.'

Jon's words about India echoed through my mind.

India isn't really a country you go to see ... India is a country you go to feel.

Suddenly, realising what I'd just said about Jon's friend, I turned to Pia with an idea.

'If this ashram is a place to go to grieve and mourn then I think I should still go there!'

'Really? Maya, are you serious? You're really thinking of going on your honeymoon alone?'

I was deadly serious. 'I think it might help me. Yes. I really do need to go there!' I insisted.

'Maya, you've never travelled so far before. I know you've always talked about travelling the world but you need to listen to me and think this through properly. I know you're grieving but you are also vulnerable. I really think this could be a mistake!'

To me, her words sounded something like a challenge.

'But I have my passport. I've already had all the travel

vaccines I need. I still have time. The flight to Delhi leaves tomorrow night from London. Look, everything's already covered and fully paid and looks non-refundable!'

Pia sat down next to me and we looked through the rest of the itinerary together.

In typical Jon style, every piece of paper, printed-out email confirmation, and receipt in his wallet was filed in date order and was covered in a splattering of yellow Post-it note reminders, all with a specific written instruction or a travel tip or a snippet of local information. All reminders of the things he'd wanted to show me and us to experience together.

Take the train to Rishikesh from Delhi
Do yoga
Meditate in the shala
Bathe in the Ganges
Chakra Healing
Cosmic Ordering
The Ceremony of Light
Tai Chi in Kowloon Park
Eat Dim Sum
Take the Star Ferry
Drink a Singapore Sling in Singapore!
Petronas Towers
Batu Caves in KL
Eat seafood in Penang!

Some were directives and one or two had people's names written on them.

I wondered who Harry Chen and Guru J might be.

Along with the notes, there was an old Polaroid photo of a group of hippies and an Indian gentleman in a huge turban and there were also lots of faded tourist brochures from Hong Kong and Singapore.

'Wow. You're right, this really is a magical mystery tour,' Pia agreed. 'This all sounds amazing. A first-class flight to Delhi from London. A week in an ashram in India followed by three nights in Hong Kong and two each in Singapore and Kuala Lumpur, followed by a week in Penang before flying back to London.' She looked at me with an expression of sisterly concern. 'But are you absolutely sure about the ashram, sis? I mean, is it really you?'

'It could be ...' I protested. 'I'm open to experiencing new things. I've read *Eat Pray Love*.'

Pia narrowed her eyes and looked unconvinced. 'The only reason I ask is that on your birthday last year, I suggested we go on a spa day together that included yoga and meditation, and you said you hated that kind of thing. I think you actually called it "mumbo jumbo".'

'But we did try those beginner's yoga classes at the new gym last January,' I countered.

'And you didn't stop complaining about your aches and pains until around April.'

'But Jon told me how he learned *proper* meditation and *real* yoga in India – not the watered-down western version of it – and how he developed a strong faith, not in a religion ... but in spirituality. And, most importantly, he learned how to heal at a time when everything in his life seemed futile.'

I remembered that Jon had also quoted Martin Luther King to me.

If I closed my eyes, I could still hear his words in my head.

To other countries I may go as a tourist; but to India, I come as a pilgrim.

And he'd been so very enthusiastic about all his amazing travels and adventures in Asia.

Arh, the sights and sounds and smells of the orient: the history ... the food ... the sultry air!

'Look here,' I said, pointing to the detailed itinerary, 'In Hong Kong, he'd planned to take me up into the mountains for a panoramic view of the cityscape. He was going to show me the Symphony of Lights laser show from a sailing junk in the harbour. In Singapore, we were to stay at the famous Raffles Hotel. In Kuala Lumpur, he'd wanted to take me to the very top of the world's tallest twin towers. And, in Penang, he told me that we'd enjoy the best food in the whole of Asia!'

My mind was suddenly in overdrive, my heart beating so fast that I needed to steady myself.

'I've decided I'm going to see it all. It's what Jon would have wanted!'

Pia wisely knew that as I'd set my mind to this there

was nothing she could do to change it and so she took hold of my hand and gave it a squeeze. 'Okay. Maybe you're right. I can see how this might help you come to terms with losing Jon and help you see life from a new perspective. And, while you're in Hong Kong, you could try to find Mum and Dad's old house.'

I felt my eyes watering at Pia's suggestion and in anticipation of seeing the house again – the gorgeous pink house where I'd been born and long dreamed of returning to one day.

'You should take the photo with you. It has the full address on the back,' Pia urged.

I nodded my agreement and once again considered all my fleeting and flickering sepia-toned recollections of living in Hong Kong. All those memories had been so richly embellished by the wonderful stories told to me in the past. After our parents died, Pia and I had split the responsibilities of sorting out their affairs. As the oldest daughter – and a banker by profession – I'd agreed to be the executor of their estate in order to settle their accounts, pensions, and insurances.

In being privy to their personal and private financial matters, I'd had to methodically search through all the yellowed copies of paperwork pertaining to my father's previous position at the port in Hong Kong. I remember how I'd held my breath and my heart had fluttered when I'd found an old document that looked like a deed and mentioned the house on Stubbs Road in Happy Valley. The house that my mother had named *Shangri-La*.

The meaning of which is attached to a book called *Lost Horizon* written by a British author called James Hilton. My mother was apparently reading this book when they first arrived and when she saw the property she was inspired to name her new home after a description in the book of '*a harmonious and mystical valley in a faraway and happy land*'.

But the old document wasn't a deed. It was actually just my father's original employment contract. It stipulated his working responsibilities and a generous remuneration package – including the provision of a house – which reflected the grandness of my father's position and high standing as General Manager of The Maritime Port, Hong Kong.

It came as rather a blow to me to realise that they'd never actually owned the house. Not that they'd ever misled me or indicated they had. I suppose I'd just presumed. I suppose I've always fantasised about there being a deed.

In my child's mind the house had always looked like a castle in a fairy tale book. A grand old colonial relic three stories high with a pink stucco exterior. And all my life, I'd dreamed of going back there someday and living in that beautiful house and having a different yet totally parallel lifestyle to my own. A life in which I wasn't a boring banker working nine to five in a stuffy old bank in this incessantly damp corner of the UK. But instead, one in which I might work as a curator in a museum or as a collector of art for a gallery or first-edition books for a gorgeous old library in Hong Kong. A life in which I'd socialise in sophisticated company down at the marina, eat dim sum for lunch in the harbour and shop in the traditional Ladies' Market on Kowloon Island.

Conversely, my sister Pia has no history with or connection to Hong Kong at all because we'd moved back to the UK while Mum was pregnant with her.

So, perhaps understandably, she doesn't get my fascination with the pearl of the Orient.

Pia also has a husband and two children to keep her busy and her thoughts fully occupied.

I'm very much in awe of my sister's skills as a home-maker and mother and I do love my nieces. Although I have to admit, I've honestly never felt any maternal yearnings to have any children of my own. I suppose it's a good thing now because that ship has long sailed.

All I can say is that I have no regrets. I'm quite sure I'm much better at being a doting aunt than a loving mother.

Concerning our parents' effects, my sister was appointed keeper of all things personal and sentimental. Mostly, it was things like old photos and memorabilia. Aside from the family photo albums, there was a beautiful and decorative lacquered box that I expect our mum must have bought in Asia. It contained her jewellery and personal things like birth and marriage certificates, and it was in this box that Pia had found the old photo of the house with the address written on the back.

A Polaroid photo that had provided precious evidence to back up my errant recollections.

I thought Pia's idea to try and find the house when I was in Hong Kong was a great one.

'Yes. Wouldn't it be absolutely fabulous if it was still there?' I agreed, giving her a hug.

Jon had been old school. He was adept at using a laptop and a smartphone, but he hadn't quite committed himself to going entirely paperless. Hence the wallet stuffed with notes.

I'm now so grateful that he still liked to print things out methodically and file them in order.

He'd not just put together a travel itinerary. To me, it felt like he'd given me some hope and some encouragement and that he was providing me with his guidance from the grave. He'd created a memory file of things to do and places to go and even people to investigate back in all his old haunts.

And I still want to experience all these things.

'Only, it's not a honeymoon anymore.' I said to Pia with great determination. 'It's a pilgrimage in Jon's memory.'

Chapter 7

The Moksha Ashram, Rishikesh

After spending the rest of the morning in my small room contemplating leaving the ashram early and heading back to Delhi, I hear my stomach groan and I realise I'm still hungry, as I'd hardly benefitted from my breakfast. I wondered what might be on offer for our vegan lunch.

In anticipation of finding a meal plan or a menu, I cast my eyes over *The Schedule* and *The Rules* once again. I thought about the noble silence and how much I'd really wanted to say hello to everyone I'd met this morning in the *shala* and at breakfast in the hope of making a friend. To me, it seemed rude to sit to eat with people and not acknowledge them.

Neither is it conducive to fostering new friendships.

I'm suddenly feeling lonely. I feel so distant from everything and I'm missing my friends from back home. The last time I'd logged onto the internet I'd had an avalanche of messages and texts from my friends. Long emails from work colleagues offering their condolences. Sympathies from the girls I sing with in the rock choir.

I haven't actually seen any of them since the afternoon of my leaving party at the bank or since I dropped out of the choir a couple of months ago because I was too busy packing up my house and planning my wedding. I appreciate all the kind words and all the offers of help.

But what can anyone do?

I want to send a message to Pia but I can't get an internet connection in my room. I suppose I'll just have to wait until after lunchtime to make some new friends here.

Just at that moment, a bell rings so incredibly loudly that I leap up from my bed.

I immediately cover my ears with my hands against the racket of ear-splitting decibels.

Have I somehow over-charged my phone and set my alarm to full volume?

I grab my phone and disconnect it from its charger but quickly realise this terrible racket is coming from a loud speaker in the hallway on the other side of my bedroom door. In my confusion, I decide it must be the fire alarm.

Oh my goodness! The place is on fire! I need to get out!

I flee from my room to run screeching like a banshee down the stairs, along the corridor, and across the terrace in an absolute panic, to join everyone at what I consider to be the muster station, except I find myself in the middle of the dining room. I skid to a halt (stubbing my toe painfully on a wooden table leg) and realise that no one else seems to be even remotely alarmed by the bell from hell. 'There's a fire! Where's the fire?' I yell at them all breathlessly.

Then, as the awful ringing stopped, everyone calmly sits down.

'It's okay. It's just the lunch bell.' I was told in a whisper by a woman opposite me.

Then the kitchen door flies open to waft the smell of warm curry spices across the room and two kitchen assistants appear carrying trays of food and baskets of flatbreads. Lunch is served to us on a banana leaf rather than plates and it's a portion of dahl curry and sliced raw carrot.

Just before we all tuck in, someone at the top of the table produces a small hand-held bell and rings it. Everyone lowers their heads in a moment of silent grace. I find myself silently seething and wondering what it is with all the damned ringing bells around here?

With prayers over, everyone begins to use their bread to mop up the spicy dahl lentils.

I do the same and have to admit that the meal actually tastes really delicious. I do enjoy a good curry and for me the hotter it is the better I like it. At an Indian restaurant, I will invariably choose a vindaloo over a korma any day. However, after my hungry enthusiasm, my mouth is burning like a furnace. Thankfully, there's a big jug of drinking water on the table to quench my thirst. I gulp down two large glasses but then feel my stomach starting to feel a bit grouchy.

When everyone has finished eating, the little bell is tinkled again. This time, it signals not only the end of the meal but also – thankfully – the morning sentence of imposed silence. The woman sitting opposite me, who had bravely broken protocol earlier to explain to me about the sounding of the lunch bell, leaned forward to introduce herself.

'Hi, I'm Belle. Welcome to the ashram. What's your name, honey?'

'I'm Maya. It's nice to meet you, Belle.' I say, thinking how ironic it is that her name is Belle, when I can still hear that lunch-time alarm bell ringing in my ears like extreme tinnitus.

Belle, I'm guessing, is likely to be the closest person here to my own age. She looks to be in her forties. She has dark eyes, a friendly face, short black spikey hair and a nasally sounding American accent. She's wearing a colourful kaftan and lots of jangly bangles on her wrists and I notice that she also has pretty henna tattoos on both her palms.

'Maya, I've been here for a couple of days. I hope you don't mind me offering you advice?'

'Please do. I'll be incredibly happy to hear it,' I assure her, curious about her words of wisdom.

'For dinner tonight, you should ask for oat porridge instead of the curry. The one thing I wish I'd known when

I first arrived here is to take it slow and easy with the spices. You can trust me on this one. You'll thank me later.'

I nod and thank her just as a sharp breath-taking cramp hits me square in the belly.

I excuse myself to dash back upstairs. In a cold sweat, I pray I'll make it to the latrine in time. I lock myself in the bathroom and squat over the hole in the ground until I can't feel my legs anymore. And, when the awful Rishikesh Runs seem to have stopped, I want to either cry or swear or both because I realise there is no toilet paper available.

Instead, there's a hosepipe with a hand triggered shower head fixed onto the end of it. This, I assume, is the famous Indian *bum gun* that I'd heard people joke about.

Once back in my room, I lay on my bed tucked up in the foetal position, groaning.

I'm really upset and disappointed to miss the mid-afternoon walk and meditation session on the riverbank. But right now, I have no choice but to stay here on my bed until I'm feeling better again. And I really should take Belle's advice to eat porridge as right now every part of me feels like it's on fire. I also realise that despite not wanting to miss out on anything, I'm completely and utterly exhausted. I've been living on anxiety and adrenalin since Jon died and I only manage to snatch a few hours of sleep at a time as my mind won't let me rest. I'm constantly going over the events of the past week and how all that has led me to India.

Once again, I'm asking myself what on earth I ever hoped to achieve by coming here and how did I ever think it might help? Clearly, ashram life is not for me. What was I thinking?

Pia's right. I hate all this introspective self-care stuff. I've never meditated before in my life. I've never done any devotional chanting and bell ringing and in-depth soul-searching. To me, well, it all sounds a bit crazy. But I'm not crazy. I think I'm just lost. Lost and very lonely.

I still think I should leave here first thing in the morning. I should head back to Delhi and bring forward my flight to Hong Kong.

I'm suddenly longing to be somewhere comfortable and comforting. I want some privacy and to be in a place where self-care comes in a bottle with a cork. Somewhere without any compulsory bell ringing sessions and a restricted diet. I want to be at the five-star hotel that Jon booked for us. It's apparently the oldest hotel in the city – 'An icon of hospitality and legend'.

Before leaving home, I looked up the website and marvelled at the images of the harbour-view honeymoon suite and gasped at the price on the booking receipt. Forgive me, but right now, I feel I need to wallow in that kind of luxury. Surely it will be a damn sight easier for me to feel sorry for myself in a place with a double size bathtub and a ginormous bed with sky-high thread count sheets and rich linens. While considering all this I must have succumbed to my total exhaustion, because the next thing

I know, I'm being woken by that damned alarm bell outside my room again. And, confusingly, it's pitch black. I flick on the light and check the time on my phone with heavy and bleary eyes. *Oh, my goodness. It's four-thirty in the morning!*

And, I will admit, a loud swear word slipped straight out of my mouth.

Even though I knew I was meant to be observing silence again.

In a panic, I grabbed randomly at some clothes from my backpack – I still hadn't unpacked – and I slid into them before joining what looked to me like the zombie apocalypse walking down the stairs and across the yard into the *shala*. Once there, I sat at the back of the room but soon realised there was a really cold, stiff breeze blowing down from the Himalayan mountains and through the ashram this morning. I'm soon shivering. My teeth are chattering.

I wished I'd grabbed something warmer to wear than a pair of thin leggings and a t-shirt.

Everyone else seems much better prepared. Most have a blanket or a shawl or a pashmina wrapped around their shoulders. I see Belle sitting just a few feet away from me. As the mantra chanting starts up, she looks my way, sees me shivering, and generously passes her shawl over to me. I feel bad taking it, but I see she's also wearing a fleecy jumper and pantaloons. I gratefully accept her kindness. Then I sit up tall so I can observe our holy guru, who is sitting at the top of the *shala*, surrounded by the warm glow of candles and wearing a heavy and colourful blanket draped over his white robes.

He's just started making the most incredible sounds from his throat.

The sounds quickly gather momentum and reverberate towards me like the wave of a great tsunami.

Om Namah Shivaya Om Namah Shivaya Hara Hara Bole Namah Shivaya!

His chanting sweeps over me and then everyone joins in with great verbal enthusiasm.

Rameshwara Shiva Rameshwara Hara Hara Bole Namah Shivaya!

This all seems a bit too much too early for me. I normally like a quiet start to my day.

But then I'm probably just feeling grumpy because there's no coffee.

I'm a creature of habit and my normal routine is to rise at 7am and drink three cups of coffee before starting work at nine and then taking another coffee-fuelled break mid-morning.

Om Namah Shivaya Hara Hara Bole Namah Shivaya Ommmmmm!

I try my best to join in with the chanting and to learn the strange words.

I'm well versed in song and can belt out a tune but to me this sounds something like a monotone rap with Hindu lyrics.

Ganga Dhara Shiva Ganga Dhara Hara Hara Bole Namah Shivaya

Jatadhara Shiva Jatadhara Hara Hara Bole Namah Shivaya

Then I suddenly hear Belle's voice. It's an octave higher than all those around me.

I suddenly want to giggle because I realise she's not chanting the words of the mantra at all. She's sing-chanting a covert conversation with me to the monotone tune of it all.

'Hey, how you feelin' this morning, Maya?'

I sing chant back to her. 'I'm better. Thanks for the shawl. It's really cold in here.'

Someshwara Shiva Someshwara Hara Hara Bole Namah Shivaya

Vishweshvara Shiva Vishweshvara Hara Hara Bole Namah Shivaya

'Hey, you wanna get out of karmic cleansing this morning?'

Koteshwara Shiva Koteshwara Hara Hara Bole Namah Shivaya

'Yes. But how?'

Mahakaleshvara Hara Hara Bole Namah Shivaya.

Everyone else seems so committed that they are oblivious to our rap-chat rebellion.

And I seem to have found a friend. Or is she perhaps a partner in crime?

A fellow flouter of the compulsory session rules?

* * *

After the hour of chanting comes the seemingly endless loud bell ringing.

Then, with the air cleared of chanting but my ears still tolling, we sit through an hour of meditation. I huddle under Belle's warm shawl trying extremely hard to 'be aware', to 'do it', to 'clear my mind' and to 'let it all go' while 'breathing' but also suffering a pounding headache. No doubt owing to the incessant bells or coffee deprivation ... or perhaps both.

Just before the meditation session comes to an end, while everyone else is in their deep oblivion with eyes closed, Belle and I surreptitiously sneak out of the *shala* together and hide behind a wall at the back of the kitchen building. Belle lights up a cigarette. 'You want one?'

I'm shocked. Smoking isn't allowed. But then neither is skipping out on a class.

And here is someone boldly prepared to break both rules at once.

'No, thanks. But do you know where we could get a cup of coffee?'

As it happens, she does, so in the shadows of the early morning half-light, we run like thieves along the line of bushes in the driveway and make sure to keep our heads down and remain out of sight. My heart is pounding with nerves and excitement. I don't think I've ever done anything this daring before. Even at school, I was never one to smoke behind the bike sheds or be one of the cool kids who played truant on a Friday afternoon instead of suffering hockey.

We make our escape through the gate and head into town.

On the main street, we find a vender selling hot chai but with a drum of contraband coffee hidden under his stall. Coffee for which we were prepared to pay a crazy number of rupees.

Then Belle and I sit together side by side on a low wall where we can watch what is going on down at the river while we sip our strong and delicious coffees as the sun comes up on this new day, casting its bright golden light onto us and everyone here.

There are lots of people already on the sandbank, where dogs and goats and cows rummage around in the rotting rubbish that has washed up and lies strewn along the water's edge. Despite this, many other people – notably students and devotees from many of the ashrams along the river in this part of Rishikesh – were sitting on the wet sand or perched on the rocks meditating. Some were enthusiastically doing salutations to the rising sun.

Men of all ages are wading into the river wearing only their underpants.

Women walking along the sandbank wear beautiful silk saris with flower garlands around their necks.

I relish the scene in front of me and enjoy the rising sun and the coffee warming me up.

Jon had enthused to me about bathing in the holy waters of the Ganges at sunrise.

I remember him telling me how he'd immersed himself

in the river every single day during his time here to benefit from the water's magical healing properties on the mind and the body and the soul. He said that pilgrims came here in their multitudes from all over the world to wash away their sins and to receive enlightenment and *moksha,* which is the Hindu word for the circle of life and death and rebirth. He told me that he had really believed, just like the pilgrims and the worshipers here, that the water in the river had a special life-affirming energy force.

He said it must permeate from the faith of the people.

He told me it had helped him come to terms with his friend's tragic death.

I remind myself that I wanted to come here to deal with Jon's death. That I too wanted to wash away my grief and my anger and my loss, and whether I believed in those mystical properties or not didn't matter because this was about Jon and not me.

'I think I should go down there and bathe in the river too,' I mention to Belle.

She spurts out her coffee. 'What? You're jokin', right? You do know that bathin' in the Ganges is like swimmin' in a soup of human excrement and all the grey powdery remains from the funeral pyres further up the river? You only have to look to see what's floatin' past!'

I'm surprised at Belle's condemnation, but I fear she's right. Now that she's mentioned it, the river does look awfully dirty.

There's a lot of trash and debris and plastic bags and

bottles and what looks like decomposing animal carcasses floating in the murky water. We sit and watch a baptism taking place in the shallows and someone fishing with a small net and then we observe a large group of people with sticks and wood who are building a bonfire on the water's edge.

I realise that the bonfire is actually a funeral pyre.

'The poor often can't afford to buy enough funeral wood, so it's not unusual for their dead relatives to end up half-cremated and floatin' down the river too. Yet some people still think it's okay to bathe in it and even to drink it!' Belle explains to me with stone-cold cynicism.

We finish drinking our coffee while watching a herd of buffalo wading into the river to stand half submerged, pooping profusely, in the muddy shallows while right beside them another baptism is taking place and a human body – wrapped up tightly in a white sheet – is placed on top of the bonfire like a Guy Fawkes. I also notice, against the vividly green water, large oily patches of bright red and orange are floating on the surface and I wonder aloud about it.

'Oh, that's toxic dye dumped in the river from the nearby sari factory,' Belle notes harshly.

Suffice to say, I've completely changed my mind now about bathing in these holy waters, even though I wanted to follow faithfully all of Jon's itinerary. But, maybe when Jon was here in 1979 it was very different and the river was much cleaner than it is today?

I must admit that looking around me I'm suffering from culture shock.

The way of living and the extent of the poverty here is making me both queasy and nervous.

India is a country that I can feel but it's also a country I can smell and taste.

I immediately have to remind myself that being pathetically untravelled and unworldly is simply no excuse for comparing what I see here with my own cossetted and comfortable western lifestyle. That what I observe as being different isn't necessarily wrong. I tell myself I've come here to nurture my spirituality and not my preconceptions and it feels wholly disrespectful to be judgemental while witnessing all this devotion and praying and bathing and yoga and meditation. In taking myself to task over this, I now feel horribly guilty about drinking the illicit coffee and conspiring with Belle in escaping this morning's karmic cleansing class. I can't help but wonder what has brought a woman like Belle to Rishikesh. What's her story?

I've quickly come to the realisation that everyone who comes here must be searching for something. Nobody in their right mind comes here just for a holiday.

But, now I have coffee and a friend, I decide to give India one more chance.

We head back to the ashram to arrive just in time for breakfast.

This morning, we are offered some kind of big steamed spicy vegetable dumpling.

On Belle's recommendation, I ask for a bowl of porridge instead, and after breakfast I feel a little more energised and ready to attend my first, much anticipated, real yoga session. Jon had always spoken about yoga like it was a superpower and how there was no better place to learn it than in India, because India was the actual birthplace of yoga. He was also adamant that only in an Indian ashram could you gain a true insight into the physical practice that embodies the philosophy behind authentic yoga teachings.

If you think that's a bit heavy, then I admit I thought so too.

But Jon had insisted that there are two types of yoga. One is physical exercise that is practiced in the west for strength and flexibility and then there's the 'real and authentic' yoga that's more of a spiritual experience and mindful medicine.

It's the latter I'm interested in.

I need to go from feeling mad to feeling mindful and I only have a week in which to do it.

I'm sitting on a yoga mat right at the back of the *shala* in a space next to Belle.

Our noble silence is being respectfully maintained once more and our teacher this morning is Willow again, the tall blonde-haired woman from yesterday whose long, slim legs are encased in a pair of billowing trousers and whose perfectly toned and enviously fat-free torso is on display in a cropped yoga top.

The sun is shining through the misty ambiance of the garden, casting beams of golden light across the *shala*. The air feels warmer now as we sit in a relaxed pose, inhaling the gently curling smoke from all the incense sticks and the sweet scent of jasmine being carried on the breeze. I'm really trying to get into the yogi mindset.

I focus on all the sounds around me from the wind-chimes tinkling on the porch, to the birdsong in the surrounding trees, the rapid-fire clicks from geckos, and the high-pitched shrieks of monkeys in the forest beyond, to the sound of people breathing on the mats all around me.

Then suddenly everyone's up on their feet, stretching and reaching up with their arms.

At least, lurking at the back here with Belle, I can benefit from watching and learning from her and from copying everyone else's seemingly effortless moves as the stretching becomes bending. Everyone folds their bodies forward to touch their toes. Heads and chins are tilted up and eyes are looking straight ahead at our yogi teacher. I feel stiff and unbending and completely awkward and I'm aware of shooting pains in my lower back, but I do my best.

I see the person directly in front of me is the tall blonde guy with the oaty-goatee beard.

He's removed the blanket from his shoulders now that the *shala* has warmed up and he's bare chested, wearing only a rather immodest pair of white silky shorts. His body is long, lean, and strong, and he moves like a ballet dancer. I watch him as he transitions gracefully from standing to bending. His loud breathing is starting to get revved up again as he folds his body.

His skin is pale and pink and already glistening with sweat.

I enjoy watching him until I see one of his testicles – also pale and pink and sweaty – hanging out of his shorts right in front of me. And, now I've seen it, I know I can never un-see it.

In alarm, I look sideways towards Belle, who is holding her pose with her eyes closed.

I do an urgent sounding little cough and her eyes pop open and suddenly she sees it too.

I really don't quite know how either of us managed to get through the rest of the morning.

Chapter 8

The Moksha Ashram, Rishikesh

Over the course of the next few days, Belle and I lurk at the back of the early morning classes together and continue to communicate using our mantra rap or by lip reading or using a type of Morse code that we've developed for ourselves using a series of finger taps on the inside of our freshly henna tattooed wrists. We also continue to sneak out of the *shala* using the guise of the pre-dawn darkness to aid our escape at the end of meditation, in order to indulge in contraband coffee and escape the dreaded karmic cleansing class.

We make sure to dodge scrotum man at mealtimes, who always sits with his legs apart and eats with his mouth open while breathing in and out like Darth Vader. We also avoid those in the ashram whom we both agree are a weird mix of strangely crazy and oddly introvert and those who never shower, probably because they prefer to bathe every day in the holy but dirty river instead, to their smelly detriment.

Belle and I seem to have the same innate temperament and dry, cynical sense of humour, as well as a freshly developed disapproving attitude, that we both blame on coffee and alcohol deprivation. We had bonded like transatlantic sisters over the various aspects of the ashram that either bored us or frustrated us. Neither of us could admit to actually achieving a state of mindful meditation no matter how hard we tried or pretended. And we'd both quickly developed a waning interest in bell ringing, chanting mantras, and karmic cleansing, while gaining an increased aptitude for anarchy and rebellion.

We colluded with each other after lights out too, even though this was of course breaking yet another ashram rule. Belle would slide out of her dorm and sneakily tiptoe down the corridor to my room where we'd sit together on my bed discussing our disenchantment with the world, while drinking vodka disguised with orange juice and eating milk chocolate biscuits.

Belle had managed to get hold of the contraband alcohol while I was busy attending an optional afternoon *hatha* yoga class. Like everyone else, I had been under the mistaken impression that she'd developed a quirky interest in making natural soaps and perfumed candles in the ashram workshop. But, as it turned out, this was just a clever ruse to sweeten her way into helping sell the hand-crafted produce on the ashram stall at the market. She'd heard that a tribe of local raconteurs were selling supplies of bootleg booze and cigarettes from underneath stalls of hippie clothing and incense sticks at the market, and all she'd needed was a way to infiltrate their trusted ranks to get hold of the vodka.

Whenever I admitted to my feelings of guilt over breaking the 'noble rules' of the ashram, Belle came straight back at me with so many reasons of justification. She insisted that everyone was 'at it' as she'd seen evidence of illicit egg eating by the supposedly strictly vegan kitchen staff. She said she'd watched them secretly burying the eggshells in the ashram garden.

She also told me that she'd seen one of the most highly revered yogis – said to be so practiced that he was able to control his own heartbeat in meditation and regulate his body temperature – smoking a Marlboro and swigging from a bottle of Officer's Choice behind the ashram kitchen. She said she'd even seen Guru J checking his phone and texting. I don't know which of these exposés shocked me the most.

But I think it's perhaps that Guru J must know the ashram Wi-Fi code.

So, if anything, meeting and spending time with my new anarchist and rebel friend Belle, had only encouraged my own personal rebellion and reinforced my errant thoughts about there being absolutely no reward in keeping to the rules and regulations, either in life in general or here in the ashram.

Once again, I was questioning the whole point of me being here, especially on Belle's last day when she said she was planning to take the train back to Delhi. I was seriously considering leaving with her even though I still had two more days left.

As we had done over the past five mornings, Belle and I escape the ashram just before the end of meditation to facilitate our illicit coffee drinking and once again, we sit on the low wall overlooking the early morning action on the riverbank. Having arrived by bus I'd been planning to take the train back to Delhi when I left here to honour Jon's Post-it note that said, *Take the train to Rishikesh from Delhi*. I didn't think it would matter if I did the journey in reverse as long as I actually did it.

And, it might be nicer and feel a whole lot safer if I was travelling back to the city with someone I knew. But what was holding me back was the fact that I still had some unfinished business here in Rishikesh. And I knew that two of those things – Chakra Healing and Cosmic Ordering – were on Post-it notes and included in my schedule over the next two days. Although I wasn't quite sure what The Ceremony of Light was about, it was written on a Post-it note too.

So, although part of me really wants to leave here with Belle, another part of me insists I must stay to follow the instructions on Jon's notes. Although, right now, I'm still holding off on the one about bathing in the dubiously cleansing holy waters of The Ganges.

Belle kindly advises me on train travel and personal safety for when I head back to Delhi.

'Buy your ticket in advance. Swami Nanda can help you with that and, when you are on the train, make sure you sit with a family group or next to another woman. Avoid men. Don't look at them and absolutely don't speak to them. Don't be polite. Don't be nervous. Be cautious. Be confident. Be assertive. Wear your Indian clothes so you fit in and that way you won't be a moving target for beggars and touts and, for goodness' sakes, make sure your phone is charged.'

I stare at her in horror. I'd managed to do the exact opposite of all those things on my way here and yet somehow I'd still survived. After spending these few days with Belle, I now suspect that despite her air of worldliness and her ballsy confidence, she's actually more angry, anxious, scared and sceptical about the world than I am.

'Okay. So, what's next for you? What will you do back in New York?' I ask her.

She sighs and shakes her head as if the weight of the world is suddenly on her shoulders.

'I need to find a new apartment as well as a way to pay for it. It's gonna be tough.'

'What happened to your place and your job?' I ask her, feeling great sympathy. I too would be homeless and professionally adrift when I returned to the UK.

She gives me an eye roll. 'I was living with someone but we broke up. I needed to get as far away as possible and, as I couldn't afford a ticket to Australia, I came to India instead.'

'Oh, Belle. I'm sorry. Do you want to talk about it? Would it help?'

She's silent for a while as she considers the option of a friendly shoulder.

But her stony-faced reticence and her firmly gritted jaw also make me think I might have over-stepped the line here in even mentioning her past traumas back in New York City.

Until this very moment, Belle and I had discussed almost every topic under the sun, except for anything remotely personal about what might have happened in our lives outside India.

All week, it had been an unspoken rule to avoid addressing anything in any way private. Clearly neither of us had wanted to broach the subjects.

I'd found it refreshing. To me, it meant we could just be who we are rather than being defined by our previous careers or our pasts. I'm sure Belle felt the same.

Except that now, on our last day together, I'm really curious to know more about her. Belle seemed to me an intensely complicated, and also a rather belligerent person, a bit like an active volcano: simmering just now but highly likely to violently erupt at any time. I suppose I want to understand why that is. And, now that I'd asked the question, with her frown and resulting silence, I think she might be wishing I hadn't.

'Okay. I'm gonna tell you. I trust you're not the kind to judge me.'

I was shocked. 'Judge you? No way. Never. You can trust me on that one, Belle.'

'Well, back in New York, I was about to get married. But it turns out, my guy was livin' a double life. An' with Lord Shiva as my witness, I had no idea. No freakin' clue. We'd even been living together. But the cheatin' bigamist bastard had a wife and a kid on the other side of town. I only found out when his wife turned up on our wedding day.'

'Oh, Belle. That is awful!' I really didn't know what else to say.

Belle lit a cigarette and took a long slow drag of it. 'I was so freakin' mad. I ended up falling out with my family over it. I lost my job over it. Then I went crazy and burned up his precious car with all his stuff in it and then, well, I left town. I had to get away. Far ... far ... away.'

'I'm sure your family must realise now that you didn't know, and this isn't your fault?'

I didn't like to ask if she expected to be arrested for arson the minute she got back.

She shrugs. 'I guess there's no goin' back. I'm just gonna accept it and move on. I gotta try an' make a new life for myself. I suppose I came to India lookin' for a way to feel better about myself and to stop feelin' cheated an' so damned angry all the time.'

'And do you feel better about yourself?' I ask her.

She shrugs again and pulls a face. I see she has tears in her eyes.

I realise I'm shivering – the heat of the day has sunk through me and through the stone wall we're sitting on – and I'm struck with the realisation that Belle and I actually have much more in common than I'd first thought. We're both backpacking brides.

Only, I don't know which is worse – her story or my own.

One thing I do know is that Belle's response to what had happened to her on her wedding day – the feelings of intense anger and the resulting bitterness – were probably, in the end, going to be far more destructive to her wellbeing than the awful event itself.

Looking at Belle right now was like looking into a mirror and seeing myself.

I decide then and there that I don't want to continue to be so angry and bitter and cynical.

'Maya, I'm still strugglin'. It's gonna take more than ringin' a few bells and chantin' a few mantras to fix me. But you've been a great friend this week. It's been fun. I'm glad we met.'

'Me too. Without your friendship, Belle, I don't think I'd have lasted this long. I want you to know you're not alone. I came here angry too. I was hoping for some peace to heal my pain. But the day starts before dawn with what sounds like a fire drill. Then I sit for an hour on a cold floor, feeling grumpy until I get my morning coffee.' I laughed but it sounds hollow.

'Can I ask you something, Maya?'

'Sure. Ask me anything.' She'd opened up to me and I feel I owe her the same.

'You're a bit of a dark horse. You don't really strike me as the kind of person who doesn't have her shit together. So I can't help but wonder why you would choose to come all the way out here to stay for a week in an ashram in India when you could have just taken yourself off to a health spa in Switzerland or something else instead?'

I stare at her for a moment while I consider both the question and the answer.

Belle alternates her glance and curiously raised eyebrows between my face and the diamond ring on my finger. 'I'm thinkin' it's gotta have something to do with that rock on your hand?'

I twist my ring around and nod. 'I needed to find a way to accept my fiancé's death. He died on our wedding day. I thought the ashram and the holy river and being in India would help me feel close to him. Close enough that I'd feel able to say goodbye and let him go. But I've failed. I'm still incredibly lost and so unbelievably angry about losing him.'

'Oh Lord. I'm sorry, Maya. If you ask me, anger is a kind of madness and feeling lost makes you kinda bitter about everything. I do hope you manage to find your way.'

It's my turn to shrug. 'I guess we've both proved that ashram life isn't a fix for everyone.'

'Anyway ...' she says, attempting to lighten the conversation while lighting up another cigarette. 'I've decided, I'm gonna take a yoga teacher training course back in New York City. I'm gonna make a fresh start. Open my own *shala*.'

I tell her it sounds like a great plan and I wish her well. 'I won't say good luck because I don't believe in it. I believe we make our own.'

Belle is a talented yogi, yet I couldn't help but think that with her attitude and fortitude, she might do better starting up her own martial arts club or a karate dojo. Not that I would ever have been bold enough to suggest it to her when her Warrior Pose was undoubtedly the very best in the *shala*.

'I really hate saying goodbye ...' she tells me. 'So Maya, if you don't mind, I'm gonna slip away this afternoon and I'm just gonna say namaste. It seems more appropriate.'

'Sure. We can always keep in touch on Facebook or Instagram. Namaste, Belle.'

We hug each other.

I've decided I'm going to give myself the benefit of my last two days here at the ashram. And maybe I can at least try to follow a few of the rules during that time ...

Maybe I could genuinely benefit from a course in

Chakra Healing and Cosmic Ordering and perhaps even find The Ceremony of Light that was mentioned in Jon's notes. I might not leave here unburdened of my grief or my anger, able to fully let Jon go and move on with my life, but I could at least honour him by ticking off the tasks on his precious Post-it notes.

Chapter 9

The Moksha Ashram, Rishikesh

That afternoon, our teacher for Chakra Healing is Swami Nanda. There are only seven of us in the class and we all sit on cushions around a central circle called a *mandala* that's decorated with fresh flowers and candles and small statues of Hindu deities.

The air is lightly perfumed with essential oils to inspire our *pranayama* – deep breathing.

Swami Nanda presses her palms together and bows her head.

'My soul honours your soul. I honour the place in you where the entire universe resides. I honour the light, love, truth, beauty, and peace within you, because it is also in me. In sharing these things, we are united, we are the same, we are one.'

Everyone replies saying 'namaste'.

And I realise and appreciate for the first time what the word 'namaste' actually means.

I'd just assumed it was a cover-all greeting, but her words truly resonate with me. They carry the most beautiful expression of human acknowledgment that I've ever heard. It brings an actual tear to my eye, as I reflect on how it perfectly encapsulates how I felt about Jon and me being soul mates. It also touches on my fear that I might never have the chance again to truly feel that way about another soul.

Consequentially, Swami Nanda has my complete attention as she goes on to explain to us all about the essence of Chakra Healing. She tells us that there are seven precious elements or *chakras* and that *chakra* is a Sanskrit word that means 'wheel'.

'The seven chakra wheels are perceived as whirling invisible energy portals between the mind and the body. They are located along the central line of a person from the base of the spine "root" to the top "crown" of the head.'

She draws our attention to a poster on the wall depicting an outline of someone sitting in lotus position with seven circled areas aligned along the spine to the head. The circles are around the tail bone, the groin, the diaphragm, the heart, the throat, the middle of the forehead and the very top of the head and each chakra has a Sanskrit name and a specific associated colour.

'Our first lesson in chakra healing is understanding that in the same way blocked arteries can affect our wellbeing, blocked energy channels — or *bandhas* — in our chakras can often lead to psychological or physical illnesses.' Swami Nanda explains.

Okay. I can imagine blocked arteries and blocked channels but whirling energy wheels?

'Blockages in our chakras can be caused by external forces and physical trauma such as injury, grievance, grief, pain, and discomfort. Imbalances can be caused by us holding onto emotional shock or disappointment, leading us to store up emotional toxins which accumulate to obstruct our energy life force or *prana*. This can lead to feelings of depression, anxiety, and lack of purpose and meaning in our lives.'

This certainly strikes a chord with me as I know how deeply I feel my grief over losing Jon.

I'm pretty sure that every single one of my chakras is blocked and imbalanced and broken. Perhaps it might be worth taking this seriously and exploring this weird science if it could help me? Swami Nanda explains how we can diagnose which of our chakras need healing and how we can clean and balance them with white light, certain crystals and meditation, but how a blocked chakra needs 'self-expression and chakra dancing' to release that blocked energy and allow it to once again flow through our bodies. A feeling of utter dread washes over me as I hazard a guess at what's coming next. Chakra dance was no doubt going to be a frantic posturing to some kind of absurd music.

'Through our dancing, our freed energy will be seen by

us through our *third eye* or what is called our *Ajna* as colours. This is where the old adage "showing your true colours" originates.'

When the music starts, it sounds like a jungle drumbeat.

Everyone stands and begins to shake themselves and move their bodies in what looks to me like a tribal frenzy. I feel terribly self-conscious because I'm not a particularly good dancer.

I prefer to sit still and listen to classical music rather than prance about to it.

Thinking back, the only dancing I've done in a long time was a slow sway with Jon at the end of a romantic evening in a restaurant where there'd been a live band. But soon, being the only one in the room *not* moving about to the banging beat feels even more awkward.

'Let us focus our minds on seeing an aura of colour through our own vibrations.'

I soon realise that no one is watching me because they all have their eyes closed.

So I start to shuffle my feet and sway my arms as the music becomes faster.

Keeping up with the beat becomes difficult. I stamp my feet and jump up and down.

My breathing gets faster until, thankfully, the music changes its beat to a sound more like a middle-eastern snake dance. Now I'm moving my body in undulating waves and I imagine I look a bit like Kate Bush performing a wilder version of her 1980s hit *Wuthering Heights*. After a few minutes, the music changes again and now it's fast and furious.

I'm panting and perspiring through the exertion but I'm really getting into it and actually starting to enjoy myself. This is great exercise. Imagine the calories I'm burning ... and it's fun!

To be honest, this is the most fun I've had in ages.

Then it all slows down once again and I'm reaching out my arms and swaying my body to the ethereal sound of flutes and harps and a slow, rhythmic drum. I'm twirling, whirling in circles, and with my eyes tightly closed I feel like I'm being lifted into a vortex of dancing bands of swirling colours. I'm suddenly feeling light-headed and quite emotional.

In my imagination I'm being wrapped up in spinning ribbons of emerald green.

I can only describe what I see through my mind's eye as something like an aurora borealis.

The music is vibrating with a humming hypnotic trance-style beat.

I'm pressing my palms together as if I'm praying and my body is swaying like a serpent.

The vibrant spinning bands of green appear to be flowing all around me. They are washing over me like a great tidal wave and, in the middle of this verdant kaleidoscope, I can see Jon and he's holding out his arms to me. I twirl and spin straight into his open arms and then we are spinning and twirling together in the dance of swirling greens. Are we amongst the Northern Lights? Are we bathing in the neon-green waters of the Ganges? Are we being brought together between life and death by Mother India?

Is this what *moksha* actually feels like?

When the music stops, I drop straight down onto the floor like a collapsed ragdoll.

I'm totally exhausted. I don't know why but I'm also sobbing my heart out. Tears are streaming down my face. What on earth has just happened to me? I'm in a state of utter shock.

And I realise this is the first time I've properly cried since Jon's death.

When I look around, I see it's not only me who is traumatised and upset.

Several others have collapsed onto the floor and are wailing and weeping too.

Swami Nanda rushes around trying to console us and offer us water to drink.

She explains how feeling incredibly emotional after performing a chakra dance is very common and entirely natural and that, contrary to how we might feel right now, this intense outpouring of emotions means that the dancing has helped us successfully connect with our chakra and see the true colours of our injured soul.

'Please don't feel upset or embarrassed. Embrace these powerful emotions!'

We close off the session in *savasana* – otherwise known

as *corpse pose* which simply allows you to lie on the floor wrapped in a soft blanket in a meditative or calming state.

Then, one by one, each of us in turn are invited to go and sit and speak with Swami Nanda.

She sits in her private corner of the *shala*, surrounded by lit candles and burning essential oils, and when it's my turn, I shuffle over to her while still a sniffling, weeping, emotional wreck. I know my eyes are puffy and bloodshot, brimming with tears.

It's as if now that I've started to cry I might never stop.

Swami Nanda immediately reaches out to me and puts her arms around me in a comforting hug. 'Oh, Maya, dear, dear girl. It's okay. It's perfectly all right to let it all out!'

I haven't been called a girl in a long time. But compared to Swami Nanda, I suppose I am.

As we sit together in a heavy cloud of patchouli, she gently coaxes me to speak about what I saw while I was dancing and to express to her my emotional experience, and convey what colours had been revealed to me when I danced. I find it difficult to find the coherent words to explain what seems to me to be unexplainable.

'When I was dancing, I saw my fiancé ...' I confess. 'Only, he d-d-died recently.'

She takes both my hands in hers and looks into my eyes with warmth and sincerity.

'He appeared to me in swirling shades of green. It was quite b-b-beautiful. He looked so r-r-real and it felt so v-v-very special. I miss him terribly. I w-w-want him b-b-back!'

And I weep and weep and weep like the whole world has suddenly ended.

'Oh, Maya, sweet Maya. Green is the colour of *Anahata* or the heart chakra. I feel your heart is broken. But, do not fear, my dear. Because if you allow it then I can help you.'

I try to smile through my tears to at least acknowledge her kindness.

'With respect to you, Swami Nanda, I fear there is no cure for a broken heart.'

She smiles and nods, her eyes shining brightly with kindness.

'But I can still help you with your pain,' she assures me gently. 'You see, Maya, when the heart chakra is broken it pains us greatly. We feel hurt and resentful and angry and betrayed.'

She's right about all of that because my broken heart aches mercilessly.

I do feel betrayed and the stress is making my chest feel so tight that it hurts to breathe.

'Yes. That's how I feel. Grief physically hurts.'

'Grief is both a positive and a negative energy. In its negative form, we tell ourselves we deserve to suffer in order to carry our burden of loss and so we constantly sabotage our own efforts to heal and move on. I can help you see the positive side of your grief. This will allow you to tap into your supressed feelings of being grateful for the love you have received and to feel once again the happiness of still being able to feel that love in your heart.'

She's right. My head is full of negative thoughts. But how can she rid me of that?

'Dearest Maya, your pain is born of fear. Do tell me, what is it that you fear the most?'

Sitting in this cosy golden snug, wrapped in Swami Nanda's love and surrounded by sweet scents and ageless Hindu statues depicting scenes of love and life and death, my fear suddenly feels very close and very clear to me, when up to this moment, it had been buried as deeply and as surely as my lost love.

'My greatest fear ... is of never knowing love again or being happy.'

There. I'd said it, and it was from a place of raw honesty and heartfelt truth.

It wasn't just Jon that had been taken away from me ... it was my love and my happiness.

'Maya, you have chosen the correct path in coming here for help and guidance, but I fear you got lost along the way. I can show you how to overcome these negative feelings that overwhelm you now, but you must trust me. Do you think you can do that?'

Everything about Swami Nanda tells me I should trust her with my broken heart.

She looks like a little Yoda and is a wise and kind old soul.

I wipe my tears away with the back of my hand. 'Okay. Yes. I can. Let's do it.'

'It's important to remember this next step is all about opening your heart and having faith.'

My heart is already broken open ... but faith? Oh dear, did she rightfully suspect that being faithless was my shortcoming? I would try. I would try my best to have faith.

'Maya, I want you to turn your third eye away from all negative energies. They are and have all week been trying to draw you away from us. You must choose to ignore negative. This is not hard to do because all energy – including all the energy within you – is always equally negative and positive. So you should consciously choose only to see and to acknowledge the good in the world and around you. Choose light over darkness. See beauty rather than ugliness.'

I nod my agreement. I came here to trust in *something* and so what do I have to lose?

'Come into the garden with me and together we will work on healing your *Anahata*.'

Along the way we walked together slowly down a steep sand covered pathway, Swami Nanda chatting to me constantly and asking me questions. Her voice sounds like a little chirruping bird in the ashram garden. I can see her face flushed with pleasure in her surroundings. 'Maya, look around you. Tell me what you see.'

All around were flowering shrubs and the sand pathway was free of weeds and tendrils. The garden here was very different from the one at the front of the ashram where the land had been left to nature. 'I can see flowers and this garden is well tended. Do you look after it yourself?'

'Yes. It's my greatest passion. Tell me, Maya, do you have a garden in England?'

I consider the small paved terrace at the back of the house that I've just sold. When I first bought the house, I was told that the terrace would be a wonderful place to sit in the summer, but in reality it never got any sunlight in any season and so was a dark, damp space instead. Then I think of all the houseplants I've neglected and killed over the years.

But then I realise I must take my thoughts consciously away from negative and only focus on the positive, as Swami Nanda instructed. So I think fondly of my mother's garden in Hong Kong and I remember how it felt to breathe in the sweet scent of her beautiful roses.

'When I was a child, my mother used to grow pink damask roses in our garden,' I say. 'I remember they were beautiful, and the scent was intoxicating. They're my favourite flowers.'

Swami Nanda looks at me with round eyes that crinkle in the corners in absolute delight.

'Maya, did you know that the damask rose is one of the oldest varieties and it is almost exclusively used these days to make rose essential oils? And that the complex perfume of the rose awakens our capacity to deal with emotional wounds? That is the reason rose oil is used to open the heart chakra. I think it's no coincidence you remember this particular rose today!'

I didn't know this and I'm suddenly in awe of the connection between the rose and my heart.

She explains how many of the plants here were grown for their unique and special properties. She pauses to point out the dark leaves of *Peet Bhringraj* – a plant that could be ground down to use as a black hair colourant. And *Indian Sorrel*, which is used in the kitchen to make mango chutney. She goes on to tell me how many of the plants here in the garden provide the ashram with Ayurvedic medicine. All around us there are trees and shrubs and vibrant flowers and wildlife. We stop to observe a bee buzzing on a sunflower. We watch a small purple sunbird with a long beak hovering at a lily trumpet. This part of the garden really is something of a hidden gem. It's warm and scented and sheltered by the sloping ground between the ashram and the riverbank. We pause to close our eyes and inhale sweet wafts of the breeze while we listen to birdsong.

It's a short but steep walk through the garden to the little *shala* at the end of the path. It looks to me like a little gazebo fashioned from bamboo and palm fronds, but it takes us a really long time to get there. We stroll so slowly, stopping often to look up into the tree canopy and admire the monkeys who are sitting on branches or hanging from vines. Some have tiny cute babies clinging onto them. And, just as we reach the *shala*, I realise what this slowest of walks is meant to represent. *Consciously choose only to see good things. Choose light not darkness. Look for beauty rather than ugliness.*

Inside the *shala* there is an altar or a *mandap* decorated with flowers and offerings.

There is also a statue of a beautiful Hindu Goddess.

Swami Nanda lights the candles. 'This is Parvati. She is the goddess of love, power and renewal. Parvati is the wife of one of the most worshipped of all Hindu Gods, Lord Shiva. We will call upon her today to help us and to guide you in opening up your heart chakra while we meditate together.'

I watch as she takes a small bowl and carefully pours rose essential oil into it while stirring it with a sprig of hawthorn. It looks like she's mixing a magic spell and I have no doubt that there are things going on here – in this supernatural setting – that are beyond my understanding.

She chooses some rocks from an ornate box laid at Parvati's feet. Rose quartz and green malachite and pink rhodonite. She lays them out on the *mandap*. Then she turns and gently lays a piece of green silk fabric over my shoulders. She anoints me with the rose oil and then we chant about opening my heart and feeling free and being forgiving of myself and others.

We practice slow yoga together focussing on *Urdhva Mukha Svanasana* or Upward Facing Dog and *Setu Bandha Sarvangasana* or Bridge Pose to open the *Anahata* heart chakra and to release pain and fear. Swami Nanda continues to chant with great emphasis on the Sanskrit words and I soon join in. The rhythmic sound we make together is exactly like the sound of a beating heart.

Lam vam ram, lam vam ram, lam vam yam.

I try hard to imagine my heart opening and divine energy whirling through my chakra.

I close my eyes and inhale the aroma of the sweet rose essence, focusing on the sound of distant bells ringing out from the many hundreds of ashrams along the river. Then I allow my thoughts to drift back to my mother's rose garden. I see myself sitting in sunshine on the immaculately clipped lawn and I watch her as she cuts roses for displaying inside the house.

The air is filled with their perfume. I breathe in and I breathe out again.

And, although I still feel a great depth of sadness within me, I also feel *something* else.

I feel lighter and uplifted somehow. I feel calmer. I feel much less fearful and far less angry.

But, in all honesty, despite her best efforts, my broken heart is still far from healed.

Swami Nanda makes us tea blended with hawthorn and lavender and infused in rose quartz.

We sip it hot from dainty china cups decorated with flower sprigs.

'Swami Nanda, how will I know when my heart chakra is fully healed?' I ask, knowing I'm leaving in twenty-four hours and it might help to have an indication of timescale.

But she gives me a riddle instead of an answer.

'When your kind heart is filled with love and you are feeling truly happy again, then you'll know the divine energies have healed you.'

I smile and thank her but in that same moment my heart is filled with disappointment.

How could my heart – kind or otherwise – ever be filled with love again?

It's impossible.

Chapter 10

The Moksha Ashram, Rishikesh

The next morning, after not skipping out on any mantra chanting, bell ringing, or meditation, and having cleansed my karma with warm salty water like a pro and then practiced real yoga, I attend a class run by Guru J on how to attract all the positive energies of the universe into our lives. This phenomenon is what is commonly called Cosmic Ordering.

I've been curious about this class all week; it was on one of Jon's notes, but it also came highly recommended by Swami Nanda. Also, not so long ago, I'd read an article about it in a glossy woman's magazine. It's apparently practiced by celebrities these days and many successful people credit cosmic ordering for all the luck and happiness and success in their lives. The article claimed that by just focussing hard and thinking only positive thoughts, you could attract positive energy (and Swami Nanda says it's everywhere) and use this energy to manifest abundance, or whatever you feel you need in your life, simply by ordering it up from the universe.

I imagine it works in the same way as when you order something from Amazon.

You simply decide that you want it. You order it. Magically, it arrives!

Imagine, the power of simply wanting and wishing and manifesting your desires! We'd all have our dreams coming true left right and centre. All our hearts' desires would materialise on demand in a puff of pink smoke.

I've tried this myself many times before and it hasn't worked.

As a little girl, I wished for a real pony. I wished so much it hurt.

But there was still no pony. Obviously, I'd been doing it all wrong.

Apparently, according to the magazine, you must absolutely believe it will happen for you.

And just having even one teeny-tiny cynical little doubt at the back of your head will effectively command a negative energy to cancel out your order. If all this has been covered by a glossy magazine and now I'm studying it in India, then maybe there's something to it?

But, I think, just like real yoga, this is something that can only be properly learned in a land of ancient magic and very mysterious ways.

And I'm pretty sure that Guru J – the man, the myth,

the legend – knows the secret to how it's really done. He's entirely likely to have taught this skill to The Beatles, who are reported to have left Rishikesh on a creative high and with dozens of new songs written while they were in the ashram and with the new *White Album* in the works. This went on to be the biggest selling Beatles recording ever securing twenty-four times the qualifier for a platinum sales award. That sounds like some amazing cosmic ordering to me. I'm excited and I'm far too desperate for doubts.

I've already decided I'm going to believe in this if it kills me.

To start off, we all sit in lotus position on cushions around the *mandala*.

Under Guru J's leadership we chant *Oooooooo- mmmmmmmmmm shanti shanti*.

Then our esteemed Guru takes some time to explain to us about this amazing phenomenon.

'There is a new conviction that is becoming a trend amongst people in the western world,' he tells us, sounding somewhat amused. 'Writing books and making TV shows to inform the population that with an opti- mistic mindset we can all manifest our hearts' desires. But, let me tell you, this is nothing new, because cosmic ordering has been used by people in India successfully for millennia.'

Guru J asks us to close our eyes and carefully choose our heart's deepest desire.

He tells us it should be something we feel we truly deserve to receive.

He also suggests it should be a noble desire, rather than a material object, as that always worked best. I realise me wishing for a pony hadn't been a noble enough goal.

'Peoples of the western world who are trying to manifest a new car, a new house, a better job or a million-dollar lottery win – and failing – are mistakenly trying to attract mere objects.'

Unlike when I was a child, I wholeheartedly believe that my heart's desire now is a noble one.

I don't need materialism. I simply want to find a way to live my life without Jon. That is my wish. My desire. I don't want to stop loving him. I don't want to forget him. I just need a way to accept he is gone and move on with my life without feeling so empty and sad all the time.

Right now, the thought of going back to the UK after this trip and starting a new life without him still seems impossible. To attract positive energy, I think about Jon's travel itinerary and how he's left me with a real legacy of spiritual adventure even though he's not physically here with me anymore.

Guru J rings a bell – I assume to clear the air in the *shala* of any negativity.

'With your cosmic wish in mind, thank the Divine and ask the universe to listen to you.'

I thank the Divine for the love that Jon and I shared and for his magical mystery tour.

'Visualise what you need,' Guru J tells us, his voice rising like a crescendo. 'Then for ask it!'

Afterwards, we are all given a small square of paper and a pen to write down what we've asked for.

Guru J explained that this small square of paper should be folded up and kept safely on our person until later this evening when we will all attend *Aarti* down on the river-bank at sundown.

I have no idea what this *Aarti* is or what exactly it entails and I just hope it doesn't involve anything remotely sacrificial. I'd seen evidence of burnt and smouldering offerings on the river bank this week and the smell was truly awful.

'If you believe wholeheartedly and in utmost faith that your request is both noble and justified then it will surely be granted. Leave the rest to cosmic order. But do not leave here with any divine doubts in your mind or your heart!'

I focus once again on Swami Nanda's wise words about only seeing the good and positive.

The desperate part of me is hopeful this will work.

After class, we all say *namaste* and bow to Guru J.

As everyone is making their way out of the *shala*, I tentatively approach my guru.

In my hand, I am clutching onto the photo from Jon's wallet that I'd brought along with me in anticipation of an audience today with the great man himself. He raises his bushy white eyebrows in surprise as I speak to him and press my palms together to bow to him.

'Namaste. Maya, it's a pleasure to meet you at last.'

I'm surprised he knows my name as I've had no real contact with him all week.

'I was wondering if you might remember a man called Jon Howard?' I point Jon out to him in the photograph. 'That's him in this photo from 1979.'

I also indicate the guru in the centre of the picture. 'And I think this might be you?'

He studies the photograph for a moment and then smiles before handing it back to me.

'I'm sorry. I don't remember a Jon Howard. And that's not me. It's my brother, Guru Juri.'

I'm disappointed, but the likeness between this guru and his guru brother was uncanny.

Curiously, he took another longer peek at the photo in my hand. 'Ah ... actually, this was taken in the old *Maharishi Mahesh Yogi Ashram*. It's just across the river from here but of course it's a ruin now. It's also known as The Beatles Ashram. You know, I met George Harrison. He stayed on longer than the others to study astral travelling under my brother's esteemed mentorship.'

'You mean to say that The Beatles didn't stay here at *our* ashram?' I exclaim in horror.

Guru J wobbled his head. 'No. But they did put the whole of Rishikesh on the map.'

I was not only disappointed but also disillusioned. If The Beatles hadn't stayed here in this ashram and this photograph had been taken elsewhere then maybe Jon hadn't stayed here either.

And to think, all this week, I'd been sitting in the *shala* trying hard to meditate while thinking that Guru J had been Jon's Guru and so we had a special connection. I'd also been walking around thinking I was walking in Jon's shadows and seeing the same sights in the same place as him. To find out he'd probably never even been here at all made everything I'd done this past week seem like a futile waste of my time and effort. Had Jon, while arranging our honeymoon, found his original ashram closed and been forced to choose somewhere else for us to stay at random or had he simply chosen this particular ashram for its special name – Moksha?

Because I remember Jon saying he'd experienced *moksha* while bathing in the holy river.

Guru J raises his hand and beckons me closer. 'Please, Maya, sit. Swami Nanda tells me you've recently made promising spiritual progress and that your heart chakra has responded well to healing. I'd hoped to have a talk with you today now that your wayward friend, Belle, has left us. I rather suspect that she's led you astray over this past week. Am I right?'

I sit, feeling guilty. Is it true? Had Belle led me astray?

Guru J seems entirely serious. I swallow hard while recalling all the illicit coffee and vodka and the playing of truant. I suddenly want to cry. I'd been caught red handed in breaking all the ashram rules. I felt truly terrible.

'You know, Maya, I don't believe we meet anyone by accident or coincidence. I believe that people come into our lives for one of two reasons.' He sticks two bony fingers in the air in front of me and counts on them. 'One. They need to learn something from us. Or, two, we need to learn something from them—'

'Oh my goodness. I'm sorry, Guru J. I've not been entirely respectful,' I interrupt.

He leans forward and takes a firm hold of both my hands. 'My question to you is this: who do you think has learned from whom this week?'

His hands are warm but his skin feels dry and paper thin, his bones fragile.

'Maya, you should know that speaking in anger is no way to speak to the Divine. They hear you and they sympathise; they want to help you. Swami Nanda is here and I am here to help you too. This is the reason we have met.'

Oh my goodness. How did he know that I'd spoken in anger to the Divine?

'And, as you're leaving tomorrow, I feel it's important you take part in *Aarti* tonight.'

'Yes. I do plan to attend the *Aarti*. Only, forgive me, but I'm not actually sure what it is?'

'It's an ancient and divine ceremony. It's also known as The Ceremony of Light.'

I gasp in relief. This was the last task on Jon's notes left to do in India!

Guru J continues to explain the ceremony. 'For thousands of years, people of all religions and walks of life have come to the Ganga to experience the power of *Aarti* because it treats afflictions of the heart. The light dispels darkness and the word *Aarti* means 'remover of pain'. Do you see how this can help you, Maya?'

'Yes, Guru J. Thank you. *Ommmmmm … shanti shanti!*'

I humbly back away and go back to my room to pick out something to wear for the *Aarti* and to pack up my backpack ready for leaving tomorrow. While doing so I can't help but reflect on my week and my experiences here at the Moksha Ashram.

What lessons had I learned here and what was it that I was taking away with me?

Faith? Belief? Spiritualism? Knowledge? Understanding?

I hear myself sigh with resignation because I'm still feeling doubtful and disillusioned.

There was no connection to Jon here. My heart chakra is still broken.

I now even have doubts and misgivings about cosmic ordering.

I heavily suspect my faith only existed here and when I leave I'll be no less absorbed by my grief than when I arrived. I've tried to open my mind. I've even given my doubts the benefit of the doubt this week. But, in truth, as much as I really want to believe, I still don't.

I can admit to feeling calmer now and less angry but I'm not entirely sure if I can credit Swami Nanda and her chakra healing crystals and rose oils or if it's because I've simply surrendered to my rage and just become exhausted by it all.

Maybe it's due to something tangible and practical like learning how to practice real yoga?

Perhaps only Belle can take the credit for helping me understand how futile anger can be. What was it she'd said about it ...?

Anger is a kind of madness ...

* * *

Just before sundown, I meet up with a group of others from the ashram who are also leaving tomorrow and together with Swami Nanda we all make our way down to the riverbank. We take a route through the beautiful garden that eventually leads down a steep pathway with lots of steps to a small area of beach. There are already lots of people waiting there. I will admit to feeling a little apprehensive as we move through the swathes of yoga students and pilgrims and the many worshipers, tourists and onlookers who have also arrived at the water's edge.

All around us are faces filled with love and devotion. There's a definite frisson of excitement and anticipation in the air and it's clear that all these people believe in the magical powers of this ceremony at the holy river. And, in being here, I feel like a terrible fraud.

I don't really deserve to be here amongst all this positive and divine energy when mine is distinctly negative and this whole event seems like nothing to me but a beautiful tourist attraction. But I'm doing my best to go along with it so as not to offend anyone on my last night.

I focus on enjoying seeing everyone happily gathered to chant and sing beneath the shadow of the enormous white statue of a handsome and serene-looking Hindu God sitting in lotus position. 'That's Lord Shiva,' Swami Nanda tells me proudly, as she sees me gazing wide-eyed in considerable awe at the white statue. As the last rays of daylight begin to disappear from the dark and undulating horizon, she urges me to look at the many hundreds, if not thousands, of lamps and fires being lit against the darkness, all the way along the riverbank.

Many of the lamps being held aloft are small and simple, but others are large and elaborate, with circular multi-tiered uplighters and blazing flames leaping into the air.

It isn't long before the air around us is thick with smoke and fumes.

Breathing in the heavy and intoxicating mix of vapours from the burning incense oils and all the paraffin wax seems to blur the lines between the real and surreal imagery of the ceremony.

It really is a spectacular sight. Holy men are gesticulating on their elaborately woven prayer mats and many hundreds of worshippers and pilgrims are wailing with devotion, chanting their mantras and clapping their hands to the songs and prayers being offered to the accompanying bells, gongs, and reverberating drums. I turn to look for Swami Nanda.

I see her standing amongst a group of people a couple of steps away.

She gestures to me and to the rest of our group to come and select one of the carefully handcrafted little boats that have been fashioned from a leaf by one of the many sellers here.

The sellers are also offering sprigs of flowers and candles to put inside the little boats.

Soon everyone, including myself, has bought their little boat and our offerings.

I watch everyone around me from our *shala* placing their pieces of folded up paper containing their divine wish into their little boats. Then I watch an old woman place a small photo of a young child into her boat along with a flower bud and a lit candle. She's crouching down, thigh deep in the holy river, weeping and singing quietly to herself as she sets down her miniature craft into the stream of current that will take it away and down the river.

Seeing all these tiny candle lights flickering and moving away on the dark rippling currents, while everyone looks on with such faith and devotion and hope, is incredibly beautiful.

The emotional symbolism of it – despite me being a hard-hearted cynic – does not escape me.

When it is my turn, Swami Nanda summoned me to the water's edge.

'We call this boat a *diya*,' she tells me gently. 'Inside it you will place all your heartfelt feelings of grief and loss and pain. The flower is your offering to the Divine. Your lit candle represents your Light of Truth. Your divine wish is your prayer.'

She gives me an encouraging smile and a bow of her head.

Standing waist deep in the dark and swirling waters of the Ganges, I set down my little boat.

I carefully light my candle with the lighter that Swami Nanda has produced for me.

'Maya, let go of this *diya*. Let it carry away all the pain from your heart so that you can live in peace and joy. Trust that you and your beloved will one day be reunited. That all love is eternal and can never die. Let it go now. Set down your *diya* into the flow of the holy river.'

I listen to Swami Nanda's sweet voice and her words. I hear the prayers all around me.

I set down my little boat onto the water and I watch through my tears as its flickering candle flame floats away from me to join thousands of other tiny lights on the river. I think about Jon and our love. I think about my painful feelings of loss and anger.

And I let them go.

Then suddenly, in the unblinking moment when I realise my *diya* is finally out of sight, I swear something strange and unworldly happens to me while I stand in the holy water, surrounded by these swathes of love and devotion and prayers and mantra chanting, something I cannot properly explain. I've being jolted by something.

Something so powerful that it fizzles through me like a shock wave. It makes me gasp.

It completely takes my breath away. It feel as powerful as the static electricity that zapped though me on that very first day when Jon and I met and shook hands in my office.

I can only describe it as some divine power connecting me to the river.

In that moment, I truly believe there is something more than life and death.

I begin to laugh and to feel what I can only describe as deep joy and incredible gratitude.

I realise how lucky I am to have known such a great love in my lifetime.

We'd only had a few short months together but when love is eternal it lasts forever.

I know without any doubt in my heart that I haven't lost Jon.

He's still with me because I carry him in my heart.

But now my heart feels light. I feel embraced and comforted.

Is this my divine connection? My Moksha? My *something?*

I do know that in that special moment I *feel* India all around me.

And I no longer see my sorrow as a terrible punishment, but as a very precious gift.

Chapter 11

The Rishikesh Express

Rishikesh railway station is on a quiet branch line and so travelling back to Delhi by train means first taking a much slower train to the bigger and much busier station at Haridwar Junction. When I arrive at Haridwar, despite the early hour, I can see it's already packed with passengers who are intent on cramming themselves into or onto the first train of the day. But, unlike my fearful impressions of last week, this week I can see some sort of order where once I only saw chaos. I can hear voices yelling words of greeting rather than spouting aggression and mayhem. Right now, my terrified inauguration into India feels like it was a lifetime ago.

The station building is attractive in its old colonial style and is painted brick red and bright white. The train, standing at platform three, with its boxy carriages and traditional livery, is the exact same one that I would have arrived on a week ago, had my original travel plans worked out. But this time, I already have my ticket in my hand, booked online thanks to Swami Nanda letting me have the Wi-Fi code. It had apparently always been available to anyone upon request because the rule about no internet only applies to the *shala* and not the entire ashram. It was a high-speed connection too.

And to think that on Belle's word alone I'd been paying a ridiculous amount of rupees in town to get online for just a few minutes on a connection so slow it only ever allowed me to fire off a quick email to my sister and never to get onto Facebook or Instagram to upload any of my photos. How very frustrating!

Swami Nanda advised me to avoid the very first train of the day to Delhi as it's the cheaper option and so understandably the choice of many. But it stops at every station en route and therefore the journey takes over eight hours.

I need to get from Rishikesh to Delhi in half that time as my flight to Hong Kong leaves tonight so I've paid just a few rupees more to take the Rishikesh express train, more affectionally known as the *Yoga Express,* that will depart in half an hour from platform nine.

I buy a cup of delicious hot chai and sit watching the latecomers arriving for the first train.

Some pour out from other trains screeching into other platforms. I see hawkers equipped with mobile kitchens clashing with passengers on the bridges, offering fragrant breakfast options of *momos* (steamed dumplings) and *dosas* (pancakes with a spicy filling) to those who are breakfasting on the go. Those who spill from trucks and tuk-tuks in the station carpark I see rushing straight into a general store on the opposite side of the street to stock up on essentials for their long journey. Then with their snacks and drinks hurriedly bought, they dash back across the street, dicing with death and traffic, dragging their luggage and often very small children, racing past all the roadside stalls selling flower garlands, trinkets, candles, and incense sticks, in through the station's main entrance doors, passing under an enormous statue of Lord Shiva, all while dodging several other garlanded statues and a life-sized effigy of an elephant, to join the jostling, colourful, and enthusiastic masses in the ticket line.

I consider how far I've come in such a short time and how much less intimidated I feel now in large crowds, on packed trains and around strangers, when just one week ago this would have all seemed impossible for me. If I believed in such things, I'd say it's a miracle.

Like a pro traveller I calmly regard the sights and sounds all around me.

When the first train departs, leaving the station with as many people holding on to it as are contained inside it, I take this as a cue to head to my platform before the next last-minute crush.

I join in with the surge and hold my breath against the pungent aromas of stale beer and cigarettes, and whatever everyone around me has eaten for breakfast this morning, as we all inch forward across the causeway. My backpack suddenly feels heavier on my shoulders, as I wane and ebb in the tide of people now walking at a snail's pace up the steps and across the pedestrian bridge. I feel someone behind me touching my hair, so I retaliate by turning to give them a glare, only to receive a delighted smile in return. Someone on my right side is elbowing me in the ribs but I stand my ground with gritty determination and discreetly check to make sure I still have my phone, cash and passport on me.

I see the station's clock showing only minutes to go before departure.

I finally break free and escape onto the platform, showing my ticket just as a shrill whistle pierces the air. I climb up the steps onto the train and into the carriage to find it's filling up fast with saffron-robed monks, migrant workers, local families, and backpackers like me.

I quickly scan the available seats and the faces of the passengers already seated. On Belle's advice I look for a safe seat amongst a family group or next to another woman and I immediately spot a young blonde-haired woman with an empty seat next to her.

I head there to place my backpack on the overhead shelf and slide quickly into the seat beside her. Scoring a seat close to a working ceiling fan suddenly feels like winning the lottery. The woman looks at me and gives me a friendly smile and so I introduce myself.

'Hi, I'm Maya,' I say and she tells me her name is Maddy.

I'm guessing from the distinct twang in her accent that, like Belle, she's also an American.

Maddy immediately spots the henna tattoo of a lotus flower I have on my wrist and she shows me she has a similar one. As the train starts moving out of the station, she keeps our conversation going by telling me that she's just spent a month in an ashram in Rishikesh (there are actually over a hundred ashrams in the town and all along the banks of the holy river) and she's now headed to Delhi for a couple of days' sightseeing before moving on to Agra to see the Taj Mahal and then on to Jaipur before heading south to the beaches of Goa.

'Ah ... so you're doing the Golden Triangle!' I'm impressed. She's probably in her mid-twenties and has the whole world in her hands.

'Yeah. I know they're the busiest and most visited cities in India, but I really want to go.'

'And why not? I'd love to go too. But, regrettably, my own itinerary doesn't allow for it.'

I ask Maddy how long she expects to be in Goa and where else she plans on travelling.

'I'm planning to do a yoga teacher training course while I'm in Goa. Then, I'm kinda hoping that teaching yoga will fund my travels for the rest of the year. I'm told there's lots of studios and holistic retreats needing qualified yogis throughout Asia, although I'd eventually like to end up in Australia, before heading back home. Then I'd have literally travelled the world.'

'Good for you. I wish I'd done a gap year when I was your age,' I tell her encouragingly.

To my surprise she suddenly turns away to look out of the window and from her reflection in the glass, I can see she's biting her lower lip to stop it trembling and looks to be fighting back tears.

Despite her confident chatter and her exciting plans, she suddenly seems overwhelmed.

I feel a great rush of empathy for this young woman because now she looks to be just as lost and lonely and scared as I was only a week ago. My heart aches for her and I'm reminded of the wise words of Guru J, who insisted we don't meet people by accident as they are meant to cross our path for a reason. That you need them to help you ... or they need you to help them.

Does Maddy need my help I wonder? How can I best help her?

'You know, they say there are two types of visitor to India,' I declare, to continue our chat.

She turns to me, trying to smile at what she anticipates to be a joke, but she's stifling back a sob. 'Is it the tourist and the traveller?' she suggests to me.

'No. It's those who are lost and those who are found,' I tell her empathetically.

'Yet not all who wander are lost ...' she countered, quoting Tolkien to me with her eyes shining through her tears. We laugh together. She's blinking rapidly to try to hide her embarrassment and then looks down at her clasped hands. I realise she's staring at the small sapphire ring on her finger and she's twisting it around and around anxiously.

Right now, I'm feeling hyper-sensitive to her resonating energies.

'So, Maya, tell me how long you expect to be travelling in India?'

'Oh, I'm not. I mean, I've been here for a week, but I'm leaving for Hong Kong tonight.'

'Oh, how fabulous. Hong Kong will be amazing! Are you there for business or pleasure?'

'I'm actually on my honeymoon.' I tell her with what I hope is an engaging smile.

She looks at me while wiping away an errant tear from her cheek.

Our conversation has stilted with confusion and so she turns away to look out of the window again. I pop in my earphones and decide to listen to the mantra I've downloaded.

I also want to rest a while and block out the multitude of voices and background noise on the train, so I can continue to train my thoughts on being mindful. But, instead, I'm thinking about this woman sitting next to me. Maddy seems so lost but what can I possibly do about that? How can I help? I run my fingers over my chakra bead bracelet in desperation.

* * *

After travelling for another hour, we get chatting again.

'Maya, I've just been thinking ...' she tells me. 'If your husband is travelling in another carriage, then let me swap seats with him. Then you can both sit together. I really don't mind.'

'Oh, that's very kind. But there's no need. You see, I'm on our honeymoon but alone.'

She looks at me with wide eyes and an open mouth. 'Oh, Maya. I'm so sorry to hear that!'

'Thank you. But to explain, my fiancé died a few weeks ago, just before we got married. And, as the honeymoon was all arranged, I decided that for better or worse, I should go on it anyway because it's what he would have wanted me to do. And, after being here in India, I've learned that I'm never really alone or without him because I'll always carry him in my heart.'

I press my palm to my chest and realise how far I've come in just one week.

Thousands of miles physically, light years emotionally. I almost feel euphoric.

'Oh, goodness. That's incredibly brave of you. I had noticed your beautiful diamond ring.'

'I can't bring myself to take it off,' I admit, 'But staying at the ashram has really helped me to come to terms with what happened and my feelings about losing him so very suddenly. What about you, Maddy? I couldn't help but notice that you too are wearing a ring.'

I indicate the diamond on the third finger of her left hand.

She exhales as if releasing stress and shakes her head as though trying to clear her thoughts.

'My fiancé ... well, he didn't die.'

I see her blush and struggle to find her words. 'Like you, Maya, I'm still trying to find the courage to take it off and it's not because I'm feeling especially sentimental but mostly because I'm not sure whether to throw it away, give it away, or sell it. I bet it's worth quite a bit.'

'Well, if it doesn't have sentimental value I'd sell it. It'll help fund your travels,' I told her.

'I'm kinda worried that if I sell it then I'd be inviting bad karma,' she explains.

I smile and nod and think it's very perceptive of her to think of the karma aspect.

'You could sell it and give the money to charity?' I offer as an alternative solution.

She smiles. 'Yeah, I like that idea. You know, Maya, until we got talking, I was feeling very alone. In the ashram, with all the silence and the quiet time for contemplation, it's been really tough making any real connections with other people. I've found it quite isolating.'

'I'm so glad you said that because I felt the same way,' I say with a laugh. 'I felt like the noble silence was akin to giving people the silent treatment. If you can't talk for most of the day then it's hardly conducive to making new friends!' I tell her how I'd met Belle and we'd communicated secretly and Maddy laughs and says she thinks it was all very ingenious.

I still feel it was more disingenuous and so I still feel terribly guilty.

Maddy takes out a bag of sweet Indian Petha candy and offers me one.

It was then I realise her issue was simply that she'd wanted to talk and had no one to listen.

'Maya, I hope you don't mind me saying this but I honestly thought I was dealing with the worst kind of wedding day tragedy ever. But now I feel yours is so much worse than mine.'

Perhaps feeling she hadn't phrased that comment sympathetically she quickly apologises.

'Oh ... my goodness. I'm sorry. That sounded terrible. I'm actually embarrassed right now.'

'It's okay. Really,' I assure her, deciding this might be the perfect moment to offer her my help. 'Look, Maddy. Would it help you to talk about what happened?'

She shrugs as if reluctant to share her story with a stranger, but her eyes say something different.

'Oh, Maya. Thank you but it's a very long story.'

'And we are on this train for a very long time so go ahead. I'm listening.'

'You're right, I would like to talk about it. I hope you don't mind me saying this, because I mean it as a compliment, but you remind me so much of my mom.'

'Come on. Tell me about him. What's his name? How did you meet him?'

Chapter 12

'His name is Theo and he is ... was ... the most amazing man I've ever met. And by amazing, I mean good-looking, smart, funny. He honestly rocked my world.' Maddy shook her head as if she couldn't quite believe how mistaken she'd been and then she shrugged her slim shoulders.

'And I fell for him big time. I mean, he literally knocked me off my feet when I bumped into him at my cousin's birthday party. And, all that corny cliché stuff about falling in love at first sight, well that actually happened to me. My stomach fluttered. My heart flipped. I just knew ... I mean, I thought, he was ... the one.'

I nodded and sighed. 'Yes. I'm afraid love at first sight is a very real thing.'

Tears sparkled in her eyes. 'I was so happy. I thought my life would only make sense if I shared it with him. We dated for a while. I moved in. He proposed. I cancelled all my own plans for the entire summer and for the rest of my life and said yes to him. I was such an idiot!'

'What plans did you cancel?' I asked, thinking this was something she particularly regretted.

'An archeologically internship in Egypt. It was meant to be the experience of a lifetime. And a chance for me to go on and do my PhD afterwards. What on earth was I thinking?'

I raised my eyes in real surprise. 'Wow. And what got you into something like archaeology?'

'I lived with my dad in Arizona until I was sixteen. Then, for the sake of my education, I moved to London to live with my mum. I worked hard at college and went to university to study Geology. And then, after getting my degree, I went on to do my master's in Anthropology. I've always loved history and science and I've worked towards getting an internship like this all my life. Then ... I just let it all go.'

'Is it really too late? Couldn't you get back in touch and ask to do the internship?'

'They've already offered it to someone else. I was told to apply again next year.'

'Okay. Well, at least that's something. It also explains why you're now doing a gap year.'

She nodded and twisted her ring around her finger again.

'So ... tell me what happened on your wedding day?' I ventured.

'I was just about to leave for the church with my mum and my bridesmaids when I heard a couple of pings from my phone. I distinctly remember saying I wasn't going to look at my phone again for the whole day. But then I was worried it might be a message from my dad. He'd already messaged an hour before to say his flight had got in late and he was going to meet us at the church. And then Cassie, my best friend and chief bridesmaid, passed the phone over to me.' Maddy gritted her jaw and her eyes turned cold as she recalled the details.

'Only it wasn't my dad this time. It was a text from a number I didn't recognise. I opened it anyway and I read it and it said: *Congratulations. You're welcome to him.* And I felt my heart skip a beat. I was confused, wondering what it was all about.'

'You're welcome to him? What did that mean?'

'Well, at first I thought Theo had a jealous ex-girlfriend who was out to try and spoil our wedding day. But then I saw a series of screen shots and I realised they were all text messages between Theo and another woman. Some were dated a couple of weeks before and some only a few days ago. I decided that this couldn't be *my* Theo.'

Poor girl! I sighed and couldn't help but think back on what Belle had told me about her wedding day too.

I'd thought my own wedding day situation, although unique, had never happened to anyone but me. This was clearly not the case. Wedding day disasters must happen all the time.

'I cringed at reading the filthy words he'd used in his texts to her,' she admitted to me.

'But how did you know it was for real?' I queried. 'How did you know it wasn't just a cruel hoax? Maybe a bitter ex-girlfriend? How did you know for sure he'd been cheating on you?'

'Because there were photos of Theo and the woman together. After seeing them, there was no doubt in my mind that he'd been cheating on me. And that I'd been a complete and utter fool to fall for him and to trust him.'

'Oh, Maddy. I'm so sorry this happened to you.' I reached for her hand and wanted to cry.

'But I think what happened to you was far worse, Maya. It must have been terrible.'

'Yes, it was terrible.' I realised she was trying to deflect back to me but I really wanted to give her this chance to fully voice and explore her feelings.

'Tell me, what did you do? How did you explain this to your guests?'

'Well, I was completely devastated. It felt like my whole world had imploded. Without any warning, the happiest day of my life had become the worst. I remember how I threw the phone down and ran into the bathroom. I remember Cassie asking me if someone died. When I came back out of the bathroom, I was a mess. My brides-maids and my mum were passing around my phone and reading the awful texts. Then, of course, they rallied around to try and console me. They were incredibly angry. They wanted to kill him. They said they wanted to cut off his balls. My mum told me to call him and tell him the wedding was off. But I wanted to think.'

Her voice was starting to falter now and the tears were welling up in her eyes again.

'I needed a moment to think about what to do. You see, my father had taken time off work – something he never did – and he'd flown in specially on a long flight from Arizona. All of our guests, family and friends, some of whom had also travelled great distances, would be dressed up to the nines and making their way to the church right at that moment. The minister would be standing at the altar dressed in his robes. The choir would be tuning up and the organist setting out all the sheet music we'd chosen. My cousin Jane would be gargling honey and lemon water in preparation for singing 'Ave Maria'. And afterwards, everyone would be expecting a big fat fabulous wedding reception with Champagne and wine and gourmet food prepared by a team of top chefs.'

I could see she was right back there in the moment. Remembering how it had unfolded and how she had felt. The weight of all that responsibility and expense.

If she hadn't had the opportunity to talk about what had happened, maybe this would help?

'I was thinking about the flower displays and imagining all the tables beautifully set and our carefully chosen wedding favours laid at each place setting. How the ice sculptures would be en route. The six-tier wedding cake on display. At great expense everything would be ready and absolutely none of it was refundable. How could I possibly cancel? How could I possibly cancel a huge wedding like that with just one hour to go?'

'But you didn't go ahead with the wedding?' I handed her another tissue.

The one she was gripping on to had disintegrated and been squished into a small ball.

'No. I had no intention of marrying him. But as well as being upset I was incredibly angry.'

I sighed. 'That I do understand. It's apparently the first emotion when experiencing grief.'

'Well, I was raging. The blissful love-bubble I'd been inhabiting had well and truly burst. The wonderful life I'd been imagining for myself as one half of a happily married couple had disappeared in a puff of lies and infidelity. And to think how I'd so readily given myself to this cheating no-good lying excuse for a man. How I'd trusted him so implicitly. And, not only that, how I'd somehow so easily and so carelessly thrown away all my own plans and life-long personal ambitions just to be with him. Was I mad? What on earth had I been thinking?'

She was ranting now. I stayed silent, recognising the pain as the same raw pain I had experienced. I knew she needed to get this out.

'So ... I decided I needed to do it my way. I needed to look in to Theo's eyes when I told him what I knew. And I wanted all our family and friends there to witness it. So we patched up my makeup and we headed out to the church. I remember sitting in the back seat of the limo, my mum squeezing my hand as we approached the church. My heart was thumping. I could hear the bells ringing. I guessed that most people were already in the church, but I could see there were a few guests hanging back hoping to catch a first glimpse of what they expected to be the blushing bride. Then our car came to a halt at the kerbside. I turned to ask my mum if she was going to be okay. I was concerned she wouldn't be able to see this through after she'd worked so hard and spent so much money planning this whole thing. I told her it was crucial that she played the part of proud mother-of-the-bride for a while longer yet. At least until I could look into his lying cheating eyes one last time. But that wasn't even going to be the hardest part of this ordeal. I knew that was coming up next.'

'Your dad?' I guessed. She'd said he was meeting them at the church.

'Yes. I could see my dad, smiling and waving at us, standing proudly in his brand-new suit and tie. He was all ready to open the car door and link his arm through mine to escort me, his only daughter, his little princess, down the aisle.'

She paused for a moment to catch her breath and mop her tears.

'If my dad had only known then what we knew, he'd have dragged the lying scumbag out of that church, kicking and screaming into the churchyard and put him into one of the graves. I had to force my face into a smile as my dad helped me out of the car. Cassie, Joanie, and Ella were climbing out of the limo behind us.

'At the church gate, Cassie held on to my bouquet while my mum fussed over me, straightening out my dress, arranging my veil, checking my makeup and blotting any sign of recent tears with a tissue. My dad just stood there looking at me in awe and wonder.

'"You look so beautiful, my Maddy-moo!" he told me and I just wanted to burst into tears and throw myself into his arms. Mum hurried off inside the church to play her part and take her seat. I locked arms with my dad, and we walked through the gate and towards the church.

'Inside, as the organ struck up with 'Here Comes the Bride' all our guests, exactly one hundred family and friends on each side of the church, all stood in their pews and turned to look at me. I kept my gaze forward and I focused on what looked like an endless walk to the end of the aisle where Theo was standing next to his best man.

'My heart was aching and my legs felt like they were encased in lead as I walked. My dress, chosen with such care and consideration for what was meant to be one of the most special days of my life, felt like it was nothing but an over-the-top, flouncy fancy-dress costume. And my smile felt as fake as my fiancé as I walked towards him on my father's arm.

'As the music stopped, my dad parked me in front of the minister at Theo's side and I glanced over my shoulder at my mum in the first pew and my three bridesmaids, who were standing supportively close to me, looking stoic rather than serene. Cassie stepped forward to take my bouquet and to slip my phone into my right hand. "Dearly beloved we are gathered here today ..." the minister began to say. I concentrated on watching the minister's moving lips so I didn't have to look at Theo. I knew if I turned to look at him, I'd risk losing it. That I might actually hit him. I remember I could feel the heat from Theo's hand next to my hand. And I took a deep breath and almost choked on his sickening cologne.

'Time seemed to last forever. Words were spoken slowly. A hymn was sung tunelessly. I was too hot and then I was too cold. Sweating and then shivering in the agony of anticipation. Then, eventually, we got to the part where we faced each other to say our vows. In the age-old tradition, Theo was to be the first in saying his part. I braced myself. This was the part where I got to look at his handsome face, look into his eyes, to see if I could see something I'd never seen in them before: lies. My heart sank when I saw he had the audacity to smile at me. I didn't smile back. I felt sick as he lifted my limp hand in his and held it. He was clearly unnerved by now and silently questioned my cool response to him.

'But I didn't care. I just wanted this over and done. He started to repeat his vows and I just thought *blah blah blah ... you bastard!* I waited for him to finish so I could have my turn. When the minister urged me to repeat the words after him, I dropped Theo's hand and turned to our congregation, making sure I raised my voice enough to be heard clearly all the way to the back of the church. And I said: "Family and friends, there will be no happy ever after today".'

I stared at Maddy in rapt admiration. 'Oh wow – and how did everyone react?'

'There was an immediate gasp after which all mouths remained open and all eyes remained popped. Heads and hats and feathered fascinators all bobbed up and down and swung from side to side as everyone looked to each other and then to me and to Theo for an explanation.'

'And, what did Theo do?' I asked.

She had described the scene so well that I was both horrified and cringingly captivated.

'Theo's face went pale when he realised I'd been holding onto my phone and he demanded to know what was going on. Then he tried to grab my hand and snatch my phone. And I said to him, "It seems there's been quite a lot going on and behind my back." Then I read out loud every single cheating text message – even saying the filthy words that really shouldn't have ever been said in a place of worship – and Theo finally showed his true colours to me by turning a cowardly yellow and then completely green before he turned to flee from the scene. I watched him go, swiftly followed by his speechless brother, his blushing mother and his irate father. Those in the pews watched too, before turning to me with disbelief and pity on their faces. I desperately tried to hold myself together if only for my pride. But you know, I wasn't so much distraught, as I was angry and disappointed.

'Theo isn't the man I thought he was and, before you throw me a pity party, I want you to understand this was not just about *him*. This is now about *me*. That's why I decided to travel and to come to India. This is about coming to terms with what *I* have done!'

I heard her tone switch from cries of sadness to one of great strength and determination.

'This is about how I somehow went from someone sensible to someone stupid. How I turned from someone credible to someone so cringeworthy. How *did* I get so wrapped up in thinking I was *in love* that I lost any semblance of good sense? How can I ever respect or forgive myself for getting it so very wrong?'

'Maddy. Stop. This is not your fault. You mustn't blame yourself!' I insisted.

'But Maya, all this will have been for nothing if I can't see where I go from here. I've let *myself* down so badly. And, if falling in love is an act of self-sabotage, how do I know for sure I won't mess up like this again? How do I know I won't let my guard down again and one day allow my life to systematically unravel just because someone good-looking and charismatic happens to walk into the same room as me and shows me some attention?'

I guess she had a point. There was a lesson in all of this for her and it was a valuable one.

'I had my whole damned life set up and then I just let it all go. Everything I'd worked so hard for – for years! – and I did it for *him*. Like it was all suddenly and inexplicably worth *nothing* to me anymore. So perhaps the real question now is: how can I ever trust myself again? That's what I'm determined to work on, so nothing like this can ever happen to me again!'

Maddy sat back in her seat and looked almost triumphant after her tirade.

It really does go to prove how everyone we meet is carrying a burden of some kind that we know nothing about. Sometimes helping someone requires sacrifice and a grand gesture but at other times, if we are prepared to open our hearts, offer a listening ear and a portion of our time, then maybe that's all that's ever needed?

'I've felt so comfortable chatting with you, Maya. I just want you to know I feel incredibly fortunate to have met you today. You are a very kind-hearted person. Thank you for listening. I guess I was bottling it all up. You were right, talking about it has helped me.'

I smiled and felt a lovely warm glow inside.

I took her hand and squeezed it. 'It's been a pleasure and I'm sure you'll be absolutely fine.'

'Erm ... Maya, I was just thinking. I know you said you were planning on travelling to Hong Kong straight away but, well, if you did want to see more of India and join me then I'd more than happy to share this journey with you. Why don't you think about coming along?'

I was taken by complete surprise at her lovely and generous offer and for a moment I found myself stalling and stuttering a few words of thanks while I considered the possibility. How I would have loved to see the Taj Mahal and the Red Fort at Agra, all the special places in The Golden Triangle. And, as I'm almost in Delhi, it seems a real shame to miss out on seeing all the main sights. They were all so close.

It was indeed a very tempting offer. But I was already shaking my head.

Jon had planned this itinerary and I didn't want to divert from his plan for us.

However tempting the detour, I'm on Jon's magical mystery tour and it's important, indeed imperative, not to get distracted. I must follow and complete this very special journey.

'Oh, Maddy. Thank you. I'd love to come but I honestly can't. I have a flight to catch.'

When we reached Delhi, we left the train and hugged each other on the platform. We swapped emails and social media contact details and promised to keep in touch and remain friends, so we could provide each other with emotional support if we needed it, as well as to find out exactly how both our backpacking bride stories would eventually unfold.

I walked away realising that in meeting both Belle and Maddy, I'd heard two very different wedding-day disaster stories other than my own. But I'd also witnessed two very different personal reactions to the fallout. Belle was still holding on to being an angry anarchist, while Maddy was determined to walk away from this guarding her heart and with a lesson learned.

So, where does that leave me? Which mindset will serve me best?

Which attitude will I choose in the fallout from my own wedding-day story?

* * *

It's a thought I'm still mulling over as I enter Terminal Three at New Delhi Airport, a modern and incredibly busy terminal with artful, symbolic *mudras* or 'hand gestures' sticking out from the walls that make me feel like I'm being given a figurative thumbs-up as I head to the security checkpoint. But when I get there, I see there's some kind of commotion and delay happening.

Two holy men dressed in their saffron robes are being addressed by a posse of security guards. They are standing to the side of the scanning machine and being asked to identify their luggage. I watch as, pointing out their small suitcases, they both look quite terrified. When these suitcases are opened up I see that there are indeed forbidden items inside to be confiscated. Specifically, large bottles of shower gel in excess of the 100ml allowed in cabin luggage.

I feel very sorry for them as they are ordered to hand over their oversized toiletries.

With the waiting over, we all move through the security

line. At the other side, I find my gate. There's still an hour to go before departure so I sit to wait. A moment or two later, the same two swamis arrive and sit on the empty seats in the row next to me. I hear them chatting away to each other and they still seem really upset at having lost their shower gel.

I hear some Sanskrit words I recognise like *saucha* and I realise they're worried about cleanliness. Something about 'what will we do if we can't wash?' and 'we won't be able to attend the *dhyana*.' They both sit anxiously rubbing prayer beads and looking extremely glum.

I recall seeing the poster in the *shala* showing a pair of hands held in a prayer pose.

Wash to symbolise purity of body and soul.

I realise and appreciate their predicament. If they're not used to travelling, then they probably won't realise that now they're through security, they can go and buy new toiletries.

Or maybe they don't have any spare money?

I remember that monks aren't allowed to carry cash. They rely totally on *alms* from others.

I look around and wonder what I can do to help without offending them.

'Excuse me?' I said tentatively, 'Do you need soap?'

They turned to look at me and blinked in surprise at me speaking to them.

'We are humble pilgrims. We need to prepare ourselves for prayers. Do you understand?'

'Yes, I understand. You have to wash to symbolise purity of body and soul.'

At the bottom of my bag, I find two wrapped cubes of the organic soap Belle had made in the ashram workshop and had given to me. I place the soaps on the chair seat between us so as not to risk us touching. Some holy men are not allowed to touch a woman ever, even accidentally. They look down at the soap and then back to me in absolute delight.

It's so nice to see a smile on their faces. It really warms my heart.

'Thank you. You are very kind in opening your heart to us.'

I blush. That's twice in one day I've been told I'm kind-hearted.

One of them produces a wallet and I immediately feel terribly embarrassed.

They obviously do have some money, but I really don't want to be paid anything.

'Oh, no. Please, that's not necessary. Honestly, I'm just glad I could help.'

From a selection in his wallet, he places a picture card down on the chair.

'Please accept this divine gift in return for your kind heart full of love and your gift of soap.'

I shift in my seat and feel uncomfortable but when I glance down at the picture card, I immediately recognise the twelve-petalled lotus flower with its six-pointed star that is the symbol representing *Anahata*, the heart chakra. I also remember Swami Nanda's words about divine energies and karmic healing and get a strong, strange feeling tingling down my spine.

When your kind heart is filled with love and you are feeling truly happy again, then you'll know the divine energies have healed you.

I can also hear hushed whisperings and a few gasps as people around us gathered to eavesdrop on what was happening here. I can feel my face glowing like a furnace.

'Look, the swami have promised to grant her a wish!' People were saying in excitement.

The swami smiles at me serenely in encouragement. 'You should make your wish.'

'Hey girl, what are you waiting for?' shouts a wide-eyed young guy with dreadlocks.

'Ask for next week's lotto numbers!' suggests an old man sporting a bushy white beard.

'Do it! Make the wish ...' urges a tiny Indian woman who was sitting opposite me.

I pick up the card and hold it to my heart. I close my eyes and I wish.

I know my wish should be a noble one to even stand a chance of coming true.

And, this time, instead of asking the Divine for *a way* to live my life without Jon, I ask for *a reason* to live my life without Jon.

Chapter 13

Hong Kong

Before embarking on my magical mystery tour, I'd never flown long haul before and I'd certainly never travelled first class in seats that were more like luxurious survival pods stocked with Champagne. I didn't ever realise that I'd feel so cossetted and comfortable, and I have to tell you that I've certainly made the most of it all, just as Jon would have wanted me to.

I've drunk the Champagne and I've enjoyed the finest cuisine; I've read the glossiest of complimentary international magazines and watched the latest movie and, if I hadn't been so excited to get to my next destination, I would have been very happy for this flight to have taken much longer than five hours because I've been so spoiled.

A shiver of excitement rushes through me as the captain announces we have started our descent into Hong Kong International Airport. The cabin crew are now busy checking that everyone is wearing their seatbelt. I focus my attention out of the small porthole window and on the bird's-eye night-time view of the thrilling city below us with its multitude of tall buildings sparkling against a backdrop of mountains and mist. I can hear Jon's voice in my ear.

Before they built the new airport, you had to fly in through the high-rise buildings and the wing tips of the plane would be practically rapping on the windows of people's apartments!

I remember my parents telling me the same thing. How amazing but scary that must have been for all concerned before they built the airport out on a nearby island. I peer down to see a sparkling galaxy of city lights below me. My ears are feeling the change in pressure as we descend. A frisson of exhilaration fizzles through me as I see that the famous high-rises are swathed in calligraphy and there are advertising hoards streaming up and down and the flickering lights and colours are being reflected in the inky shining waters of Victoria Harbour. And there are so many boats I can see moving between Hong Kong and Kowloon.

The Star Ferry, I hear Jon saying, is *the traditional way to get to the Kowloon peninsula and over to the night market on Temple Street and the famous and most popular Ladies' Market.*

I'm so very thrilled to have this dream come true and right now it's all thanks to Jon.

Might I have come here on my own if I hadn't met him and he hadn't instigated all of this? I'd like to think so. But when? And would I have come here via India?

Perhaps. I've always wanted to see the Taj Mahal. I've promised it to myself sometime very soon. Jon roused in me a curiosity and an interest in many other parts of India with his amazing stories of life in the ashram and the life-affirming spirituality. He'd made Rishikesh sound like a supernatural place. And, despite my initial scepticism and my experiences of culture shock, what I'd found there in the end was beyond supernatural.

I'll admit that it had been difficult for me to comprehend, understand, and accept what had looked to me to be strange ways and a diverse attitude to life and death. I'd been shocked in many ways by the things I'd seen there but I'd also been educated and enlightened. Because, I remind myself, India isn't somewhere you go to *see*. India is somewhere you go to *feel*.

Which leads me to wonder, how will I truly feel about Hong Kong?

It is surreal to arrive somewhere I'd once belonged and yet to be a stranger.

We disembark from the plane through a passenger transit tunnel straight into the arrivals lounge and I'm fast-tracked through the first-class channels in the comfortable chill of air conditioning that is absolutely no preparation for the heat and humidity outside the airport terminal. I walk quickly to appease my legs after sitting for several hours and, after I've retrieved my backpack from the luggage carousel, I walk into a wall of heat at the meet-and-greet area to rendezvous with my taxi.

I'd rung ahead to confirm with the hotel which flight I was arriving on and to let them know that I'd appreciate them sending a car. What I didn't expect was a chauffeur in uniform holding up a card bearing Jon's name, and I realised that perhaps I should also have mentioned I was travelling alone.

Mr & Mrs Jon Howard
Welcome to Hong Kong

I'm escorted to a shiny, emerald-green Rolls Royce parked at the kerbside and whisked through the neon-lit night to arrive at the hotel's impressively enclosed grand forecourt, where I see many more of these signature green Rolls Royces and an army of page boys, all dressed in white and standing to attention. My door is opened by a boy carrying a silver platter who is eager to offer me an ice-cold towel with which to refresh my travel-weary self.

My culture shock is back but this time not at the poverty but at the obvious privilege.

I decide that I am both fortunate and blessed to know the difference between the two.

The hotel lobby is astonishingly beautiful with a marble floor and elegant décor featuring marble statues, not of Hindu Gods or Buddhist figures this time, but instead Chinese lions and dragons.

This is nothing like the ashram. A fuss is made over my

arrival. I'm ushered to a comfortable chair at the executive check-in desk and I'm offered a drink. I ask for water.

A couple at another executive check-in point are being served very good Champagne.

All around me are smartly dressed people wearing suits and cocktail dresses, all obviously dressed up at this late hour to enjoy the bars and restaurants in the town. For me, it has been a long day of airports and travel, and I'm keen to be shown to my room so I can relax.

I pass over my booking confirmation and the receptionist casts her eyes over it and smiles.

'Congratulations on your recent marriage, Mrs Howard. I see you're in our honeymoon suite. Let me get you checked in. I'll need your passport, please. Is Mr Howard arriving later?'

I swallow hard. 'Erm ... no. I'm alone. I'm Ms Thomas and Mr Howard did make the booking for us both but ... well, he couldn't make it. Is that a problem?' I hand over my passport and she turns her attention and her blushes to her computer, tapping rapidly on the keypad. Thankfully, her recovery is both fast and professional.

'Oh ... no problem at all. I see you're also named on the reservation, Ms Thomas. Are you still happy to occupy the honeymoon suite or would you like me to change that for you? I do have another suite free, if you'd prefer it, but of course it's entirely your choice.'

'I'd very much like the room that Mr Howard originally booked for us, please.'

The valet takes care of my backpack which he insists on placing on a fancy luggage trolley. I assume that he and his trolley are more accustomed to transporting a stack of pristine designer suitcases than a rather dirty looking backpack, but he graciously doesn't show it.

We go up to an extremely high floor and I follow him along a carpeted hallway until, with a flourish and a smile, a card is used to open the door to my suite. I'm escorted inside. I'm sure he's more accustomed to showing this room to couples rather than one solo female, but again he courteously doesn't show it, and instead busies himself by flicking a switch to illuminate every lamp in the room and then helpfully explaining where the air-con controls are, how to use the TV, and where I can find the mini bar. I sigh with pleasure.

This is all more beautiful and more luxurious than I'd been expecting or even dared to hope. The interconnecting rooms are large, the carpets deep, and the furnishings gorgeous.

I've never stayed, or expected to stay, anywhere like this in my entire life.

And, joy of joys, there's a coffee machine and a glimpse of a sumptuous bathroom.

Most impressive of all are the floor-to-ceiling windows off both the sitting room and the other side of the open double doorways into the bedroom area. I rush over to the windows, drawn to them like a moth to a flame, because I can see that the dancing colours of the

Symphony of Lights show that plays at 8pm every night here is happening right now below me in Victoria Harbour.

The windows allow for a private viewing of this most spectacular light-to-music extravaganza. The only thing missing of course, owing to the thickness of glass, is the accompanying music.

I watch in awe as buildings on both side of the harbour glitter with colourful light beams and multimedia images. I gasp in delight and decide, with great anticipation of fulfilling another of Jon's Post-it note instructions, that tomorrow evening I will experience this performance in all its glory from the middle of the harbour on that old wooden sailing junk.

The one with billowing indigo-red sails filled to the brink with tourists taking flash photos.

I turn around with a huge excited grin on my face to see that the enormous bed in the adjoining room has been beautifully decorated with red rose petals in the shape of a heart and the words 'Just Married'. My smile suddenly slips away as my heart drops into my stomach. Perhaps this was why the receptionist had tactfully offered me an alternative room?

'Madam, would you like me to open your Champagne?' My attentive valet asks, indicating a bottle of Cristal resting in an ice bucket.

It had been pre-ordered by Jon. A 1996 Rosé. I'd seen the receipt for it in his wallet.

I respond with a perhaps overly enthusiastic squeal. 'Oh ... absolutely!'

I'm determined to enjoy all of this as Jon intended. And, as soon as the cork is popped and the sparkling pink nectar poured into a crystal glass flute, I slip the valet a handsome tip and indicate that I'm incredibly happy and he may now leave. Once I'm alone in all this cosseted luxury, I sweep the rose petals into a paper basket and flick off my flip flops to jump onto the bed and wallow in its comfort.

The bed is huge and so soft that it feels like I'm floating on a soft white cloud in the sky.

After wallowing, I go and stand by the window again, sipping my delicious Champagne.

'Thank you, Jon ...' I murmur, raising my glass to the last of the lights and to his memory.

Then, feeling travel weary, I check out the bathroom and oh ... deep, deep joy!

The bathroom is like something from the *Homes of the Rich and Famous* magazine that I'd read on the plane with its decadent and vast space presented in marble and glass and porcelain.

Behind the double vanity is a wall of mirrors. The soft lighting around them is absolutely exquisite because, even with my humidity-tousled hair and in my baggy blouse and trousers, right now I look more boho-chic than hippy vagrant. I squeal again on seeing an array of complementary luxury toiletries and turn to fill the bathtub and then refill my champagne glass. In a soft white towelling robe, feeling elated and giggly with the sheer extravagance, I take a few selfies reflected in the bathroom mirror to send to Pia.

I really feel I have to share this with someone and my sister is now my one and only.

I lie in the bath for about an hour amongst the scented bubbles until I finally feel calm and relaxed. After a week using the shared bathroom in the ashram, private wallowing in such gloriously glamourous surroundings is wholly appreciated and enjoyed. I know I will sleep well tonight.

And, if I dream of Jon, then this time I know I won't be upset.

I'll simply be delighted and very happy to see him again.

* * *

I slept for eight dreamless hours solid and woke up feeling amazingly refreshed.

The very moment I opened my eyes and recalled exactly where I was – not in the ashram but in the city of my birth and the place of my hopes and dreams – I bounded out of bed to do my morning stretches and yoga routine. Then, I made a cup of strong coffee using the fancy machine in my room and sat on the bed to open Jon's wallet and carefully study my itinerary once again, and to familiarise myself with the variety of Post-it notes stuck to the hotel receipt.

One stated *Victoria Peak* and then *Ride the Peak Tram*. There was an old brochure for the Peak Tram showing the steep track up the mountain.

Another *Eat dim sum* and another *Tai Chi at Kowloon Park*.

I love dim sum. But Tai Chi?

Well, I'm sure it's on the agenda for the very same reason as 'Real Yoga'.

It's part of the grand plan because Jon first learned Tai Chi here in Hong Kong.

But, by far the most mysterious Post-it note was one I couldn't quite fathom: *Divine Number Nine*.

Divine number nine? How very odd. What did that mean?

Should I be thinking of picking up a lottery ticket? Or perhaps going to the horse races?

Jon had mentioned there was a famous racecourse in Happy Valley. Could that be it?

And, in Happy Valley of course, I had my own exploratory mission to complete. I'd brought the old photo of my parents' previous home with me and I needed to find out if it was still there. I pop the photo and Jon's wallet into my day bag. I shower and dress and, setting aside my loose-fitting hippy outfits and baggy harem-style trousers that I'd worn in Rishikesh, I picked out a pretty cotton blouse and some cropped capri trousers along with my most comfortable shoes. I intended to do a lot of walking today, hiking in valleys and mountains, so I knew I had to choose practical over stylish.

Breakfast was taken in the private executive club lounge. A pot of coffee, fruit and yogurt, lightly scrambled eggs on toast and, of course, fine shavings of truffle and delicious smoked salmon with a garnish of caviar. Why not!

After which, I go and seek advice from the hotel concierge on how best to navigate the city and see the sights. I decline the services of the complementary chauffeur and signature Rolls Royce, I think because I'm perhaps suffering from a bout of high-life imposter syndrome. I'm simply not used to being ferried around by chauffeurs. I explain that I'm especially keen to explore the sights at my own pace and much prefer to walk or use public transport. My explanation was met with only lightly masked astonishment.

I'm provided with a street map and routes carefully explained to me and, wearing sunshades, a hat, and my comfortable attire, I venture out into the narrow, crooked, steep streets of Hong Kong. I pinch myself as I walk. Am I dreaming or am I really here?

I find myself in the tremendously crowded and bustling Central Area.

Small shops line the street and they are also in all the nooks and alleyways between the tall buildings. Each seems to be a thriving independent family business and a store or café or a food-on-the-go stall. As it's breakfast time, the streets are awash with people drinking tea and coffee, local breakfast specialities being offered at every turn to hungry residents and visitors alike. It all looks and smells amazing and even though I've already eaten a hearty breakfast, my senses are being tempted by the aroma of coffee, sweet buns, and fried dough sticks. I resist and promise myself I'll sample these culinary delights later and I walk until I find the main street to follow to Western Market and the bus station where I join the orderly queue.

It's so refreshing to find an orderly line and everyone waiting quietly and patiently!

The bus I catch takes a winding route away from Central Area and The Causeway to Garden Road. I was tempted to go and explore Happy Valley first thing this morning in search of my *Shangri-La*, but I'm taking the concierge's advice to go up to the peak first instead. I'm told that by mid-morning, as the heat rises and the mist rolls in from the sea, my much-anticipated view of Hong Kong and the islands is likely to be totally obscured by cloud.

As the bus makes its way steadily and slowly uphill with the engine rumbling and the gears growling, I'm focussed on peering through the window at the interesting and beautifully appointed residential homes on the steep sides of the surrounding mountain slopes. I check my map. From my lofty vantage point I can see the Victoria Gap and Happy Valley, where my parents had lived and where I was born. It looks more built up than I expected as the whole valley is full of towering high-rises.

As I stare down at the area where I intend to spend tomorrow exploring, I wonder in which Hong Kong district had Jon lived. He once told me that he'd had an apartment close to his place of work *where the old and authentic meets the new and dynamic.*

Nowadays, it seems the landscape is filled purely with the new and dynamic.

The bus rolls into the station at the Peak Tram Terminus. I'm particularly looking forward to the experience of riding on the world's steepest funicular tram – one of Hong Kong's top tourist attractions and an exciting way to reach the top of the mountain. Apparently because it rises so steeply up the side of the mountain all the high-rise buildings it passes look to be leaning over! Of course, it's actually the passenger who's on a gradient and not the buildings.

It feels rather strange and a little disconcerting to be tipped back into the wooden bench-style seats by sheer gravity but once at the top, the view from the sky terrace is incredible.

It's relaxing to walk around in the less humid air up here and to stand, as I do for quite some time, gazing down at the views of the city skyscrapers far below and then across to the many green and undulating islands scattered across the vista like pieces of a giant jigsaw puzzle waiting to be joined together. I take a deep breath and think of Jon and his life here. I think about my parents and the decade they lived and worked in Hong Kong.

I might have made this trip alone, but I certainly don't feel alone.

This is the place where my life began and, in many ways, it still feels like home. How strange that I still feel connected to Jon and to my own past here in Hong Kong.

I'm really enjoying myself on this new stage in the magical mystery tour and I'm already in great anticipation of my next experience: dim sum for lunch!

* * *

I take the return trip on the funicular and walk back into the city, wandering along the narrow, steeply sloping streets through the suburbs.

Walking is undoubtedly the best way to see and to fully experience this amazing city. I marvel at all the strange, unfamiliar sights around me.

There are rows of plucked ducks hanging by their necks in glass cases. Chicken feet fry in vast boiling woks. Stalls sell baskets of something that looks like hair but on closer inspection might be a type of fungus, and strange dried fish and other desiccated sea life, like sea cucumber, starfish and spiny urchins. There are also stalls selling top designer luxury goods.

I browse Louis Vuitton handbags, Ray-Ban sunglasses, Rolex Watches, Gucci, Chanel, Prada. All are at prices that suggest they can't possibly be the real deal even if they seem to pass muster on close inspection. I'm both amused and terribly tempted to buy one of these knock-off handbags for Pia. My sister has always been the stylish one of the two of us. Would she be able to tell the difference between a counterfeit and the real deal I wonder?

When her husband had asked her what she'd wanted for her 'big birthday' a few years ago I remember she'd asked for a handbag and Peter had thought this a perfectly reasonable request – until he went out to buy it for her. He told me he'd been so shocked by the price that he'd had to put it on his credit card and pay it off in instalments over the next year. It would have amused me to see if she could tell her £2000 Gucci handbag apart from a $20 one.

There seemed to be Chinese pharmacies everywhere too – small shops selling seeds and herbs and traditional Chinese medicines – all of which add to my sensory overload on the exciting streets of Hong Kong.

It takes me a couple of hours to reach the main street again and the old part of town that looks to cater well for history buffs, art lovers and for those hunting for souvenirs and the chance to indulge in shopping sprees. I stick to window shopping and taking in the atmosphere and aromas until my feet are complaining and I'm flagging with hunger.

I'm delighted to come across Dim Sum Square almost by accident, and I take a seat in a busy café. The menu is a huge numbered picture board on the wall. You order by simply ticking the numbers on a checkbox on a smaller paper version of the menu handed out þy the person who was also serving endless cups of steaming black tea or *yum cha* from a large pot.

I quickly tick off some delicious bite-sized *siu mai* –

delicate steamed wheat balls containing ground pork; chopped shrimp in mouth-watering flavours of ginger and soy sauce garnished with crab roe; *har gow* – classically translucent dumplings with fish; and *char siu bao* – light and fluffy buns stuffed with barbeque pork. Each came in simple bamboo baskets of three or four bite-sized portions and with as much *cha* as I could drink.

The food is served quickly and without fuss and it doesn't disappoint. Every bite is a deliciously authentic steaming mouthful of dumpling heaven. No wonder Jon wanted me to try them here and why he said they were the best in the world.

* * *

After lunch, I head slowly back through the steep narrow streets lined with old residential apartment buildings so tall that they seem to be swaying, moving and breathing with a life of their own. Then suddenly I'm back on to the chaotically busy main street where trucks and cars jostle for pole position at the junctions and scooters scuttle by making popping and buzzing sounds like the strange insects I saw being cooked in cauldrons on the street corners. I'm completely charmed by the old double-decker trams shrieking on the metal rails embedded in the street. These trams, I'm told, are the most popular and inexpensive way to get around, and they are locally and affectionally known as the *ding ding*.

To save my legs, I hop aboard a *ding ding* and ride the tram down to Central Pier.

From there, I planned to take a trip across the harbour on the Star Ferry to visit Kowloon Island, where I would find my next exciting Post-it note experience: *Tai Chi in Kowloon Park*. This particular note was actually stuck to an old, faded Star Ferry brochure.

As I wait at the harbour point to step aboard one of these iconic green and white ferries, I read that the Star Ferry has been carrying passengers across the harbour for 120 years and that the four original Star Ferry boats where called *Morning Star, Evening Star, Rising Star* and *Guiding Star*. Their names were inspired by one of my favourite British poems, Alfred Lord Tennyson's 'Crossing the Bar', which I knew well from my school days and could still recite from memory.

Sunset and evening star,
And one clear call for me!
And may there be no moaning of the bar,
When I put out to sea.

Inside the old brochure, I'm amazed to find that there's an old ferry ticket dated 22nd October 1997. It escapes me and flutters onto the floor. I quickly stoop to pick it up and on the back I see Jon's swirly ink pen scrawl.

Harry Chen still owes me a chip.

How curious. What kind of chip did he owe Jon? I thought of French fries as 'chips' but some people call potato crisps, chips, too.

With the ferry boarding, I stuff the brochure and notes back inside my bag and sit on a wooden seat that will allow me a good view of the harbour. I make sure to have my phone ready to take lots of photos of what is one of the most photographed views in the world, one I've longed to see with my own eyes for as long as I could remember.

And it doesn't disappoint. In all its glory, this is the famous Hong Kong cityscape.

So, it seems, dreams really can come true …

Chapter 14

Kowloon Island

Just thirty relaxing minutes later, after crossing Victoria Harbour, I'm on Kowloon Island, where I've got an even better view of the harbour and the cityscape. I wander along from the busy docking area to the popular traffic-free paved walkway towards the promenade so I can watch the boats on the busy waterway and take more photos.

After a while walking and enjoying the pleasant afternoon sunshine, I reach the park where a group of people are already stretching and practicing Tai Chi on an expanse of grass.

It seems that I've found my next Post-it note mission: *Tai Chi in Kowloon Park.*

I watch the zany band of participants moving under the guidance of a tall, dark-haired man wearing what looks to me like a pair of my hotel's complimentary luxurious white silk pyjamas. He moves gracefully, unlike his followers – an assortment of men and women of many different nationalities and of all ages, shapes and sizes.

It looks as though they're all doing a version of the chakra dance but in slow motion.

I've never done any Tai Chi before, but Jon, of course, had been a Tai Chi master.

There is a noticeboard on the lawn encouraging anyone passing to join in with the class and I see there's a collection box. The fee is whatever one would like to pay as all proceeds go to local charities.

Suggested donation: HK$10

I'm especially keen to try all of Jon's Post-it notes and as I'd really enjoyed learning real yoga in India, I've already decided that I'm going to fully embrace this new task and give Tai Chi a go. Who knows, at my age perhaps Tai Chi is more my thing anyway?

With a deep breath, I walk forward, put some money into the collection box, and take my place on the grass to limber up and do a bit of stretching. Then, with my feet apart and knees slightly bent, I follow the master's lead.

I stretch out both my arms and launch myself into the synchronised flow of slow and deliberate body movements, swooping slowly and dramatically as if I were throwing away an invisible bucket of water. It feels quirky but it also feels good to be outside in the warm air attempting something creative – if not terribly energetic – and enjoying the therapeutically humid breeze flowing over my body.

The master throws me a warm smile when he spots my attempts and I feel myself blushing.

Thankfully, this is nothing like the hedonistic wild abandon of the chakra dance.

'Lift your left leg and reach up with both your hands into the sky,' he encourages us.

We all stand on one leg for a while and I manage this quite well, all thanks to the hours I'd spent last week practicing my tree pose. But, to be honest, it didn't seem to matter if anyone wobbled about. It wasn't meant to be in any way competitive.

It just feels really good. Joyful.

I try to follow the sequence of movements that follows as best I can. I let my gaze drift from left to right as instructed. I move my arms ever so slowly up and down again. I concentrate hard and copy the master, rocking back and forth, shifting weight from one leg to the other and then gracefully and slowly sweeping our arms in alternate directions.

'This movement is called "The White Crane Spreads His Wings",' the master explains to the class. I don't think I look anything like a crane doing this movement.

I think I look more like 'Fat Pigeon Crash Lands'.

The master takes the time to explain the symbolism. 'The White Crane is known as the movement of divinity.

This is because it connects us to the nine divine and intricate movements of Tai Chi.'

I catch my breath. Hold on. Wait a minute ...

Did he just say 'nine' and 'divine' in the same breath?

The master tells us that our goal in Tai Chi is to 'move in a connected and divine manner', that 'nine is a most auspicious number in Chinese culture. It stands for completeness and eternity'.

I'm a bit blown away by the numerology and symbolism. *Divine Number Nine!* Did Jon's mystery note have something to do with Tai Chi? He'd specifically led me here to Kowloon Park when there are so many places to do Thai Chi.

A coincidence? Was perhaps this task more about *who* rather than *where*?

Was this man known to Jon? He's more my age. Even if he didn't know Jon, he still might be able to help me with the Post-it note I'd found in the old Star Ferry brochure.

It's worth asking the question. I mean, what do I have to lose?

* * *

At the end of the class, I linger and hover for a while until everyone else has finished chatting to the master and have packed up and left. Only then do I go over to introduce myself.

202

'Hello. I just wanted to thank you for introducing me to Tai Chi today.'

He smiles at me, presses his palms together at his chest and bows.

I quickly do the same.

'Welcome. I'm Master Chen. I'm glad you enjoyed your practice.'

Oh my goodness! His last name is Chen!

I'm so excited that my breathing has quickened and my heart has started pounding.

Was he Harry Chen? What are the odds?

Without the swaying curtain of bodies obstructing my view, I'm actually taken by surprise at how incredibly attractive Master Chen is close up. His smile is generous and warm. I see he has a nice-looking cluster of fine smile-lines on the outer edges of his strikingly bright jade-green eyes. His teeth are very white against his smooth, tanned skin. His cheek bones are high and sharp, making for a rather gorgeous Eurasian fusion and I decide he must have been blessed with both Chinese or Hong Kong and western parentage. His dark hair is peppered with a few silver streaks that are catching the afternoon sunshine.

Master Chen is a very handsome man indeed. Movie-star handsome, in fact. I realise I'm gazing at him so curiously that he might consider me rude.

But, in dragging my eyes down, I find I'm now staring at his smooth, muscled chest and admiring his honed and sporty physique, all thanks to his belted silk wrap-top which is hanging casually open. Another surprise to me is his accent. He sounds quite distinctly British.

I feel a vibrant heat spreading across my face as I realise I'm blushing like a pink flamingo.

Oh dear. *The Pink Flamingo Spreads Its Embarrassment.*

'Erm ... I wanted to ask you something, if you don't mind?' I ventured.

'Sure. Ask away.'

'I was wondering if you are Harry Chen?'

He raises his eyebrows in astonishment and then laughs in what sounds like disbelief.

'Actually, I'm Henri. But, a long time ago, the people I worked with used to call me Harry.'

'Do you by chance remember an Englishman called Jon Howard?'

As soon as I mention Jon's name his face lights up with delight.

'Jon Howard! Yes, of course. We are old friends. Is he back in Hong Kong?'

I shake my head and frown. 'No. I'm sorry. He died recently.'

Harry/Henri's smile drops. 'Oh, I'm so sorry to hear that. My deepest condolences.'

I nod and bite my lip to stop it trembling. I'm overly hypersensitive to those words now.

'Thank you. I'm Maya, Jon's fiancée. He died the day we were to be married.'

He reaches out to me. 'Oh Maya. That is awful. I'm so

deeply sorry to hear that. I knew Jon well and for a long time. Tell me, what can I do for you?'

I nod and fight my new compulsion to cry as he touches my arm supportively.

I can feel the tingling warmth of his hand seeping through my sleeve.

'I know this might sound a bit strange, but Jon left me a travel itinerary and a note about doing Tai Chi here in the park, and there was also a note with your name on it.'

He smiles and slowly shakes his head. 'Not so strange, actually. Jon had a real passion for the martial arts. We first learned Tai Chi together here under the guidance of our Grand Master.'

'Is he – the Grand Master – still alive?' I ask him tentatively, thinking it would be nice to meet him too. It feels like such a special privilege to be meeting Jon's friend from his past.

'No. Sadly, he has also passed away. But at the grand old age of ninety-six, I hasten to add.'

I nod. Ninety-six was indeed a grand age compared to poor Jon who had only been sixty.

'So how long have you been teaching Tai Chi here at the park?' I ask him.

'Ever since the Grand Master passed away. He asked me to take his place here on the promenade to keep the tradition of Tai Chi in the park going. I promised I would. Except, with all my other commitments, these days I only manage one or two afternoon sessions a week.'

'Well, I'm sure everyone who comes here appreciates you keeping this going,' I tell him.

'I appreciate you coming to find me, Maya, although, of course I'm very sad to hear the news about Jon. He was a good man and a great friend. We'd known each other since we were both at boarding school in the UK. It's such a shame we eventually lost touch. I suppose it *was* all different back then, without social media, I mean. The world was a much bigger place than it seems now.'

'Well, he obviously hadn't forgotten you,' I assure him.

Henri checks his watch. After all the realistic fakes I'd seen being sold cheaply in the shops and street stalls today, I can't help but wonder if it's real. But then, nothing about Henri Chen looks fake or disingenuous.

I suddenly wonder if I'm keeping him from all the other commitments he'd mentioned.

'Maya, it's three o'clock. Do you perhaps have time for a cup of afternoon coffee?'

I hear myself sigh with relief that he has the time to continue our conversation. He seems easy to talk to about Jon and for me to share with him the reasons I am here.

'Oh, yes, absolutely. There's always time for coffee and new friends!'

We gather up our things and walk together across the grass towards a nearby café.

Henri orders our coffee while I take a table outside in the warm sunshine. When he sits down opposite me, he gives me a charming smile and asks more about Jon and how we met.

I give him the speedy version of our love story because I really want to talk about Jon's life here in Hong Kong. Henri tells me how, after graduating in 1995, he and Jon had come over to Hong Kong together to go into banking. Pointing to a high-rise directly across the bay now dwarfed by those more recently built on the harbour front he told me, 'That building was our office back then and we worked on the fortieth floor.' He laughs at his memories. 'I remember the day we all got these brand-new computers – they were still great hulking desktop machines in those days – all with the new-fangled Windows system installed. But, of course, Jon soon had his screen plastered with all his usual Post-it note reminders!'

We laugh together over Jon's compulsion for the yellow stickers.

'Jon was like an elder brother to me. But, after the big stock market crash when millions of dollars were lost overnight, Jon moved on to Kuala Lumpur and the last I heard he was in Singapore.'

He seemed so sad at losing Jon – something I empathised with and appreciated.

Then there was a moment of silence as Henri looked at me over the rim of his coffee cup.

Taking this as a cue that it was my turn to speak, I explain a bit more about Jon's travel wallet and the 'magical mystery tour' and how this whole trip had been arranged by Jon as our backpacking honeymoon. I tell him how I'd just been in India, staying at an ashram, failing at learning how to chant and meditate properly while under the mistaken belief I was walking in Jon's and The Beatles' footsteps. I complain about all the rules and there being no coffee or wine. I laugh and make it all sound quite amusing in order to lighten up the conversation.

But then I also tell him how I've been practicing authentic yoga every day. How chakra healing and cosmic ordering had helped me to focus on positive energies and how taking part in the Ceremony of Light on the holy river Ganges had been profoundly healing for me.

'I didn't think it was possible. But ... well, in the end, it was a truly amazing experience.'

He listens with sympathy in his green eyes and a knot of concern fixed on his brow, studying me carefully over his coffee cup again before clarifying his thoughts.

'So, let me get this right, Maya. You are actually on your honeymoon. But alone?'

'Yes, that's right. After Jon died, I decided I needed to do this and that it's what he would have wanted.' I suddenly realise this conversation is getting way too dark and intense, teetering on tackling the subject of my grief, so I quickly change the subject. 'Henri, earlier, you mentioned that you have other commitments. I understand you live here in Hong Kong but what is it you do now? Are you still in banking?'

'Oh, no. I took early retirement a couple of years ago.

Now I have my boat. When I'm not practicing Tai Chi in the park, I'm sailing on the sea or I'm racing across the oceans looking for adventure!' His green eyes shine with excitement when he mentions his boat and sailing.

'It sounds like it could be rather dangerous adventuring to me!' I exclaim.

'Ah ... but wine hath drowned more men than the sea.' He quoted to me, still laughing.

I laugh too. 'Jules Verne?'

He shakes his head. 'Thomas Fuller.'

My heart swells like a great wave. I do admire a man who knows how to quote great literature.

I realise why Jon and Henri/Harry had been such good friends in the past. They were obviously very alike. Not physically, of course, as Jon had been smaller and neater in stature than his tall and wide-chested friend. But they were obviously both well-travelled and well-educated men and clearly they'd both had a penchant for adventure in their lives.

'I imagine, based in Hong Kong, you're ideally situated to sail anywhere?'

'That's absolutely right,' he agrees. 'In fact, I've got a sailing team arriving in a couple of days to help me skipper my rig in next weekend's Blue Sea Classic Race. Experienced sailing crews will happily come in from all over the world to bag a big race like this one. Some of my team I've sailed with before and others come highly recommended. I'm racing to win this year.'

I'm even more impressed. 'And where is it you are racing to exactly?' I ask him.

'Across the China Sea from Hong Kong to Singapore.'

My eyes shoot open at the mention of Singapore, as I'm in Singapore next weekend, too.

'How long do you expect it will take you to sail there?'

'Two days. We leave on Saturday and should arrive early on Monday morning.'

'So it's not just a hobby. You're a competitive sailor?'

'Yes, absolutely. Do you like boats, Maya?'

I laugh. 'Well, I took the Star Ferry across the harbour to get here today. Does that count?'

He laughs again. He really does have a delightful laugh. When his smile reaches the crinkled corners of his eyes, they twinkle the same way Jon's had, and it makes my stomach flip.

'Sure. That counts. Only, I was wondering, Maya, if perhaps you'd like to meet up again later this evening? Because, if you haven't seen it yet, I'd like to show you our famous Symphony of Lights show. The very best place to see it is from a boat in the middle of the bay.'

I'm taken aback by his kind offer. 'Oh, wow. Thank you, that would be wonderful!'

Henri looks pleased. With our coffee now finished, we stand to leave.

He touches me lightly on the arm once again and I feel my heart quicken. Perhaps a rush of enthusiasm about seeing him again so soon?

Why not? A charming friend of Jon's would be an exciting companion to take me sightseeing.

'Shall I pick you up from your hotel?'

Suddenly, I was embarrassed about where I was staying. It was, I was sure, the most expensive hotel in the city, and for some reason I didn't want Henri to make any assumptions about me. 'Oh, no. There's no need. Just tell me where and when and I'll see you there.'

'Okay. The Yacht Club at Causeway Bay at 7pm.'

'Then I'll see you there!'

* * *

I take the ferry back across to Hong Kong Island, gazing dreamily up at the skyscrapers on the harbour frontage and at the building that Henri had pointed out to me as the place where he and Jon had worked together. I see it's now the HSBC building. I'm pleased about the prospect of seeing Henri again. But only, of course, I reason, because he is my connection to Jon here. Certainly not because he is incredibly attractive and he has his own boat.

It was simply wonderful to talk with someone who knew Jon years before I did.

I wonder what I should wear tonight? What on earth do people wear on boats? It was warm and humid at night and so perhaps I'd only need something light. But then it might be cooler and breezy out on the water? I decide on my white trousers and my cashmere V-neck sweater. Classic but casual.

I wonder what Henri's boat might look like.

What did I know about boats? Nothing at all. In fact, other than this ferry boat, I can't recall ever being on one before now.

Looking down from Victoria Peak this morning, I'd seen some extravagant looking vessels in the water between the islands and in the marina. If Henri is into boat racing, then he might have a sleek speed boat with fast engines or perhaps even one with great voluminous sails. Whatever type or size Henri's boat turned out to be, one thing was for sure, tonight was going to be a wonderful experience and I was looking forward to it very much.

* * *

Back at the hotel, I take a long decadent bubble bath to soothe my tired and aching legs, sore from walking so many miles today. I wash my hair and, having worn it pulled back today in a ponytail, leave it loose and carefree for tonight. The high humidity was making my naturally curly hair lie in tousled coils and I've decided not to fight it. I simply apply a slick of pink lip gloss and a flick of mascara, before slipping into my flat-soled plimsoles.

After glancing at my reflection in the ever-so-flattering bathroom mirror, I'm ready to go. But, suddenly and unexpectedly, I started feeling somewhat uncomfortable and nervous.

About what, I ask myself? Henri? His boat? Because Jon has been dead only three weeks and this felt like I was going out on a date?

I give my reflection a stern glare, point a finger, and speak to it out loud.

'This isn't a date. I'm actually doing this for you, Jon!'

As I ride the elevator down to the lobby, I tell myself – and therefore Jon – that tonight I would simply be enjoying the company of a new old friend on his boat while seeing the much-anticipated light show in the harbour. And there was absolutely nothing wrong with that.

When I reach the lobby, I ask the concierge about calling a taxi for the ten-minute ride down to the marina. But this time, rather than a taxi, she absolutely insists on bringing around one of the hotel's complimentary green Rolls Royces for me and just moments later it glides up to the door. I'm told it's all part of the service and a perk of staying in the hotel and she wouldn't hear otherwise.

I can't help but feel embarrassed because, once again, I felt like a terrible imposter climbing into such a luxurious car.

What would Henri think when he saw my grand entrance? Would he consider me showy and pretentious arriving in a signature Rolls Royce? And it was such an ostentatious giveaway as to exactly where I was staying since the hotel's logo is on display on the side of the car. Would he think I was insanely rich or in some way trying to impress him?

As the car draws through the gates of the marina in the half light of dusk, I catch sight of a tall, dashingly handsome man in a pair of pale chino shorts and a blue polo shirt, and see it's Henri. I peer through the darkened car window and am immediately distracted by how very different he looks out of his white-silk-pyjama outfit.

He meets me at the kerbside and has opened the door before the driver even has a chance.

I feel myself blushing as he looks at me in the same appreciative way I'd looked at him.

'Good evening, Maya!' He kisses me on both sides of my flushed face in the French style, momentarily grazing my hot cheeks with his smoothly shaven jaw, while at the same time offering up an intoxicating whiff of his zesty cologne.

'Good evening, Henri. So nice to see you again and on such a lovely night.'

He escorts me towards the marina, to the dock where he said his boat was moored.

We walk along a wooden walkway past lots of impressive looking boats. Some are enormous, modern, sleek yachts and some are catamarans with huge sails.

We walk past all these luxurious vessels right to the very end of the dock where I spot a small wooden boat. When we stop at its mooring, Henri gestures to the little boat with a nod and a smile. And, I must admit, it wasn't at all what I'd been expecting.

To me, this didn't look like a race boat. It had neither big engines nor large sails.

To me, this looked like an old tugboat, with its battered livery and oily mooring ropes.

I gaze at it for a moment, wondering what to say about it. For some reason, this boat reminds me of *The African Queen* – the old wooden boat from the movie of the same name that starred Katherine Hepburn and Humphrey Bogart (it had been my mum's favourite film and so was one of mine too) – except this boat was sitting so low in the water I feared it had actually sprung a leak and might be sinking. Good heavens!

'Isn't she a beauty?' he prompts, rubbing his hands together in anticipation of my praise.

Should I perhaps admit that I'd been expecting something more erm ... seaworthy?

'She's very ... nice,' I tell him, thinking my white trousers will soon be ruined.

Henri bursts into peals of laughter and I realise he was having me on. This was a joke.

'This actually isn't your boat at all, is it?' I clarify, waving my finger.

'No. It's not. I'm sorry, Maya. It was a bit naughty of me. But when I saw this old cruiser, I couldn't resist!'

'Well, for a minute there, you had me worried for your seafaring safety at the weekend!'

As it turned out, Henri's boat was one of the ones we'd already walked past, a sleek, modern yacht with an expansive teak deck, gleaming bodywork and two huge white sails flapping above us in the warm evening breeze.

Henri's boat is called *Super Typhoon*.

'Well, I do feel you have more chance of winning with this one. She's impressive.'

'She's a performance cruising yacht. Built for beauty and speed,' he tells me proudly.

And, like a true gentleman, he holds my hand and guides me carefully across the gangplank.

'Let me give you the grand tour,' he offers and together we stand in the mid-section, below the main mast with its vast sail, where there's a comfortable open seating area.

Towards the back of the boat, I can see a huge steering wheel and a high-tech instrument board. The rest of the deck extends out towards the narrowest point at the front.

Everything, from the deck to the rails, looks immaculately clean and highly polished. I would never have imagined that a racing boat would be so beautifully accommodated. There's even a small but perfectly equipped galley kitchen. As we investigate a gangway, I pop my head into lots of small cabins containing single crew beds as well as a few larger sized bedrooms with en-suite facilities, double beds, wardrobes, and even plush sofas.

It's incredible. 'So, do you actually live on here all the time?' I enquire.

'Yeah. This is home for me. I sold my apartment two years ago to buy her.'

'Well, it's fabulous Henri!'

'Come on. Let's go back up on deck. It's time to cast off. The sun's almost down.'

Henri suggests I stand with him at the helm when we set sail. Except, I didn't quite anticipate how much the boat would roll and pitch and rock about in the water, and soon I'm feeling a bit strange. 'Erm, I'm afraid I feel a bit dizzy,' I reluctantly admit to him.

Oh, how embarrassing! I've only been on this boat a short while and I'm already feeling quite ill.

Henri looks at me with kindly concern as I stagger over to the seating area, to sit eyeing the water slapping against the side of the boat, worrying that I might actually throw up.

'You do look a bit green about the gills. Do you always get seasick?'

'I don't know!' I wail. 'Like I said earlier, I've only ever been on the Star Ferry.'

'Well, right now, there's a swell because we're at cross-currents entering the harbour,' he explains. 'Sit tight. I promise we'll be in flat water soon and you'll be back to feeling okay!'

He looks like a man who keeps his promises. So I try to relax, and not to feel so sick.

It's horribly disconcerting to feel everything in the world around me moving.

Once we enter the harbour, where I can see the Star Ferry boats still going back and forth across the straits between the Tsim Sha Tsui Pier and Kowloon Island, and the larger tourist boats jostling for a good position to see the light show, the water was indeed much calmer and there's so much going on around us that I'm distracted from feeling wobbly.

I see the big old tourist junk with its indigo red sails that I'd watched from my window last night, incredibly rowdy and crowded tonight. I realise and appreciate how fortunate I am to have such a special view of the show from Henri's yacht.

When Henri is satisfied that we're in a prime position, he drops anchor and quickly produces a small tray of aperitifs from the galley, opening a bottle of Champagne that he'd had chilling. I'm so excited as he pops the cork and offers me a foaming flute.

Never in my wildest dreams would I ever have expected to come to Hong Kong and experience this kind of fabulousness and luxury. I'd known from Jon's itinerary that I was staying in the oldest five-star hotel in the city but never would I have expected to be standing on a luxury yacht in the harbour with a very handsome consort and a glass of Bollinger in my hand. Once again, I have to pinch myself to check this is real and not a dream.

To think that this time last year Jon had yet to walk into my office and my life.

I'd been working nine to five in that stuffy office, feeling trapped and dissatisfied with my life, imagining an alternative life abroad and spinning the globe on my desk while dreaming of travel and adventure. All the while knowing nothing of how things would eventually turn out for me.

Of course, I still don't know how things will turn out for me, but I'm determined to take the advice of Swami Nanda and make this all about opening my heart and having faith in the future.

I've decided I'm going to take one day and one adventure at a time and seize every moment.

'Henri, I want to thank you. This is really fantastic and so much fun!' I tell him gratefully.

'Well, Maya, if you don't mind me saying, I think you might need a little fun in your life.'

I take in his raised eyebrows and his raised glass and I have to agree with him.

'Then let's drink to having fun!' I say as we toast and sip from our champagne flutes.

In that moment, at exactly 8pm, the sky lights up and my breath is taken away as the spectacle around us starts with a booming and melodious musical creation that Henri tells me was composed especially for this show by the Hong Kong Philharmonic Orchestra. The whole of the harbour area is a giant musical stage. My eyes are dazzled with lights as I gaze up at the far-reaching streams of light being beamed vertically into the sky, where they brighten the darkness and the clouds above us, highlighting their silver linings. Moments later, more laser beams are projected into myriad dancing, changing colours to pulse and bounce across the water on to the buildings surrounding where the lights leap and burst to the choreographed musical score. It's incredibly uplifting and I watch in childlike wonder while gasping with delight.

If this happens here every night then I can only imagine what happens on New Year's Eve!

Time seems to stand still while I pause next to Henri on the gently swaying deck.

When I turn in excitement to point something out to him, I see that he seems more interested and amused in watching me watching the show, than in watching the show himself.

I suppose that's because he must have seen it all a million times before.

Whereas I hardly dared to blink in case I missed a second of it.

Just then a giant explosion of light and a booming crescendo of sound signalled that the spectacle was over for another night and the sound of the music was replaced by the sound of cheers from both of us and from those all around us.

'I'm guessing you enjoyed it?' Henri chuckles. 'Your eyes were so wide that you reminded me of that song 'Lucy in the Sky with Diamonds'!'

I blink to try and clear my speckled vision from all the reflected residual light.

'Oh, so you're a Beatles fan, too?' I ask, recognising another similarity to Jon.

Henri tops up my Champagne glass. 'Yes. Actually, it was Jon who got me into The Beatles. I remember he had all their songs on vinyl and eight-track tapes. He was a big fan.'

I raise my glass again. 'What shall we drink to next?'

'Let's drink to friendship,' Henri suggests, looking me in the eyes with great sincerity.

I nod and smile and happily chink my glass against his once more. 'To friendship.'

Once we've finished our drinks, Henri begins steering the boat back around to the marina.

I'm sad that the show only lasted ten minutes. I'd wanted it to go on and on.

Now that the water is calmer, and I'm buoyed up on happiness and alcohol, I'm really enjoying myself, and can't seem to get enough of staring at the lights and colours of the illuminated cityscape. Henri explains to me that the harbour gets dangerously crowded at this time of night with so many boats around. And I can see this is true. The bigger commercial vessels are now blasting their horns at the smaller private pleasure-boats. Some of them are hosting booze cruises and others are darting around on what look like collision courses with the Star Ferries. We make our exit from the waters of the harbour slowly and this time I stand beside Henri at the helm as we head back to the marina, chatting and reminiscing about Jon again.

Or rather, I did, as a result of Henri's mention of The Beatles.

Chatting distracts me from feeling queasy as the dark water all around us slaps a little more violently against the sides of the boat and the two glasses of Champagne fizz and churn in my stomach. Henri listens attentively as he steers the yacht, but it's a matter of concern to me that he now wears the same frown on his face that I saw earlier today.

Perhaps he's thinking about his big race at the weekend, or maybe he's getting tired of me talking about Jon all the time? I decide to change the subject in case it's the latter. 'So, Henri, except for when you were at boarding school in the UK, have you always lived in Hong Kong?'

'Yes. Most of my life. I was born in France. My mother is French. My father Chinese.'

To me, this perfectly explained his incredible good-looks. There is something rather gorgeous about his wide green eyes, his olive skin, and his amazing bone structure. I quickly give myself a mental reprimand for even thinking the words 'incredible' and 'gorgeous' to describe my new friend.

When we arrive safely back at the mooring, Henri asks me if I'm feeling hungry.

'Only, there's a very good restaurant on the marina. They do a great sweet and sour dish.'

I honestly don't feel hungry so I feel a little reticent. Being invited onto Henri's yacht to watch the light show in the harbour is one thing, and fine by me, but going for a meal afterwards in a restaurant feels like a step too far, as though I am signing off on this being a proper date.

I politely decline and he looks momentarily disappointed before offering to call me a taxi.

I suddenly remembered about the old Post-it note that I'd wanted to show him. 'Oh, before I go, I wanted to show you something. I found it inside Jon's travel folder.'

I quickly fish the note out from the bottom of my bag.

'I found this attached to this old Star Ferry brochure. It mentions you – or, Harry Chen, at least – and I was hoping you might know what it means?'

Henri stares down at the note with disbelief on his face and then he looks bemused.

Harry Chen still owes me a chip.

'Oh, my, I can't believe it. He actually kept it all these years!'

'So ... you do know? You know what kind of chip it refers to?'

'Yes. I do. And I still have it in my possession to this very day.'

He disappears for a moment below deck and returns with a coin purse. From the purse, he pulls out a large, shiny, golden coin. At first impression, it looks something like one of those big gold-wrapped chocolate coins you give children at Christmas.

We slide into the seats on deck with a table between us and conspire under a light emanating from the mast. Henri places the coin down in front of me. It's stamped with an imprint of the number fifty in numerals, an image of a flower – a lotus flower – and the words 'Casino Lotus Macau'.

'This chip is one of two that Jon and I won in Macau on a night of serious gambling and drinking back in the late 90s.' I can see from the smile playing on Henri's lips and the light shining in his eyes that he's remembering a night that must have really meant something to him. I desperately want to know more. I've heard of Macau because Jon had mentioned it to me once. He'd described it as a mecca of casinos, gambling, and glitz in an autonomous territory once ruled by Portugal which is now, like Hong Kong, a special administrative region ruled by China.

'Macau? Yes, I've heard of it. So ... it's not too far from here?' I query.

Henri shrugs. 'Not far at all. Just an hour away by boat.'

'And this isn't a coin. It's a fancy gambling chip?' I pick it up and find it surprisingly heavy. 'Can you tell me what you remember about that night?' I urge him.

Henri rakes his fingers through his short dark hair and laughs. 'Sure. I remember how back then we'd both had a pretty tough week on the trading floor. But it was payday, and as we were hot-headed, cashed-up professionals who were always looking for the next adventure, we decided to head over to Macau to try our luck on the roulette tables.'

'What happened? Tell me about roulette.'

Having never gambled or been inside a casino myself, I'm fascinated by the concept of winning and losing, and how that might be something that could be swayed by cosmic ordering.

Henri laughs again. 'Well, with poker or blackjack or craps, you have to possess a certain kind of seriousness and a degree of knowledge of the game. Whereas, for a pair of chancers like us, roulette is easy because there are no secrets to learn – it's a game of pure chance and luck.'

Chance, luck ... and fate, perhaps?

'We somehow managed to crash a party at The Lotus Casino and it turned into a wild night.' Henri continues. 'The Champagne was flowing and the roulette wheel was spinning. For some reason we were winning more than losing for a change. And, when it was over, in the early hours of the next morning, I do recall that we caught the first ferry back and went straight into work. In those days, we really thought nothing of burning the candle at both ends.'

'And so, this chip was your winnings from that night?'

'Yeah, well, I thought so. But Jon maintained this chip belonged to him. Hence the note.'

He leans in to tell me more and, in that moment, with our faces just inches apart, I find myself looking deeply into his eyes and catching my breath at the intensity with which he returns my gaze. 'You know, there's a famous old story about a man who used to gamble at The Lotus. He wanted to win so badly that he sold his soul to the devil in exchange for the secrets of their roulette table. That's why the game's also known as "the devil's wheel". His lips curve into a boyish smile and his eyes shine with mischief. 'And that's why the numbers on the wheel add up to 666.'

'Tell me more about the chip? Did you have to sell your soul to get it?'

'No, nothing like that, because lady luck was on our side that night. We came away from that table with not one but two of these "lucky" golden chips.'

'Lucky? Why are they said to be lucky?'

'Because that night they had a bonus on their value. But I remember that what happened next wasn't so lucky.'

'How so? What happened?' I'm completely enthralled by this story.

'Well, when we got back to Hong Kong, I had both chips on me. So, I flipped one over to Jon. But as he was still quite drunk he missed catching it and it went straight into the harbour.'

I gasp. 'Oh no! What did he do?'

'He insisted that it was *my* chip I'd lost and not his. That I still owed him a chip. I guess he must have written it down on this Post-it note in case he forgot about it when he sobered up.'

'That is a wild story. I wish I'd known Jon back then,' I say wistfully.

Not that I could ever imagine myself being as wild and adventurous as him.

Back then, during the time Henri and Jon where having such fun, I was a bored and boring twenty-seven-year-old woman – working in a bank, dressing in scratchy tweed suits – whose idea of fun was watching stock prices and whose only focus in life was the dream of eventually buying my own house and moving out of my parents' home.

Oh how I wished I'd just packed a backpack and used my savings to travel and to live!

Henri looks thoughtful. 'You know, if it hadn't been for the big crash, I'm sure Jon and I would have gone back to The Lotus the very next chance we had to spend this chip and give the wheel another spin. But the rest, as they say, is history.'

'The big crash? Is this the day you spoke of when Hong Kong reverted back to China?'

'Yeah. It was the prelude to all the protests and riots we still see today and the very start of a banking crisis. All the financial institutions closed their doors, the casinos shut down, and everyone prayed for a currency exchange-rate recovery.'

'And was there one?'

He shakes his head. 'No. Instead there was a commercial meltdown. The government at the time couldn't stabilise the currency and all our investors' dreams – together with our jobs – went up in smoke. Up until that point, Hong Kong had been booming, everyone making and spending lots of money, but it was the beginning of the end of an era. I stayed because Hong Kong is my home and I'd just met my now ex-wife. Jon took a chance and jumped ship. I can't say I blamed him.'

We both sit in silence for a moment, reflecting.

I want to ask him more about his marriage but that seems far too personal a subject.

'And ... you and Jon never saw each other again?' I venture instead.

'No. I'm afraid not. Like I say, it wasn't so easy back then with no Twitter or Facebook.'

Henri slides the golden chip in front of me. It shines under the mast light and lights up both our faces in a golden glow.

'Maya, the coin is yours. I've finally repaid Jon his chip and now he can rest in peace.'

I stare down at the chip and wonder what I'm supposed to do with it.

'If you don't mind me suggesting it, I really think you should take yourself over to Macau tomorrow night and put it on the roulette table at The Lotus. Give it a spin in Jon's memory. Have some fun, win or lose. That way, we'll have both done right by him.'

'But this chip is decades old!' I remind him.

'Ah, but you can be sure a casino will always honour its debts and its chips.'

My heart skips a beat. It did seem kind of fortuitous once again seeing the symbol of the lotus flower. I'd seen it in the ashram. I'd seen it when I'd been offered my divine wish by the swami at the airport in Delhi. Now here it was again in Hong Kong.

Was it linked to my fate somehow?

I'm tempted to do as Henri suggested because tomorrow is Friday and my last day here before I leave for Singapore. He also made it sound like the right thing to do in Jon's memory.

Win or lose. It sounded like a great adventure and something that could be a lot of fun.

And, Henri was right. I really needed more fun in my life.

'I assume the 'fifty' stamped on it means it was worth fifty Hong Kong dollars?' I suggest.

'Yeah, I think so. Plus whatever the bonus was on that night. You never know, with inflation, it could be worth a small fortune now,' Henri suggests with a grin.

'Fifty Hong Kong dollars is actually worth less than five pounds GBP. So, if you're right, it could be worth a *very* small fortune indeed!' I say, laughing at his infectious optimism.

He shrugs his shoulders and challenges me with his sparkling green eyes again.

I touch the chip with the tips of my fingers and I smile, remembering another of the cryptic messages Jon had left me on a Post-it note. The one that I still hadn't figured out.

Divine number nine!

'You know what? I think you're right. Going over to the casino and spending this chip would be a wonderful way to honour Jon.' I breathe, feeling a heated thrill rushing through my veins.

Henri wriggles his eyebrows at me playfully. 'Atta girl! Go spin that devil's wheel!'

'But I can't go alone. I've honestly never been inside a casino in my entire life. Henri, if I'm going to do this ... then you're going to have to come with me to Macau tomorrow.'

Chapter 15

Hong Kong

I would have completely understood if Henri had declined accompanying me on the Macau trip today. After all, tomorrow afternoon he sets off on his boat race. He'd already explained how all his race supplies were being delivered to his dock first thing this morning and that he was meeting his crew members who were arriving on a flight at noon. Yet he had still agreed to come along tonight!

It was a shame we couldn't make a whole day of it, as there is obviously so much to do and see in Macau – it's not called the Las Vegas of Asia for nothing – but, that said, leaving later in the afternoon actually suits me better too, because today is my last full day here in Hong Kong and I still have something of great personal importance to do.

This time, my plans aren't in Jon's agenda or mentioned on any of his Post-it notes. The only information I have to go by is written on the back of an old photograph.

1975
Shangri-La, Stubbs Road.
Happy Valley, Hong Kong.

I'd looked up the street name in advance to make sure Stubbs Road still existed and – happily – had found that it did. But would the beautiful pink house with the walled garden and tall wrought-iron gate where I'd been born half a century ago still be there? I'd read that the area was popular with ex-pats and had been extensively redeveloped to the detriment of many of the original homes and historic buildings.

Happy Valley, despite its rather twee name, is actually a sprawling lowland area just a few miles inland behind Causeway Bay and between the mountains and Victoria Gap. The area is famous for its racecourse. *One of the oldest institutions in Hong Kong*, according to Jon.

The concierge tells me to take the Number Fifteen circular bus from Central and the journey should take just half an hour. In Victoria Gap, I decide to get off the bus at the very top end of Stubbs Road because the map shows the road runs around the outer perimeter area of the racecourse.

I'm feeling a little intimidated and lost already while standing on the pavement in the morning heat and I'm not entirely sure this is the best place to start my search. I showed my photograph to the bus driver in the hope he might recognise the house if it was on his route, but he'd just shaken his head so now I find myself completely surrounded by towering high-rise apartments.

I look both up and down the road and realise there are no discernible landmarks to guide me except for the race-course itself, which is likely to be the only thing still standing that was here forty-five years ago when I was here last. I continue to walk along the pavements as the morning sun rises steadily in the sky, but I see there are no single homes on this road anymore.

After an hour of walking and searching for a wrought-iron gate and the old pink house, and after showing the photo to everyone who passed me on the road, just in case they happen to be longstanding locals who might recognise it, I finally have to accept that my beloved childhood home is both long gone and long forgotten.

There are now likely to be hundreds of homes built on top of what was once our Shangri-La. I'm crushingly disappointed. I feel tearful. But I have to accept that with real estate in Hong Kong said to be amongst the most expensive in the world, and building plots at a premium here, it makes total sense.

I take a few snaps of the area to send to Pia anyway. At least I can tell her I tried, and she can see for herself exactly what Stubbs Road looks like now – a truly modern metropolis. I make my way back to the bus stop wondering if I'd even been wise to pursue this nostalgic endeavour.

All I'd done was set myself up for disappointment and all I'd achieved was bursting my own idealistic Happy Valley memory bubble.

For so many years throughout my childhood this house had still existed in my imagination. While growing up in dull and rainy Manchester, I'd fantasised about coming back here and finding the house bathed in sunlight, the garden still full of fragrant pink roses. I'd hoped that somehow and someway I'd once again call Shangri-La my home.

But now I know for sure it doesn't exist anymore.

And that makes me feel incredibly sad and empty ... as though I am now ultimately and truly homeless.

The nearest bus stop is just across the street from the entrance to the Jockey Club.

It's a tall modern building with offices and, as I'm here right now and looking along the length of the road I can see no sight of a bus, I consider that it might at least be worth going in with an enquiry about the whereabouts of the old house and what might have happened to it. Maybe there would be someone there who knew it once?

It couldn't hurt to make just one last attempt to jog a local memory, could it?

Inside the reception area there is a young woman behind the welcome desk.

She smiles and greets me but I know she's far too young to know this area from decades ago. I decide to show her the photo anyway, since I'm here, and she suggests that I take a seat.

She takes my photo into the back office and I hear her asking for someone else to help me. That someone else turns out to be a much older man who introduces himself as Mr Lee after striding up to me while holding out my photo, an encouraging smile on his face.

'Hello. I believe you are looking for this place?'

I spring to my feet. 'Yes. Hello. My name is Maya Thomas. This is the house where I was born. I've been exploring the area and I wondered if you might know if it still exists?'

I suddenly realise that I'm wringing my hands and I sound like I'm pleading with him.

'Yes. It still exists. I know it very well. This really is a wonderful old photograph!'

As he hands it back to me, my jaw drops open and my hopeful heart skips a beat.

'My parents took it before we left Hong Kong when I was five. You say you know it well?' I realise I'm shaking with happiness and I'm just about to ask for directions when Mr Lee indicates a display cabinet against a wall. He leads me over and I see it contains horse racing trophies, memorabilia and a book entitled: *The Rich History of Horse Racing in Hong Kong.*

He takes out the book and I wonder what this has to do with the house.

Mr Lee flicks to a section about The Jockey Club

Museum and then taps a neatly shaped fingertip on the page. 'Look. Here's your house. It's been our museum for the past thirty years.'

I stare at the picture in the book and think my eyes must have grown to the size of saucers.

This was without any question the house I'd always known as Shangri-La!

'It's just a short walk away from here,' Mr Lee tells me. 'If you turn right and walk up the hill, you'll see it right in front of you. It looks just the same now as in your photograph.'

On hearing this news, I stutter my thanks with tears brimming in my eyes, my chin wobbling with excitement, anticipation and great relief. I'm so delighted that I kiss Mr Lee on his cheek. He laughs and blushes with embarrassment, but he also seems delighted.

'I should warn you, Miss Thomas, that we are currently in the process of packing up and moving our exhibits and memorabilia into a newer and larger purpose-built museum at the racecourse. I hope it doesn't bother you too much to see the place in some disarray while you look around. The building will soon be empty.'

'Empty?' I repeated. 'Do you mean ... vacant? Is the house ... for sale?'

A million synapses seem to pop in my head at the idea of this house being on the market.

Oh, my goodness. What if I bought it? What if I could actually live here?

Every fantasy I've ever had about buying this house flashes through my mind.

I dare to wonder if I had cosmically ordered this. Was that even possible?

No. Of course not. That's not how it works. Hadn't Guru J said that wishes had to be noble and not about possessions or material things? Besides, hadn't I seen in my research that even the smallest apartments on Stubbs Road were selling for a million dollars? It was highly likely that this house would be worth zillions of dollars in today's market. Zillions of dollars I certainly didn't have.

Besides, Hong Kong was now part of China and the immigration rules were likely complex. I don't know if being born here means I would be allowed to live here for any length of time.

I sigh with resignation at the lovely idea of it but buying the house isn't realistic, practical, or indeed possible.

'Oh, no. It's not for sale,' Mr Lee tells me adamantly.

I sigh with anxious relief. Thank goodness. Because if it's not for sale then I don't have to torment myself over an impossible dream.

If it's not for sale, then I don't have to be upset over not being able to afford it and having to see someone else with incredible amounts of money coming along and snapping it up. Problem solved.

'We've had lots of enquires, of course. Historic houses like this one are highly sought after these days. But this house has been owned by the racecourse for the last thirty years, and I'm told they have no intention of selling it.'

'I understand. Well, thank you again, Mr Lee. I appreciate you giving me this information and, as I haven't seen this house since I was five, I'd really love the opportunity to take a look around. I'm so excited it's still here and looks the same. Seeing all the new high-rises along this road, I had started to think it might have been pulled down a long time ago, and well ... I have so many happy memories of this beautiful house!'

Mr Lee gives me a look of delight but also sympathy and his genuine interest makes me want to continue to explain my reasons for being here, revisiting this house.

'You see, I grew up in the UK but I've always wondered what it might be like to come back here and find it. It might sound a little crazy, but I've always imagined myself actually living here again.' I realise I'm rambling and gushing and therefore embarrassing myself. This man certainly didn't want or need to know my private thoughts and secret longings.

'How wonderful and how very interesting!' Mr Lee exclaims joyfully.

'So, I go out of here and turn right up the hill?' I clarify.

'Yes. That's right. You can't miss it.' Mr Lee insists.

I walk quickly up the steep hill, despite the escalating heat of the late-morning sun shining down on the street and on my head, until in great excitement I see and recognise both the wrought-iron gate in the photograph and the pink house of my dreams.

I stand in front of it and look through the gate into the garden. It really does look the same, except perhaps for the large bay windows on either side of the front door. They had clearly been replaced with newer and modern versions but in the same design. The garden looks more mature as well, the saplings that had lined the driveway now tall, mature trees.

I can hardly contain my excitement as I take some photos with my phone and then swing open the creaky gate and start up the path feeling like I'm walking on air and in some kind of dream world. The front door is open so I just walk inside to find the grand hallway lined with photos of horses and jockeys.

I look through into the reception rooms on both sides of the staircase and see they too are still full of racing memorabilia – saddles and riding clothes, whips and riding caps. In the middle of the hallway, on the strangely familiar black and white tiled floor, are lots of cardboard boxes. As I am taking it all in, a middle-aged man appears from a door beside the grand central staircase, greeting me with a curious hello and an explanation about the move to a new location.

I explain my reasons for the visit and my conversation with Mr Lee and he too encourages me to take a good look around. 'Take your time. If you need anything just give me a shout. I'll be in the back rooms.'

I thank him and wander slowly around the rooms. I'm the only visitor and being alone in these rooms makes this feel even more surreal. I feel as though I've been whizzed back in time. I imagine my mother standing at the table by the window arranging her roses in a vase. In my mind's eye I see my father sitting in his armchair reading the newspaper. I breathe in the smell of the place and let my eyes soak in the view of the side garden and the same expansive view across the familiar square of green clipped lawn where I remember playing as a child. Then I wander towards the rear of the house to gain access to the back garden and find the caretaker busily packing up exhibits into boxes.

'Do you know if the rose garden still exists?' I enquire tentatively.

He helpfully escorts me to the patio doors, and I step out onto the patio and walk across the lawn, following the scent of damask roses on the warm breeze.

With every step, my subconscious memories are being stirred and awakened and this all seems increasingly familiar territory to me. When I reach the rose garden, I see it's now past its best but there are still some late blooms flowering. I bend over to smell a pale pink rose and feel its soft velvety petals tickle my nose. I inhale its sweet musky rose scent and close my eyes to allow myself to be transported through time and space to my childhood. Just then, I hear a voice call my name.

I turn to see Mr Lee from The Jockey Club. He seems

hurried and a little breathless as he approaches. 'Miss Thomas!'

'Yes. What is it Mr Lee?'

'Miss Thomas, I was so struck by what you told me about this house and how you were born here and lived here as a child. I was really touched by you saying how you'd always hoped to come back and how you've imagined living here again. It is such a lovely, very touching story. And, well, it struck me that you might like to rent this house?'

'R-r-rent it?' I stutter.

'Yes. You see, it will soon become available to rent. You can take it on a six-monthly renewable lease. I'll need to check with our head office and confirm to you the rental price. But, if you want it, I could offer it to you. Your visit is so timely that I can't help but think the hand of fate is at work here. Do you believe in fate, Ms Thomas?'

I'm stunned. This is so totally unexpected that it makes my head feel dizzy.

Timely? Coincidence? Chance? Fate?

'I've been looking at rental applications all morning, but I feel you would be by far the most deserving candidate.' Mr Lee assures me with a congratulatory smile. 'It can also be taken fully furnished as we still have all the original furnishings for the house in our storage facility.'

Oh my goodness … did my wish just come true?
Did I order this up from the cosmos?

'Mr Lee, thank you! I really don't know what to say. I'm completely taken by surprise and you are very kind but I need a few days to think this through.'

Mr Lee looks at me with his brow furrowed as though he thought I was being a tad ungrateful.

'Okay. I can hold it for you over the weekend. But only until Monday morning.'

I know that on Monday morning, having spent the weekend in Singapore, I am supposed to be flying to Kuala Lumpur and then on to Penang in Malaysia before heading back to London.

'Thank you, Mr Lee. I'm sure you can understand this is a really big and important decision.'

I search the bottom of my handbag for a scrap of paper, my hand catching on a yellow Post-it note.

I see it's the one with *Tai Chi* written on it.

I scribble my email address onto the back of it for Mr Lee.

'Please email me all the details of the lease and I promise I'll get back to you by Monday.'

I leave the house in a bit of a daze, my brain racing through all possibilities and scenarios.

Could I live here in Hong Kong for six months?

Well, actually, the arrival stamp in my passport says I can.

And I currently have nowhere to live back in the UK. So, why not stay here for a while? I'm retired now. Why not finally live my dream? Six months in Hong Kong in this beautiful house of nostalgia would be wonderful. And I'd have Henri Chen as my Tai Chi Master.

What would Pia say? I think she'd say: *why not try it? What do you have to lose?*

I'd miss her and the family of course. But I'd have plenty of room for them all to come for a holiday!

I'd also miss my friends in the choir and my ex-colleagues from the bank. But in truth, they are always so incredibly busy, and they are all married anyway so I can't expect they'll miss me too much in return. Besides, we can all stay in touch on Facebook and Instagram.

This could be a fresh start. I could still hold Jon in my heart but live a whole new life. This could be my chance to move forward and my reason to start to live again. My divine wish!

Perhaps, before I get too excited, I should wait until I find out how much the rent costs each month. I've no idea what rents are in this area and it might simply be too much.

I walk back down the hill to the bus stop and silently argue with myself about jumping into a hasty and regretful decision. Just because I have the proceeds of my house sale in my bank account right now and my investments and redundancy money tucked away, doesn't mean I should fritter it all away on paying rent. I've always been a believer in buying and investing in property and not renting it. I'm also still ten years away from being able to draw my private pension and that's a scary thought. Scary because, at fifty years old, I'm hardly highly employable anymore.

I'm not just retired, I'm also redundant. No one wants a middle-aged woman greeting clients and advising them on their investments when they can have fresh young faces straight out of university instead. Not to mention the economics of paying them a fraction of what I was earning as a senior account manager. No. The sensible thing would be to go back to the UK to settle down, buy myself a small house and appreciate what I've built for myself as a nest egg over the years. A safe situation.

I have to be realistic and realise that all this talk about moving to Hong Kong is nothing but a pipe dream.

Chapter 16

I catch the bus going back into the Old Town and head straight to a café for lunch. I drink lots of chai and eat dim sum again while flicking through my phone. Despite having convinced myself that living in Hong Kong and renting anywhere is a bad idea, I still can't hold back my curiosity or my compulsion to browse real estate rentals in Hong Kong online.

I want to get a proper idea of what kind of prices the big old beautiful houses in The Gap rented for these days. There weren't many examples but, of course, the ones I did see advertised were so ridiculously expensive that it only confirmed to me it's best to put this whole crazy idea that Mr Lee had put in my head to rest once and for all.

I decide that I need to do a bit of what my sister Pia calls 'retail therapy' instead.

I need to go shopping anyway because if I am going into a casino tonight with Henri then I need to look the part. I've never been to a casino before, but I've seen lots of movies featuring casinos and I particularly remember a James Bond movie in which he went to a casino in Macau. All the women looked incredibly glamorous, wearing what my mother would have called 'glad rags' and I know I have nothing even remotely like that in my backpack. So I amble down a few side streets until I spot a small boutique tucked away in an alley. On a mannequin in the window I see a fabulous, glamorous, close-fitting, calf-length, black silk gown with a high neck and a low-cut back. It catches my eye because it has a fine lace layer overdress that looks almost translucent against the black shift underdress. I stare at it and wonder what it might feel like to wear such an exotic gown.

I decide to go inside and when I try it on I feel like I'm wearing a slinky black gossamer cobweb. To be quite honest, I can hardly believe it's my own reflection in the mirror.

I've lost weight over the past couple of weeks and for the first time in over a decade, I can see a more sculpted face looking back at me.

As I smooth the dress down over my hips, I wonder who this strangely self-assured and mythical creature in the mirror is. The sales assistant tells me it's absolutely perfect for a casino and I couldn't agree more.

* * *

Back in my hotel suite, I still have a couple of hours to get ready so I take a fragrant bath.

While the water is running, I practice yoga in order to calm my nerves about this evening. I'm feeling both excited and terribly anxious about all that has happened here in Hong Kong.

The excitement of seeing all the sights that Jon had wanted me to experience here – meeting Henri – rediscovering my childhood home and then hearing the unexpected offer and the possibility, and of course the impossibility, of renting it. It's a lot to process over just a couple of days and strangely, my time in India seems like it happened many months ago now. My tragic wedding day seems not mere weeks, but years ago.

It's as though time and distance and my understanding of it all has become distorted.

This magical mystery tour is definitely turning out to be the adventure Jon promised!

I feel like Jon had planned for me to meet Henri. How could it be any other way? It certainly hadn't been by chance or coincidence. In fact, every Post-it note in Jon's wallet had seemingly led me straight to Henri.

And now, with Jon in my heart, I'm about to go out and experience and recreate with Henri what was, and will be again, a night of thrills gambling in a casino. How very exciting!

After my yoga practice and a quiet time of calming meditation followed by a decadent bath, it's finally time for me to get dressed, my mind now focussed very much on the task at hand.

I tease and smooth my hair back into a tight sleek chignon that I've rolled at the nape of my neck and secured with a black ribbon. Then I slip into my racy and lacy and, dare I say it, *sexy*, new black dress, and slide into my new high-heel shoes before applying a slick of glossy red lipstick. Only then does a frisson of nerves and another episode of terrible guilt consume me.

I quickly rub the lipstick off my lips. I decide it looks garish and too much.

What on earth am I doing? This isn't a bloody date!

And what if this isn't how women dress in casinos in Macau? Or indeed anywhere else? What if I'm under-dressed or in fact horribly overdressed? What if I've made a big mistake?

Is this dress too young for me? What was it my mother used to say ... mutton dressed as lamb?

What if Henri thought I'd gone totally overboard? That would be so embarrassing!

Maybe I should wear something less showy and more practical?

I eye up my comfortable ashram clothes in the wardrobe and groan in despair.

Then I take a deep breath and suddenly remember, to my horror, that I'd forgotten we would be travelling to Macau by boat. Henri had said that Macau was 'just an hour away by boat'. A whole hour at sea! Oh dear. What if I get horribly seasick on the way over there?

Henri had said all his race crew were all staying on

board the *Super Typhoon* tonight ahead of the race tomorrow. Maybe that means we'll be taking the public ferry over to Macau. That might take even longer than an hour!

I really should have thought to buy some seasickness pills today when I'd had the chance.

I pick up my phone to check how long the Hong Kong ferry takes to travel to Macau and it's then I see there's an amber alert been given for high winds and the possibility of high swells on the open sea tonight. I feel my stomach roll over with nerves once again. Oh, my goodness!

I'm supposed to be meeting Henri down at the marina at 6.30pm. What if I chicken out and don't go? I could feign an illness and simply call it off?

Except I don't have Henri's phone number and I can't bring myself to just not turn up. That would be terribly rude and very bad mannered.

Besides, thanks to the hotel's signature Rolls Royce, he knew exactly where I was staying.

I check the mirror again and see the reflection of the mystical woman who isn't afraid. The woman who insisted on travelling alone so soon after losing the love of her life. The woman who managed to travel solo across Northern India having never travelled outside of the UK before. Who had happily broken all the rules of the ashram and then risked immersing herself in the holy river Ganges. The woman who was strong and determined and who wouldn't let anything, or anyone, stand in her way of completing this important mission, this mighty pilgrimage, this loyal quest in Jon's memory. I grab my clutch bag and leave the room before I can change my mind again.

I ask the concierge to call me a car to take me down to the marina and I also ask her if she knows how I might get hold of a couple of seasickness tablets. I'm asked to wait a moment.

She soon returns with a packet of pills. 'We recommend taking two, madam.'

'Then I'll take two right now as I'm heading out on the ferry shortly. Thank you.'

* * *

When the Rolls drives through the gates at the marina, I see Henri standing in the same spot as last night, in anticipation of my arrival. He's a delightful and thoroughly unsettling sight in his own glad rags. I climb out of the car into a stiff but warm breeze blowing in from the sea and into his outstretched and waiting arms.

He greets me enthusiastically with another of his double cheek kisses, dousing me in a sensual waft of his manly citrus cologne. I have to take deep calming breaths to settle my escalating heart rate.

'Henri, you look wonderful in your tuxedo!' I gush in absolute honesty.

'And, Maya, you look fabulous in your gown!' He tells me, looking quite taken aback too.

I do a little twirl and find myself giggling with excitement and anticipation.

It feels so special to be dressed up and in the company of such a charming man.

I tell myself that Jon would approve, then try to silence the little voice inside that is chiding me at being overly impressed with Henri's looks and how well he has polished up.

I see Henri quickly check his watch. 'We have time for a quick drink before we leave.'

As an escalating wind whips around us, he slips my hand into his to escort me just a few metres along the wharf to where the yacht club has a private bar and restaurant.

Henri opens and holds the door for me and guides me ahead of him with the lightest touch of his hand on the small of my back. With my dress cut low, his fingers happen to touch my bare skin for a moment and a wave of goose bumps tingles down the length of my spine.

'Are you feeling chilly?' he asks, seeing me shivering.

'Oh, no. Not at all!' I profess. 'It's just the draft from the air con above the door.'

Henri nods to a security man in the foyer who greets us and calls him 'Captain' as he waves us on towards the cocktail bar.

'Maya, what would you like to drink?' Henri asks as we both take a stool at the highly polished wood bar. I'm not sure if I should have anything alcoholic because I'm suddenly feeling rather lightheaded. I'm not sure if it was the sight of Henri in his tux, the intoxicating scent of his cologne, or the lightness of his touch on my sensitive bare skin that I've yet to recover from.

'Oh, just a club soda for me, thank you.'

'Okay. If you're sure? You don't want a glass of Champagne?'

'Well, I heard it's possible that the sea crossing could be a bit rough tonight. So I'm just being cautious,' I tell him, trying not to let my voice tremble in case it betrays my nerves.

'Ah, yes. That's very true. And it's why I've decided that we should fly to Macau instead.'

A sense of relief washes over me. Henri was being incredibly considerate. Especially as, being a sailor of the high seas, he was unlikely to suffer seasickness himself.

'So we're heading off to the airport soon?'

'No need.' Henri tells me with a dismissive wave of his hand.

In that moment I see that he's wearing gold cufflinks at his wrist in the shape of dice.

'We've a helipad right here at the marina. Our pilot has just messaged me to say that he'll arrive in fifteen minutes. Plenty of time for an aperitif.'

I'm a little dumbstruck at this and feeling more than a little nervous, to be honest. I'm not normally afraid of flying but to me helicopters have always looked very dangerous. I've seen too many movies in which they crash horribly.

'A helicopter!' I gasp in what sounds a bit like strangled panic.

Having just stepped over to take our order, the barman obviously thinks I'm ordering an obscure cocktail and looks understandably confused.

'Two club sodas please.' Henri instructed.

My mouth is so dry that when I take a gulp from my fizzy water, I suddenly get a terrible bout of the hiccups. How embarrassing. I haven't suffered with hiccups for years!

'I'm sooo velly excited abooot going to the cashiono!' I profess before realising that it didn't actually make sense.

'Maya, are you okay?' Henri asks me, looking at me suspiciously.

'I'm not entirely sure,' I confess. 'I took some pills so I wouldn't be seasick.'

'What did you take and how many?' he says, looking into my eyes in concern.

'Twhoo. Itch called Dramashumthing.'

For some reason my mouth won't work properly.

Hiccup! I produce the packet I'd been given and Henri shakes his head.

'Two is too many. These things can make you really high and drowsy.'

'Oh, no I'm snot sweepy!' I insist. 'I'm feeling velly happy achtuchly.'

Henri's phone pings. 'Okay. That's our chopper. Ready to go?'

I slide off the stool repeating the word 'chopper' and giggling like a naughty schoolgirl.

Henri links his arm in mine to guide me out to the helipad, where a big noisy whirling beast awaits. My anxiety and fear have now been replaced by a new and vibrant enthusiasm and even with my hair flying in the air and my dress being whipped against my legs in the wind, I'm suddenly utterly fearless.

I scramble into the back seat of the chopper to be buckled in by Henri who then secures my side door and climbs into the seat next to our pilot. Soon we're lifting off, and for some unknown reason I can't help but shout out 'Thunderbirds Are Go!' in great excitement.

In the backseat of my brain, I do realise that I'm not actually feeling my normal self. I feel like I've drunk a whole bottle of Champagne rather than one glass of water.

In the very back of my mind – the bit that still seems to be thinking sensibly – I'm wondering how long the pills will take to go through my system and for me to feel normal again. Whatever normal is ... Then the front of my mind – the bit that's quite stoned at present – tells me that if normal means formal and stuffy, then maybe I'd rather be high and squiffy and maybe I don't want to be normal anymore. Oops! I realise I'm feeling rebellious and naughty again! But this time, not out of bitterness and anger, but because I want to have lots of fun. I do need some excitement in my life. I want to enjoy myself. Oh, I do feel a bit strange!

We swoop forward and fly across the harbour and I press my nose against the window.

I notice Henri also has his head turned and his eyes fixed out on the cityscape.

Below us the sea looks innocently calm as we climb higher into the sky.

'*Up up and away in a beautiful balloooooon!*' I sing at the top of my voice.

Henri and our pilot are both wearing headsets. The noise from the engine and the rotor blades are so loud that I feel I can sing as much as I like because no one would mind and nobody can hear me anyway. Although, I did see the pilot glancing back at me and then laughing in amusement, as if I was a subject of their conversation.

I wonder what Henri is saying about me now? Something along the lines of 'Oh, don't mind her, she's as high as a kite'?

Not that I care. I'm not in the mood for caring. I just feel ridiculously excited and happy.

* * *

After landing at the heliport on Macau, we take a car over to the glamourous bit of reclaimed land that's known as The Cotai Strip. Henri told me this was where Macao's best hotels, gourmet restaurants, high-end boutiques and cocktail bars could be found. They were all laid out like they were on a Monopoly board amongst the famous-name casinos such as The Venetian, The City of Dreams, The Wynn Palace, The MGM, just to name a few.

'Oh look! There's The Sands!' I exclaim with great enthusiasm.

'Yeah, The Sands was the first of the Las Vegas style hotels to arrive here.'

'Oh wow – look there's The Eiffel Tower and The Parisian!'

'You'd be hard pressed to know once you're inside these hotels that you aren't in Las Vegas.'

I'm about to tell him I've never been to Las Vegas, when he asks if I'm hungry.

'Starving,' I admit.

Henri checks his watch. 'Good. Because I know the perfect place for dinner.'

The Wynn Palace is an extravagant modern hotel with a vast lake in front of it complete with dancing fountains. Gliding slowly over this lake and between impressive giant effigies of Chinese dragons, are cable car gondolas.

'Oh look!' I yell with my head tilted and my eyes rolling. 'Gondolas!'

Henri takes my hand again as we climb out of the taxi and head into the hotel through its huge glass doors. 'Can we go and ride on the gondola later? Pleeeeease?' I beg of him.

Inside, The Wynn Palace is a bright, no-expense-spared den of luxury and modern excess. The vast lobby features breathtakingly colourful and decorative floral displays, including a life-sized carousel with prancing horses and a Ferris wheel made entirely from exotic flowers. There's also Chinese dynasty art featuring giant vases and marble statues.

Through an atrium, there's a vast, brightly lit shiny shopping mall full of top name designers.

'Handbags and shoooooeeessss!' I gasp, pulling on Henri's arm like a puppy straining on a leash. The lobby is extremely busy with lots of well-dressed and elegant people checking in but Henri leads me determinedly through the crowds in the direction of all the restaurants. He marches me past cocktail bars, a steakhouse, an Asian restaurant, a fragrant flower shop, and an enticing macaron shop (macarons are my favourite sweet things!) in order to reach the main restaurant. Henri tells me that the *Hong Kong Times* had recommended dinner at The Wynn as the best five-star meal in Macau.

The main restaurant here is spacious, with an array of tables and seating arrangements on two levels, offering a theatre-style view through a wall of windows to the outside performance on the lake, where the fountains are dancing in sync with the music playing inside the restaurant.

We are swiftly offered a table for two at the window and I'm immediately mesmerised.

Dragging my eyes away from the view, I look around us to see the room is sparkling and designed with influences from an ancient Chinese dynasty, richly adorned with warm hues of orange, red, and gold. The tall windows are framed with exquisite, russet-red velvet drapes which are held back with gold-coloured rope sashes. Interestingly, the walls feature a stunning and unique collection of mirrors.

'Look! All the mirrors are decorated with golden dragons!'

I count over a dozen gold jewel-encrusted dragon mirrors of various shapes and sizes with their claws clutching onto the frames and their elaborate tails coiling around the glass. They are incredibly beautiful; I've never seen anything quite as ornate in my whole life.

As a collection, I'd guess they were worth an absolute fortune.

A waiter appears and I encourage him to tell me more about the dragon mirrors.

'Ah, madam. They really are quite something, aren't they? They were created by a French designer in the Chinese style over a hundred years ago,' he enthused.

I look to Henri with an enraptured gaze. 'Just like you, Henri ... part French and part Chinese!' Henri laughed and shook his head in amusement.

The waiter continued. 'It took five years of sleuthing to track them all down and to bring them together in this collection that you see here before you today. Many were purchased from private sources from all over the world and some were bought at the famous auction house in London.'

I could see Henri listening politely, but I also saw him keenly eyeing the incredible feast laid out on the buffet tables around us. Like most men, he was more interested in food than conversations about decorative art.

As promised, it was a dining extravaganza. There were many dedicated food stations offering a selection of everything you could ever dream of eating: fresh seafood, sushi, salads, soups, a selection of charcuterie, rich casserole, roasted meats and poultry, seasonal vegetables. There were also desserts galore – fruits, cheeses, and chocolates.

Before we went over to see everything up close, the sommelier appeared to take our drinks order. I enthusiastically browse the wine list but to my disappointment – in that Henri being half French was sure to be both knowledgeable and enthusiastic about drinking wine – he dismisses the waiter and suggests we both stick to plain water. He reminds me that we should keep our heads clear and our wits about us in order to focus on our mission tonight at the casino. I'm sure he's also worried that I'm still under the influence of the seasickness pills.

I was having such a lovely time that I'd quite forgotten the reason we came here was to cash in Jon's chip and play the tables. Thankfully, Henri hadn't, and under his watchful green eyes and his encouragement to drink lots of water, by the time we've worked our way through the buffet and reached the desserts, I've sobered up and am fully *compos mentis*. 'Thank you for looking out for me. I feel much better.'

'You're very welcome. I'm relieved you're feeling better.'

I ask Henri why, when he'd lived so close to this absolute

mecca of adult entertainment for so long, he hadn't been tempted to come back to The Lotus to cash in the chip for himself.

'Oh, I've been back a few times. But not to The Lotus and I've never felt comfortable claiming the chip as my own. Not after Jon insisted this chip was his and mine was in the harbour.'

'That's very noble of you,' I say, admiring how he adheres to a gentleman's code of honour.

He shakes his head. 'No. Not noble. It's a matter of principle. It's actually really bad *chi* to cash in a gambling chip that's not your own. It's akin to trading your soul with the devil.'

'What? So, you're giving it to me to cash instead! What about my soul?' I protest.

'Ah, but you have his note. It's his written instruction and that makes you Jon's representative in the casino. You're actually doing me a great service in taking it off my hands.'

He laughs and wiggles his eyebrows at me devilishly.

'Well, it sounds to me like you and Jon were quite the players back then. I can imagine you were a formidable team. Butch Cassidy and the Sundance Kid or Smith and Jones or Batman and Robin!' I laugh, imagining their fun-filled capers together.

'Or perhaps Tom and Jerry?' Henri quips. 'I never did find another sidekick after Jon.'

'What about the wife you mentioned?' I query, surprised at my own boldness.

'Ex-wife,' he tensely corrects me without elaborating.

With our meal over, we quickly settle the bill and head a short distance across town to The Lotus in a taxi. Along the way, he tells me with great enthusiasm about the legendary old casino. 'The Lotus is nothing like any of these new mega casinos. It's Macau's original gambling establishment. It gives us a unique glimpse into Macau's history with its bohemian gaming rooms and its psychedelic exterior. It's really something!'

I can hardly wait. I'm so happy now that I've dressed for the occasion in my new outfit.

As Henri promised, The Lotus Casino really is something. The outside looks like a giant golden lotus flower, all lit up with twinkling neon lights. I stand on the pavement staring up at the emblem that I've somehow adopted as part of my fate on this magical mystery tour.

Inside the old casino it's small, dimly lit, and very crowded. The décor looks a little sinister in ebony and red with bold crystal chandeliers.

I see Henri looking around us with the expression of a little boy in a sweet shop.

'Last time I was here, the croupiers were still shaking the dice in their hands!' he tells me.

Taking my hand, he guides me through the room towards the cashier's cage. Along the way, we stop so he can pop a few coins into the slot machines. He calls them 'hungry dragons' and they soon take all our change without paying out.

Then we pass the crowded roulette table and I notice a sign above it that states:

No Guns Allowed
Minimum Bet $50

The entire room is noisy, hot, and sour with exhaled air and whisky.

Finally, we approach the young cashier clerk who is wearing a red silk *cheongsam*-style dress and sitting prettily behind the golden bars of the most secure section of the casino.

'Hello. I'd like to speak with the manager please,' Henri says.

She looks at him curiously. 'I'm afraid she's unavailable. Can I help you, sir?'

'Perhaps. Can you tell me the current value of an old chip?'

He places the golden coin onto the cash desk for her inspection and I watch with interest as the clerk's face immediately registers a look of surprise. She picks it up and politely asks us to wait for a moment.

Henri looks at me and grins. 'Any final bets on the value at today's exchange rate?'

'Sure.' I offer, getting into the gambling spirit of the evening. 'I'll wager the chip is still worth exactly fifty Hong Kong dollars. And look, it's the minimum bet on the roulette table!'

Henri laughs. 'Okay. I believe the chip is worth a lot more than fifty dollars considering inflation and the associated golden bonus. And I propose that if I'm the winner of our little wager, we get a fancy room here at The Lotus and stay the night.'

I'm a bit shocked at this bold presumption. Is he inviting me to sleep with him?

The thought of spending the night with him makes me blush uncontrollably.

'I believe you mean *two* fancy rooms, do you not?' I clarify.

Before he can answer, the clerk returns with the manager, who introduces herself as Jenny Li and smiles at us through the security bars.

Glancing down at the chip in her hand, she caresses it with her manicured fingers then flips it over to examine both sides carefully. 'Sir, may I ask you where you got this chip?'

'I can tell you where *and* when,' Henri says confidently. 'It was won at the roulette table in this very casino back in 1997. I'm assuming you'll honour your chips. Am I correct?'

'Yes, of course, we always honour our chips. It's just that this one is quite ... special.'

I hold my breath. The way Jenny Li is looking at the chip has my heart racing.

'It's from a limited edition issued on the night of the twentieth of October in 1997.'

263

'Ah, yes, now I remember,' Henri says. 'There was a celebration – a party – that night.'

'Yes. It was my father's fiftieth birthday party.' Jenny Li smiles warmly at Henri.

I quickly realise that the 'fifty' stamped on the chip might not represent its worth after all.

'It was a great night. I do hope your father is in good health?' Henri enquires.

'Yes. Indeed. He's now enjoying his retirement. Please, allow me to escort you up to the second-floor lounge.' She clicks her fingers and issues an inaudible instruction to the clerk in the cash chamber. Henri glances at me and gives me what I can only describe as a confident wink. He obviously thinks he's going to win our bet.

The wink gives me a ridiculous fluttering of butterflies in my stomach.

We're shown to an elevator and taken up to a much more distinguished room than the gambling area downstairs. The VIP gambling room. It looks more like the glimpse into Macau's history that Henri had promised me. *This* was a mausoleum to gambling. There are lots of faded photos on the walls and a huge, ancient-looking roulette table in the centre of the room.

The same roulette table where Jon and Henri sat on that fateful night in 1997?

I can imagine them sitting here, in the midst of a gritty but glamourous crowd gathered under the shiny brass downlighter mesmerised by the sound of the clack-clack-

clacking roulette ball as it bounced around the wheel of fortune, the crowd roaring as they placed their golden chips.

What was it Jenny Li had said about the chip while we were downstairs?

This one is quite special.

I'm now convinced I've lost our bet and this chip is of far more value than I'd first thought.

I'm also convinced I might have just agreed to sleep with Henri tonight.

The thought makes my knees weaken just as we are offered a seat in a velvet-upholstered private booth close to the cocktail bar. A waiter offers us drinks. I ask for a vodka martini because right in that moment I feel like a glamourous Bond girl living by high stakes. Henri, looking a worthy 007 in his tux, orders a bourbon whisky.

A moment later we're joined by Jenny Li, who is carrying a small briefcase. Goodness, this is so very James Bond!

I'm nervous and excited as the briefcase is put down in front of us in the booth and, following a discreet nod from Jenny Li, I click it open. My jaw drops in shock to see that inside the case there are neatly stacked piles of cash – all in USD.

'I trust you'll find this a fair exchange for the golden chip. Ten thousand US dollars.'

I gasp. Henri swears and then rubs his chin in astonishment.

There's no hiding our mutual shock and disbelief.

'I had no idea it was worth this much,' Henri stutters as he turns to me.

'Can I assume you'll give us the chance to win some of it back on the tables?' Jenny Li enquires of us.

Henri turns to me. 'Maya? This is your money. What's your game?'

'Roulette,' I say clearly.

'Ah ... the devil's wheel,' Jenny Li remarks with a wry smile.

'Yes. And I'd like to put it all on divine number nine,' I say with a wry smile of my own.

Chapter 17

The Lotus Casino, Macau

Jenny Li escorts us over to the grand old roulette table and arranges for us to be seated. We murmur our hellos and our thanks to those who make space for us around the table. I'm already impressed with how exceptionally well dressed everyone looks here. The men in dinner suits, the women draped in couture and expensive jewellery.

'Ladies and gentlemen. Place your bets.' The croupier instructs.

All attention is immediately piqued when Jenny announces to the croupier that, 'The lady would like to put one thousand dollars straight onto number nine.'

The chips are quickly counted and dropped as a stack on the nine.

A murmur rises and other chips slide onto number nine to join mine.

The wheel begins to spin.

'Ladies and gentlemen. No more bets.'

I watch the wheel and the numbers blur in front of my eyes as my heart pounds and I try to keep track of the ball as it rolls and bounces, hitting and missing various numbers, teasing those who had picked them as their wagers. The wheel slows and shouts begin in various languages from those who thought such encouragement might win them favour. Under my breath I chant '*divine number nine*' as my mantra.

I draw my breath and then hold it as the ball pops into the slot marked with the number twenty-eight.

I groan, unable to hide my disappointment. I'd felt so sure we would win by fate alone and we had been so close because number twenty-eight was right next to number nine. In less than a minute, I'd lost all that money. How irresponsible of me!

But then, as the wheel slows to a stop, the ball jerks, jumps and lands straight on number nine!

My eyes almost pop out of my head in astonishment as the whole table erupts into cheers and I blink to make sure I haven't imagined this win.

I look to Henri. He's throwing his hands into the air and yelling, 'Thank you, Jon!'

Then he's turning to me and clasping his hands either side of my face, planting a firm kiss directly onto my slightly parted lips. Despite the surprise and pressure of the kiss, I find Henri's lips to be soft, warm, and flavoured with bourbon. They don't linger on mine for more than a moment but the effect and the outcome of our bet has sent my head spinning.

I steady myself and turn my attention to Jenny to see that her face is a picture of devastation before she quickly manages to regain her composure. Then she makes a great show of clicking her fingers in the air and ordering a bottle of Champagne to be brought over to us.

'How much have we won?' I ask Henri in a fervent whisper.

'The odds on a straight are 35:1. Plus our original bet. So, we win $36,000,' he explains.

I feel my legs wobble beneath me once again. I had no clue the odds were so high.

'What do we do now?' I ask.

'We drink the Champagne and then we book the best rooms they have available.'

What we actually do next is drink the Champagne and then immediately lose six thousand dollars. Jenny looks a little relieved when she comes over to tell us she has made the penthouse suite available with the compliments of the house.

Henri thanks her and sounds pleased. 'Really? Wow! The penthouse!'

I'm just about to ask for another room for myself when Jenny announces that we are indeed on a roll of luck tonight, because the hotel is full and the penthouse was the only room available. 'So, please do enjoy your stay with us at The Lotus!'

I console my nervousness by assuming a penthouse will have more than one bedroom.

* * *

In winning so much money (and then going on to lose half of it) Henri and I have lots of fun that night. Fuelled by Champagne, we take a taxi along the Cotai Strip and go out on the town, exploring more of the fabulous casinos and all the extravagant and luxurious hotels.

We take a gondola ride inside The Venetian, an operatic boatman singing to us as we glide along the Grand Canal. Then we go outside again and I spot the sky gondola ride I'd seen earlier outside The Wynn. We rush over to sit side by side in the small cab, with the disturbing heat of our thighs touching on the narrow seat, as we glide high over the lake as the water fountain dances below. It's all incredibly exciting and, dare I say it, very ... romantic.

As we gaze over the sights and the lights, my mind keeps flitting back to the memory of that kiss in the casino and I feel terribly confused and horribly guilty about how much I enjoyed it. I'm also now extremely anxious about our accommodation tonight and the possibility of Henri and I having no choice but to share a room.

My nerves and my imagination are suddenly running away with me.

Had I realised we were having to stay over tonight, I wouldn't have asked him to come along. Did he think I'd invited him for more than just a night on the town? We both had separate and pressing plans for tomorrow and yet he's suggested we stay over. Had we been giving each other mixed messages?

Is that why he'd been so keen to race through his schedule today and meet me tonight?

I'm extremely flattered if that is the case, but I'm also concerned he might have totally the wrong impression of me. We eventually find ourselves at the Eiffel Tower at The Parisian just as a 'musical legends' tribute show is about to start. Watching the show seems like a good way for us to reset the evening and rest our legs while being entertained for an hour.

We're given a comfortable booth in the theatre and the slick and professional quality of the performances would have had you believing that it was actually Prince, Michael Jackson, Adele, Cher, Dolly Parton, and other stars of past and present up there on the stage.

The atmosphere in the theatre is lively and soon everyone in the audience is up dancing to the classic beats. Henri pulls me to my feet – so this respite ended up not quite as restful as I had imagined – and we dance in the aisle together. He's a fine dancer, moving confidently and taking the lead spinning me around before pulling me closer to his hot and incredibly taut body for our own rock and roll version of a waltz.

It's all so much fun and I'm soon hot, breathless and really enjoying myself.

After the show, Henri grabs my hand once more and we spill back out onto The Strip to wave down a taxi. I'm getting used to him holding my hand now and I find I welcome his strong hand folding around mine. It feels safe, like he's taking care of me. 'Come on, Maya, there's somewhere special I need to show you.'

I know it's getting late but just when I think our evening might be drawing to an end, it seems that Macau – and Henri – are just getting started. The taxi whisks us off The Strip, down into the old part of Macau, where in total contrast to its neon-lit, high-tech, western-influenced, concrete jungle, we enter the historic centre with its cobbled streets, ancient pastel-coloured buildings and colonial architecture.

'This old part of town is now a UNESCO World Heritage Site.' Henri tells me as we climb out of the taxi to find ourselves in a narrow warren of back streets near a ruined neo-classical church lit by yellow streetlights.

It's all breathtakingly beautiful and there's hardly anyone else around. Just us and one or two other couples strolling hand in hand in the golden hue of the old fortified walls. The narrow streets, with signs in both Portuguese and Cantonese, soon lead us into a paved square. 'Come on, let's go and get a drink and a bite to eat?' Henri suggested.

We find ourselves outside a gorgeous little Portuguese restaurant called Alfonzo's.

Inside, it's like stepping through a portal in time into a rustic little *restaurante* in the Portuguese countryside. We order a bottle of red wine and chat over the glow of a candle flame and I watch as the flickering shadows highlight Henri's handsome face, emphasising his chiselled features and the cupid's curve of his lips as he smiles.

It's so intimate and, dare I say it yet again, incredibly romantic.

In fact, I have to remind myself once again that this is not a date.

I need to tell myself that despite all the excitement of our time together these last two nights, Henri and I aren't supposed to be getting lovey-dovey and cosy together.

Have I somehow managed to lose sight of my mission to honour Jon?

Just because Henri is handsome, charming, and wonderful company, and it has been an exhilarating, memorable night, it doesn't mean I should be lustfully lingering over this candle and our time here together.

Just because Henri is, in many ways, very similar to Jon doesn't make it right.

Early tomorrow morning, we'll be heading back to Hong Kong, where we will say goodbye. Henri has his boat race across the China Sea and I have a flight to Singapore to catch.

Thinking about his boat race, I tell him I hope the sea will be calmer for him tomorrow.

'For a while it was actually touch and go as to whether the race would run after all. We had high winds tonight as a result of a tropical storm out at sea and forecasters thought there could be a possibility of it tracking across our race route. But the good news is that it's expected to dissipate tonight and so we're all clear to set off tomorrow afternoon as planned.'

'Gosh, are you sure it's safe to sail?'

'Yeah. Of course. It will be a challenge but that's what sailing is all about. I have a highly experienced crew and we expect to have a strong jet current and surface winds in our favour.'

His eyes shine with excitement in anticipation of the task that lies ahead of him.

My heart flutters with excitement on his behalf. Clearly, Henri is a bold and brave man.

'How long do you expect it to take you to reach Singapore?' I ask, while considering my own travel plans. I know I have to leave for the airport around 2pm tomorrow afternoon.

'We sail at 4pm,' Henri says. 'It's a race over six hundred nautical miles and we need to complete it in under forty hours to be in with a chance of a placing, so I'm hoping we'll arrive in Singapore around 8am on Monday morning.'

I'll admit I'm disappointed. It would have been nice to have waved him off at the harbour.

'Wow. That's a long time at sea. Did you compete in the race last year too?'

'Yeah. Last year was a big learning curve. We came sixth after sailing for forty-nine hours. This time, I'm racing to win. I really think we've got a strong chance of victory.'

He takes my hand across the table and gently rubs it with his thumb.

'Maya, I'm also really hoping that you'll be there to see us arrive in Singapore.'

I slowly shake my head. 'I'm really sorry, Henri. But I'll have already left for KL.'

I watch his facial expression drop in disappointment and my own heartbeat dips.

'That's a shame. I thought you said you were still in Singapore on Monday?'

'I leave on Monday to spend a couple of days in KL before heading to Penang.'

'Ah, right. Yes. I remember now. You're off to Jon's favourite foodie island in Malaysia.'

'Yes. It's the final stop on my itinerary before I fly home to London.'

The warm atmosphere between us has cooled so I quickly change the subject, telling him about how I'd been able to find my old family home in Happy Valley.

'I'd been hoping to see the house again after all these years and it was amazing to find it. Especially as it was hidden amongst all those new high-rises. And, of course, it was surprising to find that it's been a horse racing museum for the past couple of decades!'

'Oh, then I know it. It's that impressive pink place just across from the jockey club!'

'Yes. Incredibly, it's still pink and my mother's rose garden is also still there to this day.'

275

I bite my lower lip while I mull over whether to mention that it's currently being cleared, and I've been offered the possibility of renting the place and staying on in Hong Kong for six months or more. But I decide there's no point in telling him all of that when I've already decided to be sensible and not pursue it. I'd concluded that it was totally unrealistic to think I could make a new – albeit temporary – life here in Hong Kong.

I'd just be setting myself up for a lot of upset and disappointment later, even if I could afford it. Because what if I'd wanted to stay longer and then couldn't?

After a few moments of silence between us where it seemed like everything had been said except goodnight and goodbye, Henri takes my hand again and we lock eyes over the now dwindling candle flame. He speaks with what sounds like heartfelt sincerity.

'Maya, I want you to know this has been more than great. Meeting you has been wonderful. It's been such a pleasure. Having a casino buddy again has been a lot of fun and I want you to promise me that if you are ever back here in Asia again, you'll look me up. Doesn't matter where in Asia because I can sail to wherever it is and meet you there. Promise me?'

I sigh with pleasure and squeeze his hand. 'Of course. I promise. It's been an amazing few days and I've really enjoyed getting to know you, Henri. Thanks for everything. For teaching me Tai Chi and for taking me out on your boat last night to see the light show and especially for our adventures in Macau tonight. I've honestly never had so much fun and I've certainly never won so much money!'

He nods and smiles but also looks a little sad. 'Sure, anytime.'

'So, in the meantime, let's keep in touch,' I suggest. 'Are you on Facebook?'

He laughs. 'No. But I'm on Instagram. I like pictures of boats and nautical hashtags.'

I silently thank Pia for explaining Instagram just before I left for India.

* * *

It's well after midnight when Henri and I finally take a taxi back to The Lotus and step into the private executive guest lift to our suite on the top floor. We stand silently side by side in the lift with our eyes transfixed by the escalating floor-level display until we reached the forty-eighth floor. With every passing floor, I feel increasingly sober and more nervous about arriving at our sumptuous accommodation and finding either separate bedrooms or cause for an anxious scene.

The lift door swooshes open at a carpeted entrance hallway to the penthouse suite, where the first thing I see is an enormous vase of fresh flowers on a circular table under a magnificent chandelier. Henri and I step out of the lift and part ways to explore the vast space in different directions. I find several interconnecting rooms, a small but well-equipped kitchen, a lounge with an array of vast, squashy sofas facing a massive flat screen TV, and a dining room with what looks to be acres of polished wood table and dozens of chairs. I continue until I find two mirrored dressing rooms off two magnificent bathrooms ... and just one large bedroom with one extra-large bed.

I re-join Henri in the lounge where he's removed his bow tie and found a fully stocked bar. He's opening a bottle of cognac. 'All this space and furniture but only one bed,' I note.

'Jenny said the last person to stay here was a president. Shall we have a nightcap?'

Henri doesn't pick up on my last remark or register my concerns.

All I can think about is there being two of us and only one bed and in my overactive and now overstimulated imagination, this all feels like too much.

Is it because he's a strikingly attractive man and he looks so temptingly suave in his tux?

Is it because he's impressively well-travelled and has a sexy twinkle in his eye?

Is it because I think he would be an incredible partner in bed?

Is it because the oversized bed makes me think about Henri's manly lure and magnetism?

Or, is it because in my head and to my horror, I'm already naked in that bed in Henri's strong and muscular arms? The thought of it has me weak at the knees.

I decide to tackle the situation straight away before any more assumptions are made.

'Henri, I want you to know that although you won our little bet earlier, it's not that I don't find you attractive – because I do – but I don't intend on sleeping with you. I'm sorry. It's just, well, I'm on my honeymoon.'

He pours a small measure of brandy into two large brandy glasses with a steady hand.

'Your honeymoon?' he repeats.

'Yes. W-with Jon,' I stammer, by way of explanation.

Henri only manages to half conceal his frown. 'Ah, yes ... the pilgrim honeymoon trail.'

His tone upsets me. 'I'm sorry? The pilgrim trail? What do you mean by that, exactly?'

He approaches me and sets the glasses down so he can cup my face with his hands.

In his eyes I see his compassion but perhaps not his complete understanding.

'My darling Maya, don't you know that I'm jealous?'

Jealous? Of what? Jealous of Jon? Why would Henri be jealous of a dead man?

'But you can relax. I have every intention of taking the couch tonight.'

I breathe a deep sigh of relief. 'Thank you. I appreciate your understanding.'

'No understanding required,' Henri insists as he picks up his drink and moves away to turn his back on me. I'm guessing he's having mixed feelings but then he turns to look at me again and I see mischief etched on his face.

'But just to clarify ... you did say just now that you do actually find me attractive?'

I roll my eyes at him to excuse myself from having to qualify his flippant comment and wander into the bedroom to take a pillow and a sheet off the bed, all the while pondering further on his admission of jealousy. There's no doubt that Henri is a gentleman. He's been nothing but a kind and considerate friend to me all evening. He was really concerned for me earlier after I'd taken the seasickness pills and he'd wanted to look after me. But all of that is because he and Jon had been friends and – because of that – now he was my friend. He'd been so easy to be with tonight and together we'd had so much fun and adventure.

I really don't know why I've been so worried about being in a room alone with him.

Had I really thought he might jump on me the moment we got up here?

Or that he might have been expecting me to jump on him?

I honestly think I've been massively overthinking this and flattering myself too much.

'Here. Take these. I hope you'll be comfortable,' I say, handing over the bedding.

I honestly don't know what emboldens me, but I lean forward to kiss his cheek and say goodnight. Maybe it's the warm, wonderful, and now deliciously familiar whiff of his cologne mixed with the scent of cognac on the air between us? Or just the desire to offer further thanks for the fine friendship we had forged. Either way, it all went wrong.

Henri moves his head to the side at the last minute and I end up with my lips on his mouth instead of his cheek. And, before either of us knows what's happening, we're locked in a long and delicious kiss. He tastes of brandy and manliness and his lips are soft while his body feels hard and muscular beneath my fingers as they sweep across his broad chest.

He draws me even closer towards him as my breath quickens, my lace-covered breasts and my stiffened nipples pressed hard against his shirt.

I feel his heat and his heartbeat and my own heart pounding.

When we pull away, we stare at each other for a moment in shock.

At first, I see that Henri is just as surprised as I am and that his eyes are now an even darker shade of green. But then his expression softens and his eyelids lower in lustful repose as he looks at me. And, in that moment, all my guilt melts away and I know I desperately want to sleep with him. I can't fight myself or my desire for him any longer. There's no reason not to when we obviously both want the same thing. And, after tonight, I'll likely never ever see him again. The latter fact only makes this prospect all the more appealing to me.

A night of sex and physical satisfaction with a man who is fun and attractive. It doesn't have to be anything more and no one needs to get hurt.

We are both adults. Okay, I'm not sober but I'm certainly not drunk either.

Maybe this is more of an act of rebellion than a sound decision?

Or maybe I'm simply acting on our mutual attraction and the sexual tension that's been building between us right from the first moment we met. I'm a normal, living, breathing woman and I have a libido. I need release. I also need affection.

Before I fell in love with Jon, I'd occasionally had boyfriends with benefits. I know I could do that again tonight with Henri and we could both enjoy mutual affection and sex without the complications of commitment or love because after tonight we will be strangers.

Being faithful to Jon's pilgrim trail doesn't mean sentencing myself to a life of loneliness.

Jon wouldn't have wanted that for me.

And, after all, he's technically the one who brought Henri and me together.

Surely that's the same as giving his blessing?

Chapter 18

Henri's lips are still close to mine so I kiss him again, this time with purpose. I hear his throaty, guttural moan of pleasure as I make my intentions clear. Then we practically drag each other across the room and into the bedroom, pulling at and discarding our clothes as we go. I flick off my shoes and he lifts my dress over my head as I unbutton his shirt, pull at his belt, and unzip his trousers.

He whispers my name and words of encouragement as my hair falls over my shoulders and we tumble onto the bed together. I respond in kind and in consent as he hesitates for just a moment before sliding my panties down. Then, hot and naked in our embrace, we slow the pace and take our sweet time, taking turns to make love to each other, until we're sated and eventually, in the early hours of the morning, we fall asleep in one another's arms.

That night I dream of golden coins, spinning roulette wheels, and dollar notes.

* * *

In the morning, with sleepy eyes and a warm, lazy body, I lie next to Henri as he sleeps and I study his beautiful face on the pillow. He is so ridiculously handsome. Especially with a morning shadow of stubble. I think about how, in another existence, in another life in which I lived in Hong Kong, I would have liked to get to know him better.

All I know about him right now is that, just like Jon, he's into martial arts and was an investment banker. That he was once married. That he lives on a yacht and he likes to sail. That he likes to gamble on occasion and that he drinks bourbon and cognac and appreciates food and fine wine. That he's intelligent and articulate and he's a really smooth dancer. He's also a passionate, skilled, and considerate lover.

Perhaps I do know more about him than I thought? Perhaps it's him who knows nothing about me?

I lean carefully over to the bedside table to collect my engagement ring from where I'd placed it in the early hours of the morning. I slip it back on my finger and watch Henri's dark eyelashes fluttering on his high cheekbones, sad that once he opens his eyes it will be time for our love bubble to burst. This will all be over.

We'll travel back to Hong Kong and he'll head straight over to the marina because he'll have been watching the clock – or rather the gold Rolex on his wrist – knowing he still has such a lot to do to complete the preparations for his race this afternoon. He certainly won't have any time to think about me or that I am leaving today and how, despite my promise to look him up, we are hardly likely to see each other again. I'm pretty sure he'll forget me and our night together soon enough. But I'm also pretty sure that I'll never forget him.

Today I will go back to my hotel alone to pack up my things and head out to the airport.

And, when his boat race starts, I'll already be halfway to Singapore.

It's a real shame that it's worked out this way. I'd have enjoyed all the bonhomie and celebration involved in waving him and the crew of the *Super Typhoon* off on their epic race. It's also a shame that I'll be leaving Singapore just hours before his boat arrives.

I'm reminded of a poem I've always loved by another of Henri's namesakes – this time Henry Wadsworth Longfellow – but only now do I fully understand the poignancy behind the words.

Ships that pass in the night, and speak each other
 in passing
Only a signal shown, and a distant voice in the darkness;
So on the ocean of life we pass, and speak one another
Only a look and a voice, and then darkness again and
 a silence.

* * *

When Henri opens his eyes, he blinks sleepily and smiles happily. He says, 'Hey, good morning, beautiful!' as though relieved last night's passions hadn't been just a dream.

Then he pulls me back into his arms and folds me once again against his warm body.

He kisses my forehead and holds me tightly and I feel like I'm melting with both the pleasure of being with him now and the sadness of knowing that this is our swansong. His voice is low, soft, and direct when he speaks, giving me the impression that he's spent some time during the night thinking about our time together in this bed and in each other's arms.

'Maya, I'm wondering if you might consider delaying your flight out of Singapore on Monday? It just seems crazy to me how we'll both be in the same place on the same day and yet we'll be missing each other by only a few hours. Believe me, I'd be racing across the sea with even more purpose if I knew I could see you again.'

It all sounds wonderful and I know I'll feel truly terrible turning him down.

'We could be celebrating a great win and every great win demands a party with Champagne. Please, Maya, come on. Tell me you'll be there.'

But I just can't bring myself to change my plans.

Doesn't he realise that I'm not on this magical mystery tour to get halfway and then abandon it?

I have a duty to honour Jon's memory by following all

of Jon's notes to finish what I started. If Henri can't understand that then it's his problem, not mine.

'Henri, I can't. My flight is booked. I have my itinerary. It's Jon's plan.'

'But isn't it also Jon's plan that brought us together?' he counters.

He's using the same rationale that I used last night to justify us sleeping together.

I stare at him. This isn't what I had expected from him this morning.

I'd slept with him in the safe and certain knowledge that this was just a one-time thing. That last night had been no more than a wonderful and uncommitted conclusion to two amazing days.

'Look, call me old fashioned, but we slept together and it means something to me,' he continues, looking at my engagement ring with a frown. 'Maya, I want to be honest. I was feeling pretty jaded about relationships. Until I met you.'

'Jaded? I don't understand. Do you mean since you got divorced?'

'No, not that. My divorce was amicable. What I mean is that well-meaning friends are always trying to set me up, but I've never met a woman I wanted to see again. Until you.'

He's leaning on one elbow now, gazing at me with pleading eyes.

'So, why don't we give this a chance? Say you'll wait for me in Singapore.'

He strokes a lock of hair from my brow and studies my face while he waits for my answer.

I shudder with pleasure at his soft, slow caress across my cheek. It feels so very intimate.

'Henri, this wasn't a date. We've only known each other for two days. Slow down!'

'That's exactly my point. This isn't something I can do casually. I really want to get to know you better. All I'm suggesting is that we create a window of opportunity in which we can both get to know each other properly. Flights can be changed or cancelled, you know. Plans can be postponed. Just for a couple of days. Then we can see each other again in Singapore. What do you say?'

I stare at him and allow myself to imagine a scenario where we spend two more days together in Singapore. But those are days I was supposed to have been with Jon – not physically but spiritually – and abandoning his plan to be with Henri seems like a selfish betrayal.

'Look, Henri. I agree that this didn't feel entirely casual. Clearly, we do have something between us ... a connection. But following Jon's plan is important to me. It might not be set in stone but it is set in my heart. I'm sorry, but I feel I must continue to follow his plan.'

He frowns and shakes his head. The look in his eyes tells me he's loathe to accept defeat. Again, I see him glancing with narrowed eyes down at my engagement ring.

Suddenly, looking up at me he counters with a compromise.

288

'Okay. At least tell me that you'll think about it between now and then?'

Think about it? Change my mind? Change my plan. Ditch Jon's magical mystery tour?

'Henri, perhaps you don't understand that this is all about the journey. It's Jon's journey. And you are not Jon. Don't you see? You're just my connection to Jon.'

I realise all at once that I've made a mistake. My words had been cruel and my tone more than a little fierce. In the next few moments of stunned silence, Henri processes what I've just said to him. I fall into a bit of a panic when I see the hurt of my rejection register on his face and I scramble to better explain myself so that he might understand.

'Henri, remember when you committed yourself to teaching Tai Chi in the park in honour of your Grand Master? Well, this is my way of honouring Jon. Now do you understand?'

He nods slowly. 'Okay. Yeah. Sure. Now I understand.' He sighs deeply with resignation.

Then he pulls me into his arms and kisses me one more time.

It's a slow, deep, smouldering, incredibly passionate kiss and an emotional goodbye. When he finally releases me, he heads straight to the bathroom, and I lie alone in the bed, my mouth tingling with the taste of him and my body still pulsating with the reignited desire for the pleasure and the pressure of his hard body inside mine.

Feeling cold and lonely again, I imagine myself calling out his name and saying I'm sorry and that I will meet him in Singapore. I so desperately want him to come back to bed.

Suddenly, all the feelings I was trying to quell last night seem magnified rather than resolved. I'd quickly gone from feeling aroused and heated to feeling riddled with guilt that Jon was cold and dead and in his grave while Henri was very much alive and just on the other side of the bathroom door. I close my eyes and try to think about Jon.

If I think about Jon then I won't think of Henri.

I need to fix my mind on exactly what I set out to do and complete this journey.

I tell myself I'm not falling for or lusting after Henri. In being with him, I was just being reminded of all that I was missing about being physically connected with Jon. I try hard to picture Jon's face, but, frustratingly, it keeps morphing into Henri's.

I call to mind my meditation teachings and use my *ajna*, my mind's eye chakra, to see Jon and to reimagine all my favourite memories of being in Jon's arms: how our kisses would lead to our lovemaking and how his lips would sweep sensually from my mouth to my neck, trailing slowly and exquisitely down over my entire body.

But now I only see Henri making love to me instead.

Feeling flustered and ashamed, I give up and get out of bed to make a pot of coffee.

I use the second bathroom. When I come out, showered

and dressed, Henri is gone but he's left a note on the coffee pot about 'joining him downstairs for breakfast'. It doesn't escape me that he's used a yellow Post-it note from the desktop in the adjoining sitting room.

Feeling a tad overdressed in last night's clothes, I go down to join Henri.

He's sitting in bright sunlight at a table beside a large window that offers a fabulous view of The Strip. The weather outside looks fine today – the sky cloudless and blue, the palm trees motionless. The wind has calmed which bodes well for his boat race this afternoon.

He smiles when he sees me enter the executive dining room and immediately puts down the *Hong Kong Times* he had been reading to stand and see me seated opposite him at the table for two. Despite our previous night of gambling and drinking and debauchery, Henri somehow manages to look bright-eyed, fresh, and still incredibly dashing in his shirt and dark trousers. Naturally, he hadn't bothered with his bowtie this morning.

I, on the other hand, probably look a little the worse for wear on a lack of sleep.

I'm relieved when a waiter rushes over with a pot of hot, fresh coffee and a breakfast mug.

'So how are we planning to get back to Hong Kong this morning?' I ask Henri.

He looks at me over the top of his own coffee mug. 'As fast as possible. Would you mind if we took the hi-speed ferry back? I checked the forecast and the crossing is calm.

I can't get a chopper here until midday and the ferries leave every fifteen minutes.'

'No problem. Perhaps it's time I found my sea legs anyway.'

After breakfast we collect ourselves together and then we have a bit of a tiff over Henri objecting – in fact refusing – to take his half of the cash from our winnings last night.

We have fifteen thousand dollars left and I thought it only fair that we split it equally.

'Maya, I don't want it. I don't need it. It's not mine and Jon wanted you to have it.'

We ride to the port in a taxi in silence, each looking out of opposite windows.

My thoughts are of guilt once again. I can see a reflection in the glass of the sad and pained expression on Henri's face. It indicates that he still thinks me heartless and unrelenting. At the ferry port, we buy tickets and wait to board the ferry.

We have tickets for the VIP lounge upstairs as Henri told me I'll be far less likely to feel queasy and seasick while we're moving if I can see the coastline clearly. I trust his judgement.

We take large comfortable seats in the forward cabin and, as the boat begins to move away from the dock I assume Henri will be busy thinking about preparing for his race this afternoon. Instead he strikes up conversation again. He's obviously still thinking about us. 'Maya, do you think you might ever come back to Hong Kong?'

I process his question while staring resolutely forward out of the window.

'Do you think I need more Tai Chi lessons?' I quip, trying to make light of things.

A little voice inside is telling me to say yes but I'm not sure I should trust it.

I feel Henri take my hand in his and give it a gentle and reassuring squeeze.

I also feel his fingers brush against my engagement ring. I sense that me wearing Jon's ring is making him feel uncomfortable since we'd been intimate. If so, then I'm also finding it difficult to reconcile the conflicting feelings I felt this morning while sliding it back on my finger.

I'm also having difficulty convincing myself that what's happened between us over the past two days, and especially last night, was only about casual sex and mutual satisfaction. In the absence of a serious reply, Henri leans in and speaks to me quietly.

'Maya, I just want you to know that I'm not ready for this to be over between us. I get it. I do. You think I'm moving too fast. I'm sorry. I can slow things down. I don't want to rush you or presume that you'll ever get over Jon, or that you'll ever come to terms with what happened on your wedding day. But, if you ever feel that you could put down that torch you are carrying for him and live with his memory rather than his ghost, then perhaps, if you can't stay now, you'll think about coming back. And we can find

out if last night ... and this *something* we have found
together might lead to *something* more?'

My heart is melting from the impact of his words but
I remain staunchly silent.

I don't want to make Henri a promise I might not keep.

Because I still have my pilgrimage for Jon to complete.

Chapter 19

Singapore

At the airport, waiting at the gate for my Singapore flight, I check my phone once again, still holding out hope for a final farewell message from Henri. Something light-hearted to follow up on what had felt like an intense and awkward moment after we arrived back at Victoria Harbour from Macau. Just a few words, so I'd know he wasn't still sulking or stinging over my adamant refusal to delay my departure from Singapore on Monday.

I'll admit that after I shot him down in flames and told him he was moving too fast, I've shed a tear over the thought of never seeing him again, but maybe our final hug and kiss and our emotional bids of farewell had been the end, as far as he was concerned.

After what I said about him only being my connection to Jon, I can't say I blame him.

Should I prompt him by reaching out to him first?

Should I send out a message, an olive branch of peace between us?

I don't. Instead I send a message to Pia to let her know I'm about to leave Hong Kong.

In a message to my sister yesterday, I'd given her all the details about finding the house on Stubbs Road and I'd attached lots of photos that I'd taken both inside and outside in the garden. This morning, I see she's replied with great enthusiasm and has asked lots of questions.

I tap out my reply to her but decide to keep the details about Mr Lee's offer to myself for the time being. Perhaps I feel it's something best discussed face to face in Pia's kitchen once I'm back, while I'm regaling and amusing her with all the finer details of my adventures.

Not that I've actually received Mr Lee's promised email and formal offer yet.

This makes me rather suspect that he might have changed his mind about offering it to me in such haste, when there were sure to be other people far more suitable and deserving than myself, who want to live there. Besides, I'm inclined to suspect that if I did tell Pia about it now, she would jump on this as a once-in-a-lifetime opportunity and try to convince me to see the merits of 'giving it a go' and renting the old house for six months.

When I've now decided the idea is totally unrealistic and completely outlandish.

I mean, what would be the point, really?

I also don't feel ready to mention my trip to Macau with Henri.

It's not like I want to keep secrets from my sister. I just wouldn't quite know where to begin or what to say to her about Henri and about the time we've spent together these past couple of days.

With the benefit of some hindsight and a little distance – although it's admittedly a complicated issue involving Jon, Post-it notes, gambling chips and lots of Champagne – our one-night stand now almost feels a little sordid.

I feel sure that if I even so much as mention his name, Pia will somehow know I've slept with him, and I don't want her knowing stuff that might make her worry or disapprove of me in any way. Pia and I are both water signs. She's a Pisces and I'm a Scorpio. This means that I might believe I'm deep and unfathomable but she's entirely capable of picking up on 'vibes' that she 'feels in her water'. And, to be honest, right now, even I happen to think that my justification for sleeping with someone I'd only known for two days, when my poor darling fiancé is hardly cold in his grave, is a bit harsh and certainly bold, even for me.

My phone pings and my heart leaps because I see it's a message from Henri.

Two simple French words:

Bon voyage.

I sigh with relief and quickly reply:

Sail safe. I hope you win!

I'm staring down at our messages with a lump in my throat when there's another ping and I see this time it's an email from Mr Lee. In it, he says he's spoken to the legal person who deals with their property leases and he's taken the liberty of explaining my special circumstances and my personal association with the house. And, therefore, they are delighted to formally offer me a 'preferential person' six-monthly renewable lease at $20,000 per calendar month.

$20,000 a month!

To accept the offer, I'd need to confirm my intentions by 10am on Monday morning.

I'm reeling with astonishment at the astronomical rental figure.

But, I suppose, I'm also feeling terribly relieved.

Because it's such a large and impossible amount of money, I can now finally stop imagining and doubting and defending myself and all my impossible dreams and mulling over the possibility of living, however temporarily, in this beautiful house in Hong Kong.

It's like a weight has actually been lifted from my shoulders.

There's no way I would consider or possibly afford to spend that kind of money on rent.

Good grief! Over a period of six months that was $120,000!

I could probably buy a small house in the UK for that kind of money.

Right. Okay. Good. It's time to stop thinking about it. It's out of my hands.

No more big decisions about staying or returning or coming and going.

But, as I'm called to board my flight, I find I'm still thinking about it.

And, I'm still reeling. I had, of course, realised that real estate was expensive in Hong Kong. I'd browsed estate agent shop windows and seen that rentals were hard to come by and small apartments sold for millions. Single houses were an almost non-existent commodity here in one of the most expensive cities in the world. Particularly those with many rooms and an expanse of garden. I won't deny that it had been a fine fantasy for a while.

A few moments after take-off, my final impression of Hong Kong is a scene I know will be forever etched in my memory. As I look down through the aircraft window, the plane turns and banks low over the harbour, giving me a spectacular view of the causeway and the marina below. I can see the very place where Henri and his crew are doing their last-minute preparations for the race. There's just two hours to go now before the *Super Typhoon* and all the other boats will sail away on their great adventure across the sea. I can clearly see all the big yachts with colourful bunting on their masts and their huge white sails all set and ready to go. I read

Henri's message again on my phone and my eyes linger on his words.

I also cast my eyes once again over the email from Mr Lee.

I decide that I really should reply to Mr Lee today now that my final decision has been made. Then he can offer the house to someone else this weekend rather than waiting until Monday.

Someone with deeper pockets. It's only fair.

But in re-reading the amount of the monthly rental once again, I realise my foolish mistake.

Mr Lee wasn't talking about US Dollars at all.

He was, in fact, referring to Hong Kong Dollars.

My heart sinks and then it soars again because by my quick estimation, $20,000 Hong Kong Dollars roughly equates to $2,500 US. It's still a lot of money but as a monthly rental in a big city it's no longer impossible for me. I do the sums.

Over six months that would equate to $15,000 US.

Which is the *exact amount* of dollars I have on my person after the win in Macau.

How crazy is that? Coincidence again? Cosmic ordering?

I guess the universe really is trying to tell me something!

I'm starting to sweat and tremble and I'm restless in my seat as my mind begins to whirl.

I'm running through all the 'what if' possibilities and I find myself once again considering the serious possibility of taking on the house in Stubbs Road and the ramifications of me actually changing my mind and going to live in Hong Kong!

I desperately need to speak with and consult my level-headed sister about this. Pia will be my sounding board. I can trust her opinion way more than I can trust my own.

The one thing I do know for sure is that if I do decide to return to Hong Kong instead of taking my flight home to London, it won't be because it means I would have Henri in my life. This would be about what's best for my life and my future. I've only known Henri a couple of days and I've been dreaming of Hong Kong my whole life.

And there's no way I'll rush into things with Henri while I'm still grieving for Jon. If Henri is destined to be part of my future when I'm ready to move on, it would just be a wonderful bonus.

* * *

Over the four-hour flight, I mull over the practicalities of a move to Hong Kong. I honestly can't come up with anything that might stop me from staying for the six months allowed by my entry visa and, to be honest, I'm not looking any further than that just now. Six months would allow me to live my dream and to get a taste for an alternative lifestyle.

Six months in Hong Kong might allow me to move on with life on my own terms.

I turn my attention to our imminent landing at Changi Airport in Singapore, peering down at the sparkling Singapore River and all the iconic buildings of Marina Bay as the plane treats its passengers to a bird's-eye view of the small, diamond-shaped island on the southern tip of the Malaysian Peninsular and the swish modern metropolis below.

I'm not entirely sure what I'd expected to see here, in what was once a British trading post, but it certainly wasn't all these super impressive, slick new buildings juxtaposed against the old architecture in the colonial district. It's all so incredibly pretty.

It's late in the afternoon when I'm whisked away from the airport and through this lush tropical city in the cossetted luxury of yet another complimentary limousine. Sitting comfortably in the vast, soft leather backseat of the car, I keep my eyes fixed on the city sights.

Jon had booked us a suite at his favourite place here: the famous Raffles Hotel.

In anticipation of my stay, I'd already browsed the hotel's website, and been impressed by its history and iconic status as well as the list of legendary and famous names who have stayed there, including countless writers, movie stars, and royalty. Named after the founder of Singapore, Sir Stamford Raffles, it's reputed to be the oldest hotel in the whole of Asia and I was looking forward to the experience.

Until I met Jon, I would never have imagined in my wildest dreams staying in such a magnificent place. Jon once described walking into Raffles Hotel as 'like stepping back in time to a bygone age'.

Jon had also told me how he'd often used Raffles Hotel and its famous sidekick, The Long Bar – where the Singapore Sling cocktail had first been invented – as the backdrop for all his business dealing back in those halcyon days when he had lived and worked in the city after leaving Hong Kong.

As the car swept up to the magnificent building with its imposing façade, I hear Jon's voice telling me that Somerset Maugham himself had once said that 'Raffles stands for all the fables of the exotic east' and he had often expressed a wish to one day return here. To share in the grandeur of it all once again with me by his side.

I'll admit, though, that since leaving India I haven't felt Jon's presence at my side so acutely.

Jon had liked to look back and sentimentalise and to recall what he had called his 'former glory days' in Asia and that's why, today at least, I must put all my distractions aside and complete my important mission. My pilgrimage in Jon's honour and memory. Our honeymoon.

As I climb out of the car to be escorted by a welcoming military-uniformed doorman inside the hotel via a red carpet, I brace myself to enter another unfamiliar world. One in which I'm yet to feel comfortable or confident because – aside from this crazy and unconventional mix of both basic and luxurious accommodations – whenever I've travelled before, whether for business or pleasure, I've stayed in a Travel Lodge or a Holiday Inn or somewhere with an average of three-stars for no other reason than it simply wouldn't have occurred to me to do otherwise. But not Jon.

Jon had led both a bohemian and a conventional life. He'd lived life alternately in the slow lane and in the fast lane. He'd enjoyed the company of artists, poets, and musicians and he'd also mixed in high circles with cultured people from around the world. And here was I getting a tiny taster – an *amuse bouche* – of the life he'd once lived. A window through which to peer at the life I might otherwise have experienced for the rest of my days had he lived.

It was a bittersweet experience and there was certainly a cruel aspect to doing this alone.

I was to stay at Raffles for two nights and I had lots of Post-it note instructions of sights to see in Singapore during that short time.

Visit the Gardens by the Bay.
View the harbour from Marina Bay.
A stroll along the marina waterfront promenade.
Shopping on Orchard Road and Chinatown's street market.
A boat ride down the Singapore River.

There was so much to do in just a couple of days!

* * *

A short time later, in my beautiful suite, surrounded by blissfully serene surroundings, I want to wallow in the luxury of the space and the opulent silence for a while rather than go outside. So, I kick off my shoes, and I lie on the vast and ridiculously comfortable bed.

I have so much to consider and to think about and this is a great place to contemplate, a calm and cossetted place to arrange all my errant thoughts. I need a plan, I need to focus on my life in the present rather than living a life in retrospect and, most of all, I need to be absolutely sure that whatever I decide to do next is right.

Keen to speak with Pia, I try to call her but there's no answer. I then realise it's only nine o'clock in the morning in the UK and she'll still be on the school run. I bide some time looking over Jon's first Post-it note instruction and, with a growing thirst, I decide to stroll out from my room and along the arched outer terraced corridors, with their white painted walls and dark wood accents, to find The Long Bar in the 'Cad's Alley' so I can try a Singapore Sling.

On the wall adjacent to the entrance, there's a poster in the Art Deco style telling the story of the Singapore Sling. How it was created by a sympathetic bartender to look exactly like an innocent fruit juice, at a time when women openly drinking alcohol in bars was frowned upon. The rest, as they say, is history.

The bar had apparently been a meeting place for rubber and palm-oil plantation owners and their wives back in the 1900s. In the historic room, with its classic-movie ambiance, I sit on a stool at the bar and snack on monkey nuts from a hessian bag while enjoying my fruity drink from a long glass. The furniture is cane and rattan and there's a welcome breeze from the gentle wafting palm-frond-shaped fans on the ceiling. I find the drink refreshing but a little too sweet for me, as it contains lots of pineapple juice. Everyone in the room also seems to be drinking Singapore Slings.

When I've collected a small pile of empty peanut shells on the bar, the bartender asks me if I'd like him to clear them away for me. I'm just about to gather them up myself to save him the trouble, when he takes me by complete surprise and with a quick swipe with his hand, knocks them across the bar, straight onto the floor. It's only then that I notice lots of other shells on the floor already. He enjoys my astonishment and points to a sign on the wall.

Littering encouraged: feel free to brush your peanut shells onto the floor.

Who knew? Apparently, it's a very old colonial tradition.

Refreshed and feeling deliciously mellow from my aperitif, I saunter back to my room.

Inside, the suite feels humid so I open the French door and walk outside onto my private balcony. It overlooks a central courtyard lined with tall palm trees and is a perfect place to sit for a while, with comfortable rattan furniture and a large parasol offering a tired guest both privacy and cool early evening shade. I check my phone and see it's now just after 6pm. As there is no time difference between Hong Kong and Singapore, I know Henri's boat race will now be well underway. I close my eyes and try to imagine him on board his boat with the wind in his face – yelling 'jive ho' or something nautical – while steering the *Super Typhoon* across the sea in this very direction.

I sigh and realise that despite my display of dismissive bravado I'm missing him already.

I would have much preferred that he was here with me right now: standing on this balcony, wearing his tuxedo, his tie loose, his dark hair brushed back from his strong forehead, his face tanned and relaxed, the corners of his eyes creased as he smiles at me in that playful and sexy way that he had while we were discussing the value of the golden chip at The Lotus Casino.

Henri had said that this race was a big deal so I'm now wondering if it might be featured on local TV?

Curiously, I walk back inside to switch on the TV and to progress through the channels until I find what I'm looking for on the local news channel. They're showing recorded coverage of the start of the race and I hold my breath as the exciting spectacle is presented.

'The twenty-first Blue Sea Classic Race is now underway!' the commentator enthuses.

Lots of beautiful white-sailed yachts flowed out of the harbour in bright sunshine with the Hong Kong cityscape providing a spectacular visual backdrop. The commentator said that thirty-two yachts were competing in the race this year and my eyes dart across the screen from vessel to vessel hoping to spot the *Super Typhoon*.

But it's impossible. The main view of the race was captured by a drone camera in the sky and many of the boats look very similar in size, shape, and style. It is, however, possible to see lots of individual crew members on the yachts, dashing about on the decks dressed in shorts and bright team sailing colours and caps, while white-tipped waves splash up the sides of the boats as they slice through the water and make their way into the open sea, all jostling for an early lead.

The commentator promises more updates on the race later.

I try calling Pia again, thinking she should now be home and she picks up my call immediately, this time sounding excited that I've called, demanding that I put her on video for a personal tour of my luxury hotel suite.

Only afterwards am I able to sit on the bed and tell her about Mr Lee's offer.

I take pains to explain to her that I still fully intend on continuing to follow Jon's itinerary and completing the whole trip. But then I'm considering the idea of, perhaps, instead of returning to London, taking the option of flying back to Hong Kong and taking on the house and living there for the next six months. I explain that that was how long I would be allowed to stay on my British passport. 'And, after that time, I'll no doubt come back to England.'

She listens to me talk without any interruption, which is unusual for Pia, so I know she's giving this her serious attention, but it's impossible for me to detect whether she's feeling utterly shocked by all of this and thinking I'm being too impulsive right now or if she actually thinks this is a damned good idea. 'So ... what do you think?' I beg.

Not that I'm asking her to make a final decision for me – far from it – I just need her opinion. So, while she continues to silently process this information, I hold my breath and chew my lower lip, waiting for her honest advice.

I don't need to remind myself that no one in the world knows me better than my dear sister and, despite our age gap and the distance between us right now, I trust she'll be able to assess this situation clearly with my best interests at heart.

When she finally speaks, her words come down the phone at me like an explosion.

'Oh Maya, for heaven's sakes! Email Mr Lee straight away. Tell him you'll take the house and that you'll want it fully furnished. Just do it. Do it right now!'

I say goodbye to Pia – who is enthusiastically making plans to come out and visit me during the next half-term – and then, straight away, I send off the confirmation email to Mr Lee.

Just as the sun is starting to go down, I return to the calm and shady ambiance of my private balcony – comfortably wrapped in a soft fluffy bathrobe – to flick idly through a magazine. But I'm not reading. I'm still thinking, already anticipating my wonderful new life and my brand-new start in Hong Kong. I'm also thinking about Henri again.

I find myself sifting through every little thing that's happened over the past couple of days, turning over every word in our conversations to join up the proverbial dots to try to gain some perspective on how I really feel about Henri.

I put *Singapore Life* down on the table and close my eyes.

I recall his words to me this morning.

Carefully chosen words that were undoubtedly sincere.

'*I don't want to rush you or to presume that you'll ever get over Jon. Or that you can ever come to terms with what happened on your wedding day. But, if you ever feel that you could put down that torch you are carrying and live with his memory rather than his ghost, then perhaps you'll think about coming back here?*'

I cringe at how rude and thoughtless my own response to him must have seemed.

Perhaps, in future, I should be a lot more careful what I wish for if my cosmic wishes are to actually come true. Especially if my tendency is to dismiss them when they materialise.

My first divine wish had been to ask for *a way* to live my life without Jon. It had been granted to me during the Ceremony of Light in Rishikesh, when I'd sent all my anger and pain and sorrow sailing down the holy river in a little boat with my divine offerings. I'd felt the divine power of the Mother of India flooding through my whole body.

My second divine wish, offered to me by the Swami at the airport, had been for *a reason* to live my life without Jon. Was Henri the living breathing result of that divine wish?

If Jon had wanted me to connect with someone here in Hong Kong, then wasn't his friend Henri the perfect introduction? Henri had suggested as much last night and I had heartily agreed. And now my heart feels heavy and burdened over the harsh words I'd spoken to Henri.

My chakras of regret are tingling so much right now that it hurts.

Have I made a terrible and cowardly mistake?

All the thoughts in my head are muddled up with my fear and doubts and good intentions. Am I so completely terrified of losing someone again that I'd rather shun them instead?

Guru J taught me how to manifest my wishes, hopes, dreams, and desires, and that personal encounters are never by chance or mere coincidence because we are fated either to learn from or to teach something important to everyone we meet. But what have I learned from Henri? What has Henri learned from me?

We had come together to gamble on Jon's chip.

Was I also supposed to take a gamble on Henri?

Should I perhaps have been more honest with him this morning and admitted that all this was happening too fast and too soon for me? Should I have been brave enough to admit that I was afraid of making *any* commitment, never mind running the risk of falling in love again?

Except he'd never even mentioned commitment or love.

He'd simply acknowledged that the two days we'd spent together hadn't been time enough for us to get to know each other properly. And, in asking me to stay here in Singapore, he was simply saying to me that he wasn't ready for this to be over between us.

With the benefit of hindsight, it all seems like a terribly reasonable and romantic gesture.

I nervously wonder how he'll react to the news that I'm planning to take on the house. What will he think when I tell him I'm returning to Hong Kong?

I dwell on this for a moment and then decide I won't warn him of my change of plan or tell him about my change of heart just yet. Because after the passions of Macau and the intensity between us when we parted company at the harbour this morning, I think we both need time to cool off.

I decide I'll wait until I've returned from Penang.

Then, as Henri said, we might find out if this *something* between us might lead to *something* more.

Chapter 20

Singapore

It's almost dark here in Singapore and yet it's still wonderfully warm and only slightly humid. It's an absolutely perfect evening. And now that I've sampled The Long Bar and the famous Singapore Sling, I'm keen to explore everything the city has to offer. First up is The Gardens by the Bay and what can I say? It's a flood-lit feast for the eyes. A veritable fantasyland.

There are enormous structures and exotic themed spaces and a giant bio-dome that looks like it's floating in mid-air. There are art sculptures everywhere and dozens of 'super trees' that are not trees at all but man-made vertical gardens stretching up to fifty metres tall. As the sun disappears, the whole place is starting to light up like it's Christmastime at Disneyland.

I amble along the undulating pathways through the park, enjoying the ambient atmosphere and inhaling

313

deliciously tempting wafts of food floating on the sultry air. Unable to resist for any longer, I buy a carton of spicy noodles from a vendor and sit on a wooden bench to eat my meal with chopsticks while I gaze around me in wonder at the sparkling lights. It's difficult to comprehend the reality of where I am right now and where I was just one week ago, which was sitting on a wall in Rishikesh, overlooking the Ganges. Right now, I could be on another planet entirely.

In an hour or so, I'm told the whole of the gardens will be enveloped in a nightly musical extravaganza called the Garden Rhapsody Show. Having already witnessed the equivalent in Hong Kong with the Symphony of Lights Show, it's something I don't want to miss. So, happily, I spend the next hour strolling through the spectacularly lit gardens, before making my way across the dragonfly bridge to Marina Bay with its iconic feature: The Marina Bay Sands Hotel. It's quite distinct because it looks like three tall towers with a boat-shaped top, as if a ship sailed across the bay and ran aground on top of the buildings. I'm told there are restaurants, bars and an infinity swimming pool up there for those who wish to swim in the sky.

Gazing up at the boat-like structure makes me think of Henri once again. He's now more than three hours into his race and it's almost dark.

I wonder how he's feeling right now. I imagine him standing at the helm of his boat, steering through great waves, and once again I marvel at his courage and the bravery of all his crew.

I stroll along the marina waterfront promenade and see that children are still running in and out of the fountains. Romantic couples are walking arm in arm. Foreign tourists with impressive cameras are taking photographs of the very last rays of the sun going down on a far horizon. All along this stretch of promenade, on the paved areas beneath streetlights, under the elevated walkways and on the grassy areas down by the waterfront, there are people on mats practicing various strains of yoga and martial arts.

Some are doing power *vinyasas* – almost like a chakra dance – set to music. Some are doing zen yoga wearing headphones to cancel out any distractions. There's also a Tai Chi class, which causes me to pause so I can sit on a bench to watch.

The master is an old Chinese man and he's small, light, and lithe in his movement, quite different in his presentation when compared to Henri's precisely focussed poses and power stances. But I'm mesmerised and when the whole class performs The White Crane Spreads His Wings, looking like silhouetted statues against the darkening sky, I find I'm so choked up with emotion I can't stop tears from brimming in my eyes.

I blow my nose and decide to retreat. The park is getting so much busier and the crowds are making me feel stifled. I walk through the gardens slowly, catching glimpses of the light show going on all around, but feeling increasingly trapped in the bustling masses.

* * *

I get back to my room at Raffles around 8pm and order a club sandwich and a bottle of wine from room service. As I grazed on noodles and ice cream this afternoon, I really don't have the appetite to sample the fine dining in the restaurant tonight.

I flick on the TV again hoping to catch any updates on the boat race, but I end up idly watching a travel programme showing tropical destinations favoured by Singaporeans for holiday getaways and weekend jaunts. I had no idea there were so many beautiful tropical island paradises just a stone's throw across the water in Indonesia. All look unspoiled and idyllic with white-sand beaches, swaying palm trees and the bluest waters you could ever hope to see. Some of these islands have lush five-star hotels on them and vast freestyle swimming pools. Others are tiny tropical atolls with private villas, inaccessible except for those who are lucky enough to have their own boat or small private plane, and therefore remain the exclusive weekend lairs of the jetsetters.

Henri told me he liked to take his boat out to far-flung tropical islands and out-of-the-way places in order to discover real peace and quiet. The kind of places where he could take a book and a bottle of rum and sit on the sand pretending to be a castaway for the day. It all sounds to me like a very decadent and exotic way to live one's life. An hour or so later, halfway down my bottle of wine, I flick through the channels again.

I watch an old movie – it's not quite as good as I remembered – and then I fall asleep.

I dream of Jon once more, but this time, he isn't holding out his arms to beckon me into his loving embrace or to twirl me around an imaginary ballroom in a blissful waltz. This time he's standing in the distance, in a swirling white mist, smiling, waving to me, and blowing me a kiss. I can hear his voice clearly and I distinctly hear him telling me to be happy.

In my dream, I'm distraught and running to try to reach him because I sense he's saying goodbye to me and that I might never see him again. But it feels like I'm running on a treadmill and getting nowhere while Jon is still smiling and waving until he turns away.

I call out to him. I beg him to stop and wait for me. But my voice is mute, and despite my desperate efforts, I never get any closer to him.

When he steps back into the enveloping mist with a final smile and a wave, I know in my heart that he's letting me go, and I wake up to find I've been crying in my sleep.

He's still here in my heart, I tell myself. *Still safely here in my heart.*

* * *

I attend a sunrise meditation and ashtanga yoga session in the hotel's courtyard to clear my mind, stretch my body, and feel better. With my spirits lifted, I enjoy a delicious breakfast of coffee, juice, and eggs benedict. Afterwards, I set out with even greater determination on my mission to see and experience Singapore.

According to my itinerary, the first stop is, *Shopping on Orchard Road*.

For a shopaholic, this would have been a paradise: big, bawdy and lined with modern shopping malls. It really is – as a poster I spot claims – where the world comes to shop. I'm pretty sure you could buy anything your heart desired and at great expense.

But I'm not a shopaholic and I'm not that impressed. I browse but resist buying anything.

The next Post-it note is *Chinatown's Street Market* which sounds more like my kind of thing. Chinatown is said to be 'Original Singapore' so I'm hoping to find suitable gifts here for Pia and my little nieces. I buy a couple of beautiful silk scarves and some small lacquered trinket boxes, a handcrafted bamboo handbag and two silk fans with my niece's names on them in calligraphy. Okay. Shopping done and my second mission is a success.

I head down to the quayside. The next Post-it note states: *A boat ride down the Singapore River*. I'd spoken to the concierge at my hotel for advice on this trip before I set out. There were several options but the recommendation was to go for rustic charm and a river cruise on a 'bumboat'.

A bumboat is, I think, the Singaporean equivalent of Hong Kong's Star Ferries.

At Clarke Quay Jetty, where I can board one of these boats, I'm told to look out for the statue of Sir Stamford Raffles on the spot where the namesake of the Raffles Hotel and the founder of modern-day Singapore first set foot. I make sure to take a photo of him and I enjoy the cruise. The boat isn't overcrowded, and it's nice to sit at the back in the sunshine to catch the breeze off the water. The boat is electric and so it's a peaceful and relaxing river experience – a wonderful way to see the sights from a different perspective – and I take lots and lots of photos. But an hour later, with Jon's itinerary completed in a timely and, what feels like dutiful, manner, I'm keen to get out of the heat and the sun.

Looking for shade and a more cultural experience I head out to explore one or two of Singapore's many wonderful museums and art galleries. I stop for lunch along the way, but purposely avoid all those eateries that are busy with tourists even though I'm a tourist myself. I'm more than happy to find a tiny Malaysian café in an almost hidden alcove that appeals to me because it looks like something I would have found in the back streets of Hong Kong.

Inside, there are exposed brick walls and less than a dozen small tables with carved wooden chairs offering comfortable silk cushion seating. Only about half the tables are taken with diners and I'm immediately shown to a table for one in the corner.

The place has the vibe of a casual but chic secret city hangout. I immediately love it and I'm surprised when my first thought in browsing the menu is that Henri would have loved this too.

I order Nasi Lemak, a delicious and traditional spicy dish bursting with flavour served with rice and chilli sauce on a banana leaf. Having my food served on a banana leaf reminds me of meals in the ashram and I find myself smiling at the recent memory.

After lunch, I stroll around for several hours in the cool air-conditioned ambiance of the National Museum. It's interesting to learn the fascinating history of this island city from the fourteenth century to present day. I follow this up with a visit to the nearby National Art Gallery, housed in a grand neo-classical building that was once City Hall. It's wonderful.

And that's my busy day. Adventurous. Accomplished. Successful. Interesting.

But it also felt futile, pointless and lonely. So much so that I now question, what on earth am I doing here?

I certainly hadn't felt this way while I'd been exploring Hong Kong.

So what's different? I decide that it's two things.

The first is that Jon is no longer by my side spiritually. I just can't feel his presence anymore.

Until today, I could feel him with me every moment of every day. Guiding me. Supporting me. Looking out for me and caring for me. Sometimes I could even almost hear his voice, his laughter, and his encouragement. But I woke up this morning knowing for sure he's gone. Had he just been hanging around like a guardian angel until I knew my own mind again?

Because that's the second thing. I woke up this morning feeling upset but also reenergised.

I feel like a different and braver person today. I feel positive, calm.

I feel like I'm breathing properly and I'm thinking about life rather than death, as though a fog has cleared.

I'm seeing things clearly for the first time since the day of my wedding.

And in that clarity, I've come to a happy decision.

Singapore is a beautiful city, but it doesn't make me feel happy in the way Hong Kong does.

So I've decided I'm going to kick back and be rebellious again.

I've broken my own rules before and today I think I should do it again.

Since arriving here in Singapore, I've been racing around like a crazy person, trying to tick off specific tourist destinations while missing out on almost everything else. I haven't really been enjoying myself. So why am I following this plan and all these notes?

Setting out on Jon's quest had seemed the right thing to do at the time and, of course, I'm grateful the plans led me to Henri, but now it's not Jon to whom I feel connected and it's not his words on repeat in my head.

It's Henri's words that haunt me now.

So I've decided that I'm going to cancel my flight tomorrow morning after all. I'm not going to Kuala Lumpur to dutifully tick off any more sights and places. I'm not going to travel to Penang just to eat meals and have drinks. I'm not following a nostalgic and redundant honeymoon itinerary. I'm going to stay here instead. I'm going to gamble and take a risk.

I'm going to meet Henri when he sails into Singapore harbour tomorrow.

I take a taxi back to Raffles with a silly smile on my face and, once back in my beautiful suite, I fully appreciate the cool, orderly, and distinguished ambience of a room that yesterday felt like a gilded cage to me. I make myself a gin and tonic from the mini-bar and sit outside on my terrace in the afternoon shade. I check the time on my phone.

It's early evening. Henri has been sailing for twenty-six hours now.

I reckon he has perhaps another fourteen hours to go before he'll sail into safe harbour. With my heart swelling with excitement at seeing him again, I try to imagine him out there right now on the sea, hundreds of miles away from land in either direction, having faith in himself and his crew, and bravely taking a chance on the possibility of victory. I see Henri's brave quest as a fine metaphor for taking a chance in life and winning.

Chapter 21

The Hong Kong to Singapore Boat Race

I dress and go down for a casual supper in the library known as the Writer's Bar off the lobby, where I feel like I'd stepped back in time and fully expect to be seated next to Ernest Hemingway or Noel Coward. I'm offered a menu that looks like an old leather-bound book and I eat while happily congratulating myself for finally making what I feel is an entirely good decision to stay in Singapore and return to Hong Kong with Henri.

Back in my room, I relax on a pile of comfortable pillows on the bed while flicking through the channels on the TV, hoping that one of the local news channels will be covering Henri's race and perhaps giving out details of early placings.

If cosmic ordering is to work for me once again, then surely Henri's boat will be in the lead right now, about to break the race record and take first place, because I've put so much effort into my wishing. Finding the weather channel instead of the news, I sit bolt upright on the bed with my heart thumping because the presenter is talking about a tropical storm that has suddenly formed in the South China Sea.

There's also mention of The Blue Sea Classic Race and how 'a severe, low-pressure weather system is hampering the rescue of dozens of yachts caught up in the storm winds and high seas'. I freeze with fear. *Rescue? What? When? How was this happening?*

This doesn't make sense to me. The weather had been perfect at the start of the race yesterday and here in Singapore it's been nothing but blue skies today.

I press buttons on the remote control until I find a local news channel. They're busy talking politics but at the bottom of the screen there's a red ticker tape news message saying that a typhoon had developed 'out of nowhere' in the South China Sea.

They call it a 'super typhoon' and the storm being described by the same name as Henri's boat sends a chill through my bones.

I turn up the volume as the news anchor begins to report on the storm and I hold my breath as a meteorologist appears on screen to explain this phenomenon. 'We haven't seen a storm this powerful develop this quickly before,' he says in a tone that sounds horribly grave, 'And this immensely powerful storm is now barrelling down the same stretch of water as the yachts competing in The Blue Sea Classic Race between Hong Kong and Singapore.'

'Can you tell us why this storm is a problem for these highly experienced sailors?' The news anchor asks the expert. 'Can't they just batten down the hatches and sail through it?'

'What makes this storm so dangerous is not its size but its ferocity and the speed with which it has formed. These boats and their crews are no match for a storm of this kind because they will have been hit head on, taken completely by surprise.'

The camera swings back to the news anchor. 'All we can hope and pray for now is that the rescue effort is a success and no one loses their life in this unexpected storm.'

I yell at the screen in angst as another expert, this time a climate change activist, begins talking about rising sea temperatures creating 'perfect storm conditions' and how we all need to act now before it's too late. Well I'm in full support of fighting global warming, but at this moment I'm in desperate need of a mention of those in trouble and those who have been rescued.

As far as I'm concerned, they could talk about what caused this storm later, because right now there are lives at stake. I grab my phone in frustration and go on to social media to find out more about the rescue. Thank goodness Pia pushed me to learn how to use Twitter.

I see people using the hashtags #SuperTyphoon and #BlueSeaClassic and find worried families of the crew and those following the race tweeting for more information on specifically named boats. I see there's some information from the Hong Kong race administration offices that mentions some of the boats retiring from the race and turning inland to find safe harbour. I hope with all my heart that Henri and his crew are amongst them.

I click on the source of this information and follow links that lead me to the race website and a banner reading:

ATTENTION: STORM SITUATION UPDATE

Here I find a full list of all the individual vessels entered in the race, many of them with the words 'RETIRED' or 'REPORTED SAFE' in red text next to them. I anxiously check through the list until I find Henri's boat and, although the *Super Typhoon* is listed, there's no note to indicate its status.

In desperation, I go back to Twitter.

I type a message quickly –

Any news of the yacht called Super Typhoon?
#BlueSeaClassic

Then I turn my attention back to the TV and flick manically through the news and weather channels. It frustrates me to think that while I'd been strolling around today, happily sightseeing, ticking off Post-it notes and mulling things over in my mind about Hong Kong and Henri, he and his crew and everyone else in the race had been battling for their lives in this terrible storm. Why hadn't I thought to check on his situation sooner?

Now it's dark and late in the evening, and I still don't know if Henri and his crew are safe.

I switch from the weather channel to the local news and to my shock and horror, I see they're now showing recorded coverage from a camera positioned on the front of one of the racing yachts while they'd been in difficulty. It gives terrifying first-hand visuals of what the race crews were facing and it's horrific; the vessel in question is being thrown from side to side on a surging sea and being hit by truly massive waves. The water is wild, undulating, and foaming. The sky, or the occasional tumultuous glimpse of it that's displayed, looks to be black and thunderous. The sound coming from the recording is loud and haunting, the wind howling. Although voices of the crew can only just be heard, it's clear that they're very afraid. I have to press my fist against my mouth to silence my yelps of fear as I watch the yacht being tossed about like it's in a giant washing machine.

A message ping is emitted from my phone and I see it's a reply to my plea on Twitter from the account of one of the other boats in the race.

I hear Super Typhoon sent out a mayday distress call at 6.15pm today @SeaQuest.

I stare at the message in horror. That was two hours ago. I quickly type my response.

Do you know if they are safe? Where are they now? @MayaThomas.

I wait with bated breath for more information from the *Sea Quest*, but it never comes.

I click back to the race administration website again to find the *Sea Quest* listed. I see it's been marked as retired and safely accounted for so I assume the information is sound, and Henri had sent out a distress call. The thought that he could be lost at sea or worse fills me with petrified nausea.

There are still six yachts on the list, including Henri's, with no updated information.

What can I do? I feel so helpless!

Then, on the race administration website, I see there's a telephone contact number.

I punch the numbers into my phone but get a busy signal. I keep trying while also watching TV. Seeing the coverage of those massive waves breaking over that yacht being shown on loop on the news makes my stomach roll. Then an agonising thought occurs to me. Am I fated to lose the only two men in my life I've ever really cared about?

Am I destined to live a lonely tragic life?

Why was I being so cruelly punished by the universe and for what? What did I do?

Suddenly, I'm furious in my retaliation and raise my fist to the ceiling.

'How bloody dare you!'

But then I remember Guru J telling me that speaking in anger is no way to talk to the Divine. So, I decide to apologise. I humble myself and sit in the lotus position with my eyes closed to chant mantras and then to meditate as best I can because lives depended on it.

I evoke thoughts of calm seas, blue skies, and safe returns.

I praise Lord Shiva and ask for his love and forgiveness.

Then I use all the skills I learned and practised in India to manifest a cosmic order to the universe. I call for salvation for Henri and all the lost crew and for courage and faith for myself. Then I speak to Jon. I'm not sure if he'll still hear me but I hope and pray he can do something to help. When I open my eyes, the red ticker tape news reel is still giving weather statistics.

The super typhoon winds are in excess of eighty knots with gusts up to one hundred knots.

Information like that would mean something to a sailor like Henri but I just have to assume it's bad.

'Oh Henri! Wherever you are right now ... please be safe and come back to me!'

I really don't know what else to do or where to go next for information.

The coverage on the TV begins showing new and updated news. There's a live video feed from a rescue helicopter that's hovering over a violently boiling sea lit with a search light and littered with the debris of capsized yachts. Crew members are being shown either inside waterlogged life rafts or clinging to the sides of them.

I watch with tears streaming down my face in angst because it's all truly terrifying.

I see the helicopter is attempting to airlift casualties to the safety of a nearby ship, but the power of the wind, spray and waves is clearly making the rescue incredibly difficult.

Coverage switches to a rescued crewman on the ship, who is explaining how he'd been airlifted. He told the camera how he and his fellow crew members had been trying to sail through the midst of the storm in the hope of offering assistance to another yacht, called *Blue Moon*, which had transmitted a mayday call before it disappeared.

'Conditions got so bad we couldn't reach her. We fear she may now be sunk. Her crew are still missing ...' The man breaks off as he begins to cry. It's heart breaking.

Another yacht, called *Amazing Grace*, is reported as capsized. Footage shows the mast had snapped, falling and trapping the man who'd been steering the boat. Thankfully, a coastguard boat had arrived just in time to offer help and to rescue the whole crew. The skipper of *Amazing Grace*, a middle-aged man who looks horribly traumatised by his terrible experience, speaks to a news reporter over the video link straight from his rescue boat, saying that he's never experienced anything like it in all his years as a yachtsman. 'I've never steered through wind and rain and white water like it before,' he says. 'It was terrible. Just when we thought we were getting through it, it just kept getting worse.'

Another crewmember, a young woman aboard the *Amazing Grace*, tells how they'd had the radio on the whole time. 'An' we kept hearin' all these mayday calls from stricken boats that had been rolled and how crew were in the water. We managed to get our storm jib off just as a wave hit us. Next thing I know, we're upside down. I can tell you I thought it was the end.'

The news reporter says that the rescue service deployed to deal with this amounted to military helicopters and lots of civilian boats and large ships in the area that had responded and detoured to assist. I scour the screen for a sighting of Henri's yacht and turn up the volume on the TV to listen for any mention of *Super Typhoon*. Unfortunately, the commentators in the TV studio, who are having conversations with their storm experts over the visual coverage, don't help because they keep talking about the super typhoon storm and my heart almost stops every time they say the words.

I fear the worst if Henri's boat isn't found soon.

I've been constantly redialling the race administration offices at the marina in Hong Kong during this time and

I'm so relieved when eventually my call gets picked up. When I speak, my voice is high, shrill and breathless with urgency, I stammer out the name of the boat and Henri's name and explain how I've been told by someone on Twitter that he had been sending out mayday calls and that I'm worried sick.

'Can you please help?' I plead to the woman on the other end of the line.

'Can you please slow down and give me your name?' Her voice is so calm and methodical that I can hardly believe I'm speaking to a person rather than a machine. But right now, she's my only hope, so I do as requested. 'My name? Oh, yes, of course. I'm Maya Thomas.'

'And, you're making an enquiry about the *Super Typhoon* and Henri Chen, is that correct?'

Maybe she was specially trained to be both stern and calm in an emergency?

I'm sure she's been answering the phone for several hours, speaking to concerned family and friends.

I suppose she needed to be careful what she says and also what she doesn't say. Because no one wants to be told the worst over the phone after all.

'Yes. That is correct,' I say slowly and clearly. 'And I want to know ...'

'Ms Thomas, can you please first tell me what your relationship is to Mr Chen?'

I'm taken aback by this question. What can I say?

That I've only known him two days, but they'd been

two amazing days with a man whom I'd found attractive and utterly fascinating?

That after losing Jon, I'd honestly thought I'd never meet anyone else with whom I'd feel comfortable enough to be myself? Someone to laugh with again and with whom to feel happy.

I can't possibly say all that to her, but I have a feeling that if I don't say I'm in a close relationship with Henri then she won't tell me anything at all. She might even hang up. 'I'm his ... girlfriend.' I tell her boldly.

'His girlfriend?' She repeats, in a tone that indicates she might not actually believe me.

Maybe I needed to sound more convincing?

This situation is the same as when you call a hospital ward and ask about someone's condition and you're asked who you are in relation to the patient. To get the information you must be immediate family or a spouse and being just a girlfriend doesn't really count.

'Actually, I'm his fiancée,' I state.

'Fiancée?' She repeats back to me.

Oh, my goodness. If I'm going to have to speak this slowly and she's going to repeat everything I say and then write it down, this is going to take forever.

'Yes, that's right. Can you please tell me what information you have right now on his wellbeing and his whereabouts because, as I'm sure you can imagine, I'm worried sick about him?'

'Yes, of course. Here at race HQ we've been collecting

data and I can tell you that we've published a list of skippers and crew who are accounted for at this time on our website. I can confirm that Henri and his crew are not currently on this list. But that's not to say they are not safe. Henri is an excellent skipper and he has an experienced crew, so please don't worry too much Ms Thomas. I have your phone number now, and I promise I'll call you back the minute I hear anything more.'

I'm grateful to her for being so helpful and forthcoming and I tell her to call me Maya. Then I thank her profusely once again and repeat my phone number.

She hurriedly explains to me how she's solely reliant on updates from the rescue teams involved and how, while they do appreciate loved ones need information it's also important they give priority to the task at hand. I'm just about to hang up when she suddenly says 'wait!' followed by nothing but an eerie silence.

I fear we've been cut off. 'What? Wait? Are you still there?'

'Maya, I've just received news of the *Super Typhoon*!' she says quite breathlessly.

She no longer sounds automated. She sounds excited.

'Henri and his crew are safe and well and the vessel is intact and seaworthy. They just lost their radio communication after being flooded. They're reported to be assisting in the rescue mission of a drifting vessel called *Blue Moon*. That's all I have right now. But I'll call you back as soon as I know more. Oh, thank goodness. They are all safe!'

My relief is palpable. All I can think about is the fact that Henri is safe and helping to rescue the stricken *Blue Moon*. He's a hero.

* * *

I don't sleep over the next few hours of darkness. I drink coffee. I give thanks for the news of Henri and I lie on the bed with my phone by my side and the TV on while tuned into either the news or the weather channel in order to try to stay updated.

At six o'clock in the morning, just as the sun is coming up, my phone rings.

I almost jump out of my skin in alarm and anticipation.

It's the lady at the Blue Sea Classic Race HQ offices in Hong Kong.

'Maya, I have good news. I've just heard that Henri and his crew, together with the crew of the *Blue Moon* and another drifting yacht called *Ocean Challenger*, are safe and sound and are now all heading in calm waters towards Singapore. Estimated arrival time is said to be around ten-thirty this morning!'

I hear myself give a high-pitched squeal. It's a completely involuntary response.

'Oh, thank you. That is so fantastic to hear. What is your name by the way?'

'It's Jennifer. You'll usually find me on the reception desk at the Hong Kong Yacht Club. I know Henri well but I didn't know he was engaged. I look forward to meeting you, Maya. Maybe we can go for a cup of coffee or something stronger?'

'Sure. Thanks Jennifer. I'll look forward to it.'

Oh dear, another terrible lie. How can I possibly explain myself to her? And, if she knows Henri well, then what if she mentions I claimed to be his fiancée?

'And, Maya ...'

'Erm, yes?'

'Give Henri a hug from all of us here at the club. Tell him we are all very proud of him.'

The thought of hugging Henri again has me at the quayside at 9am. I simply couldn't wait around at the hotel any longer. When I arrive, I see it's a good thing I set out early because the harbour front is already crowded with press and media.

TV station crews are setting up their camera equipment and news reporters are speaking with great authority into their microphones about how they are waiting in anticipation of welcoming home 'the victims of the most unexpected storm in sailing history'.

News anchors have rushed over from their studios in the city centre to be here on the quayside too and they are relaying to their audiences all the terrifying facts about known losses and casualties while newspaper journalist are interviewing bystanders.

I pitch myself on the edge of a crowd of families and friends who have gathered in the warm, early morning sunshine ready to welcome home their precious loved ones, but there's no escaping the storm of news coverage that is going on all around us.

'The Office of Meteorology in Hong Kong heavily defends its position this morning after failing to predict one of the most aggressive storms ever to have formed in the South China Sea. The storm, which quickly developed into a 'super typhoon' enveloped the Hong Kong to Singapore Blue Sea Classic Race. Only three of the thirty-two yachts that set out from Hong Kong almost two days ago are now expected to finish the race. We still haven't had confirmation about those known to be missing and therefore cannot report or speculate at this point.'

I stare out to sea, focusing my eyes and my hope-filled aspirations on the horizon line, anxious to see the three boats and their white sails the moment they appear. All around me the incessant narrative from the reporters continues.

'A storm alert was issued five hours into the forty-eight-hour race with a low-pressure warning and wind predictions for up to fifty-five knots or around one hundred kilometres an hour. At that time, the consensus amongst the competitors and the race administration was that the predicted storm would be short lived and the wind speeds were well within safe sailing parameters. Unbeknownst to anyone, the competitors were sailing straight into the path of a storm that literally blew in out of nowhere, causing twenty-metre-high waves, and wind speeds double those predicted, which capsized boats, snapped masts, knocked out communications and swept many sailors overboard.'

'Seventeen yachts retired early from the race and found a safe haven in a small Vietnamese harbour. Twelve yachts are known to have capsized or sunk. Other crew members have been rescued from the sea or from life rafts.'

'We are here at the harbour in Singapore awaiting the arrival of the only three yachts known to have survived the most powerful super typhoon ever recorded in this part of the South China Sea. Weather forecasters had not indicated anything untoward in short-range weather patterns and the question now is why this super typhoon wasn't detected earlier.'

One reporter had latched on to the fact that Henri's boat was named *Super Typhoon* and suggested that naming it as such was 'crazy, irresponsible, and a bad omen'.

I have to move away. I can't stand to listen to any more.

I'd been feeling so overjoyed this morning, knowing I'd see Henri again.

I'd been so sure that my divine wishes and my desperate prayers had been heard and answered. But now, realising how many people have been hurt and traumatised, and knowing it could have so easily been Henri who had been lost overboard, it's all rather too much.

A fleet of ambulances has arrived to assist those injured onboard the three incoming yachts.

I wonder if this is an indication that they'll be arriving back soon?

Suddenly there's a great cheer from all those waiting.

I jump up and down to see through all the people now standing in front of me trying to catch a glimpse of the first sighting of sails. And then suddenly there they are.

I hardly dare to blink in case they disappear again.

Eventually they come into full view, getting larger and larger as they approach the shore.

I forget my fears about what might have been because right now all that matters to me is that Henri is safe and I'll soon see him again. The memory of his face, his smile, his last kiss, and the final words we spoke to each other as we parted at the pier haunt me. But in seeing his face again, I know I can replace them with new and happier memories.

I watch as the three yachts limp rather than sail into the harbour to great applause and an awful lot of tears. I see how the *Super Typhoon* is flanked by the other two yachts, as they sail slowly, side by side, towards what was still being considered the finish line.

The canvas sails on all three boats look tattered. Clearly, there was a lot of damage to their main frames, but the crew onboard are all waving, yelling, and looking ecstatic to see their families on the quayside waiting to greet them.

Because Henri's boat is positioned between the other two I can't see him yet.

I watch, wait, and hold my breath, hopping from foot to foot, looking to the back of the boat where he should be steering. Then, I witness something incredibly poignant.

The crews on the *Ocean Challenger* and the *Blue Moon* swiftly take down what remains of their sails and this slows them down just enough, so they are now hanging back from the *Super Typhoon*, with its sails also flapping rather than billowing in the wind.

The *Super Typhoon* is now marginally ahead.

It seems they are giving Henri and his crew their victory after all.

And now, even though my tear-filled eyes, I see Henri standing at the helm.

I see he's waving his arms in the air and looking back at the crew on the other two boats, urging them to sail into the dock with him. He looks totally astonished by what is happening here. He clearly hadn't expected this but he is the true winner of the race, even if his victory is treated as a formality rather than a celebration.

I keep my eyes fixed on Henri and my heart goes out to him. He looks exhausted and pale, still wearing a full set of florescent orange wet-weather gear even though it's now so hot on the quayside that I'm feeling scorched. I notice he has a dark shadow of stubble on his face from the two days he's spent stoically steering that boat and bravely rescuing others. My heart swells with pride and my whole body aches with relief that he's safe.

When all three yachts are secured to the quayside, the crews begin disembarking.

It's mayhem on the dock. Everyone surges forward all at once, much to the annoyance of the media and to the detriment of the ambulance squads and paramedics who are trying to reach and attend to the crews. Some of the sailors are walking wounded, having sustained head gashes or broken limbs that are wrapped up in bandages and makeshift slings.

One or two are more seriously hurt and are having to be brought off on stretchers.

From what I can see, Henri looks battle weary but otherwise unscathed.

I hold back from the crowds and watch as he's the last person to leave his vessel.

Of course, he's then immediately mobbed by the waiting media with their microphones.

'Captain Chen, can you give us your account of what happened at sea?'

'Do you realise that you won the race?'

Cameras were pushing almost into his face.

'Mr Chen, you're being hailed a hero. Will you do an interview for Singapore TV News?'

I edge forward to hear him saying he's 'incredibly thankful to be back on solid ground'.

He doesn't answer any of the questions from the media mob about his ordeal or his win and he's rescued by a paramedic who thrusts a bottle of drinking water into Henri's hand and then uses his authority to dismiss the reporters and lead Henri to a cordoned off area where there's a waiting ambulance. I follow. He still hasn't seen me.

I stand to one side and wait for the right moment to approach him.

I see him being helped to remove his heavy jacket. His movements are slow as the jacket is pulled from his shoulders, his face wracked with pain. He sips from a water bottle while sitting on the ambulance step to have his blood pressure taken and his vitals assessed by the attending medic. The paramedic seems satisfied and I hear him tell Henri to 'drink lots of water and get some rest'. When I can't wait any longer, I walk into his line of sight.

I call out his name.

'Henri!'

His head snaps up, his jaw drops open, and his tired eyes light up when he sees me.

A moment later, he's on his feet and I'm wrapped up in his arms.

'Oh Maya. I'd convinced myself you wouldn't be here. But you came back!'

'No ...' I laugh. 'I didn't come back. I never left. I needed to see you again, Henri. I wanted you to know that I've decided to stay and rent a house in Hong Kong for a while.'

He looks at me in amazement but before he can speak there's a tremendous whirling noise and the air around us is whipped up as a helicopter lands nearby.

I shade my eyes from the dust blowing in the air and see the helicopter belongs to the Hong Kong Yacht Club. The doors fly open. Three people climb out. Two men, who dash straight inside the first aid tent, and one attractive red-haired woman, who heads straight over to Henri and me, smiling at me like we know each other.

'You must be Maya ...' she says to me. 'We spoke on the phone. I'm Jennifer.'

I'm sure all the colour must be draining from my face as I shake Jennifer's hand.

'It's good to see you're still in one piece, sailor!' she says eagerly to Henri, slapping him on the shoulder and making him wince. 'You had your poor fiancée worried about you!'

'Fiancée?' Henri repeats, turning to me with a look that is both curious and startled.

I stammer something about how he'd had everyone worried while squirming on the spot.

Henri continues to study me with an expression of confusion and suspicion but he waits until Jennifer has headed into the first aid tent to join her colleagues before he speaks.

'Maya ... just how long have I been gone?'

I swallow hard and manage to squeak out. 'Erm ... it's been two days.'

He nods and then looks down at the floor and his sodden shoes for a moment.

'Okay. So, let me see if I've got this straight. Two days ago, when we last spoke, you said to me that things were happening too fast for you and you were leaving. And now, by some miracle, you've found a house in Hong Kong and we're getting married?'

When he finishes looking at the floor he looks up at

me again and he's grinning from ear to ear, his beautiful green eyes shining brightly and filled with humour again.

He's definitely taking this much better than I thought so I decide not to explain.

Instead, I simply remind him of what he said to me two days ago when we last spoke.

'Well, you said that if I stayed, we'd be able to find out if this ... *something* that we both feel for each other might lead to *something* more. Isn't that right?'

He laughs aloud and pulls me back into his arms.

Then, in a low whisper, he tells me how he did have something more for me.

And it turns out that something was a deep, smouldering, incredibly passionate kiss.

I felt my heart fill with love and I knew I was truly happy again.

THE END